Anna Eichberg Lane

Brown's retreat and other stories

Anna Eichberg Lane

Brown's retreat and other stories

ISBN/EAN: 9783743322318

Manufactured in Europe, USA, Canada, Australia, Japa

Cover: Foto ©Andreas Hilbeck / pixelio.de

Manufactured and distributed by brebook publishing software
(www.brebook.com)

Anna Eichberg Lane

Brown's retreat and other stories

BROWN'S RETREAT

AND OTHER STORIES

BY

ANNA EICHBERG KING *Lane*

BOSTON
ROBERTS BROTHERS
1893

University Press:

JOHN WILSON AND SON, CAMBRIDGE, U.S.A.

CONTENTS.

BROWN'S RETREAT.

I.

BROWN'S RETREAT flashed upon them all of a sudden.

The neighborhood went to sleep, one night, guileless and innocent,—that is, theoretically guileless and innocent,—and awoke in the morning to the consciousness that Brown's Retreat was in its midst.

There was considerable mystery and confusion attending the want of knowledge whether Brown's Retreat meant that Brown had retreated, or if it was a general invitation into the "retreat," or if Brown was a practical joker and Brown's Retreat merely a gentle stimulant to that weakness.

Edgerly was a prosperous town, with a harbor, an East India trade, and a charming collection of waterside characters. It had also a state-prison that was kept on the most desirable plan, where five hundred gentlemen were lodged who had differences with their country's laws. Once in a while, curiously enough, one of these gentlemen would escape. There were other worthy institutions in Edgerly, of which it is, however, unnecessary to speak.

Edgerly itself was built on some three or four hills, so that the narrow, zigzag streets were not only narrow and zigzag, but they had quite an abrupt slope, and some of them, had they been built as surveyors intend, would have led you, running at a smart pace, down into the very depths of the dubious-looking black water at the foot of the hill, where, at the weather-beaten wharves, with their perfume of bilge-water, some rusty-looking schooner would be lying at anchor, displaying on its bare spars a varied collection of trousers and under-garments hung out to dry, besides affording a glimpse of a decidedly untidy nautical character, mopping the unsavory deck.

Brown's Retreat was nearly at the foot of Edgerly's down-hill street. At a rough guess it was six feet by ten, and occupied one half of the ground floor of No. 7, a wooden house with depressed-looking windows, at each of which appeared a vision of somebody's baby and some baby's mother, all looking very frouzy and much in want of soap and water and fresh air.

It left lookers-on no doubt of its character, as it boldly proclaimed itself " Brown's Retreat " on a deal-board, painted in lamp-black by one whose right hand had lost its cunning, for the letters resembled Edgerly streets, being narrow and zigzag in the extreme. Nevertheless, they stared into the world over the small, dingy show-window, which revealed as a solid foundation, two quarts of dismal apples, surmounted by several rows of sticky pop-corn balls, a collection of combs and seed-cakes, a few paper dolls, a sprinkling of dead flies, clay-pipes, and shoe-strings.

Sometimes a child's face would peer out eagerly from among these treasures; a child's face, yet strangely unchild-like, with shrewd gray eyes watching stealthily,—a poor little body shivering in a doubtful calico dress, with an attempt at finery, in a string with three glass beads about her wretched little neck.

The child was small, the shop was small, and the counter was very small. The selection of wares was modest, and the greater part graced the window.

When the sign, " Brown's Retreat," appeared over

that window the neighborhood stared. Whether the invisible Brown grinned is unknown; but true it is that the mysterious child kept the little shop with much solemnity. Once in a while, when the shop was empty,—which, Heaven knows, was most of the time, for neither money nor trade was very brisk in that part of Edgerly town,—a cautious voice would whisper, " Coast clear, Popsy? "

The mysterious child would reconnoitre stealthily, and then whisper back through the key-hole of a small door in the back of the shop, half lost in the gloom of the place, " Yes, Nunc ! " Then out would come a man's head with tumbled, brown hair, an unshaven face, and undecided blue eyes, that had, however, little redeeming wrinkles at the corners, as if the man could laugh at a joke.

If Popsy whispered warningly, " Shoo, — shoo, Nunc ! " there came back a muffled " All right, Popsy ! " By which you will see that not only was there a Brown's Retreat, but there was even a retreat to that.

It was on a late November day that Brown's Retreat appeared before an astonished world ; a raw day, when the inky waves with a greasy scum, down in the harbor, had foamy white caps tossing upon them, and plebeian Edgerly went about with a red nose and its hands in its pockets, and some of the ladies had their dress skirts over their heads.

Popsy, having flashed out along with the Retreat, was much stared at and questioned ; but the only information gleaned was that Popsy had a sick uncle in the back room, who wasn't to be disturbed. It seems he had bought out the previous occupant who had failed ingloriously, with five dollars debts and assets *nil.*

" Uncle says, too, we musn't trust," Popsy added. As she spoke a low chuckle was heard through the key-hole of the back room, as if some one couldn't help laughing, for the life of him.

"Merciful powers, what's that?" asked the visitor.

"It's only uncle a-choking," said Popsy, with much presence of mind.

II.

A MAN may be a rascal, and yet possess a fine sense of humor. That was the matter with Popsy's uncle. His name was Brown, and before he became ripe for the penitentiary he had been quite a decent member of society, who even went to church once in a while. That was his misfortune. Had he not gone to church he might still have been a decent member of society instead of what he was.

One Sunday morning he wandered into a meeting-house, and heard the preacher grow eloquent on forgiving the sins of our fellow-men; how he, the preacher, loved mankind, and there was nothing his erring brethren could do to him which would turn him against them. Brown had gone into the sacred edifice more for warmth than from piety, for it was a bitter, biting winter day, and his lucky star was, just then, very dim. Being there he listened, and listening believed the eloquent words. Confidingly, and with a certain sense of humor, too, he took the reverend gentleman at his word: that night the parsonage was entered and a large number of valuables were stolen. Brown was not caught in the act, exactly, but a silver cream jug was found in his left coat-tail pocket for which he could not account; especially, as it had a strange monogram engraved on one fat side. To his surprise and disappointment the minister appeared against him; a jury without a bit of humor found him guilty, and a prosaic judge sentenced him to five years' imprisonment.

Brown did not belong to the class that novelists delight in describing—the noble convict. He was simply human, and being down on his luck and because of that unfortunate sense of humor, he had stolen, but beyond that he would harm neither woman nor child.

The late November night when he escaped, one thought had been uppermost in his distracted mind,—to secrete himself on some outward-bound vessel in Edgerly harbor, and be carried to parts unknown; very fine in theory, very hard in practice, though Brown had his friends, and there's truth in the adage, "honor among thieves."

That eventful night, when, trembling and shuddering, he stood once more under the skies, a free man, unimaginative creature though he was, he felt his own unspeakable wretchedness. With the instinct of a hunted beast more than the consciousness of a man, with a deadly fear at heart, that made him repent too late of his rash folly, he turned his back on the open country, which would have meant safety to many a man, and groped his way through miserable alleys and no-thoroughfares, shrinking at every sound and starting at every shadow, to Edgerly's market-place. The sky was black, the rain fell in torrents; and a piercing wind swept the great drops hither and thither.

"Dog's weather!" muttered a policeman, and pulled his coat collar about his ears, and was for a moment not quite as watchful as he should have been. "Good convict's weather," Brown may have thought, if the power of thinking was still left to him in the midst of cold and terror, as he crouched in an angle of the great market that stretched its granite length in dim perspective, lighted at distant intervals by flickering gas-lamps, about which the rays, falling on mist and rain, formed a dismal yellow halo. Deserted all, deserted.

Edgerly market lay quite near the wharves ; not very respectable to be sure, but Brown and respectability had long since ceased to know each other. Quite unhindered he continued his vagrant, groping way, till, being about to turn a corner, a corner with a traitorous street-lamp, he ran face to face against another man.

"Damn you !" muttered the new-comer. Then catching sight of the cowering face, he grasped the wretched man's arm with the power of a vice. " You, Brown,"—

"You, Jim," — and Brown tried to free himself and raised one clenched fist.

"None o' that, Brown ; we're friends ! Aren't you—why—you must have—you must have "—

"Cut ? Yes," Brown interposed. " I'm off, Jim. They'll be after me now, sure !" he cried, and peered anxiously about.

"From the . . . ?" Jim asked, turning his thumb in the direction of Edgerly's prison. Brown nodded, and was about to hurry on, when the other stopped him. "Yours is hard luck, old boy. Here, take this ; it'll help you on. I'll do more for you if I can, —for old time sake, ye know." Thrusting some money into the man's hand, this good Samaritan, in the guise of a common sailor, vanished.

With a ray of comfort at heart Brown clutched the money to his breast, and at last found himself in that narrow, zigzag street which led to the black water at the foot of the wharf, a street not very dainty as to its inhabitants, and very willing to give anything it possessed for miserable money. It was the most undesirable of all the streets in a great city,—a street with tumble-down, wooden houses and odd nooks ; with narrow lanes and alleys creeping out, and, here and there, dark quadrangles below the level of the street, with rickety wooden steps leading down to them, and dimly lighted by an oil lamp swinging from a wooden arch overhead and throwing a wretched glimmer on unspeakable poverty and crime. Down this street the culprit crept. He had just reached such a quadrangle, and had shrunk back from the dreary darkness and the dreary light, when he heard a bitter sobbing, and the next instant he felt something pull at his trousers. With a shudder and an oath he looked down.

"Let go, you brat!" he muttered, as he caught sight of the shivering form of a child crouching on the top of the miserable flight of steps. The child ceased sobbing and shrank back at the sudden violence of face and tone, while the unhappy man disappeared into the darkness. There is a touch of superstition in the most unimaginative and irreligious of us,—a feeling that, somehow, as we do, so shall we be done by. Fleeing, as he was, from every known peril, Brown was yet stopped in his headlong course by an unexplained feeling that a certain guiding power—Brown would call it "luck," in an unvarnished statement—might, in retribution, forsake him as he had forsaken the child. So he retraced his steps to where she had fallen on her face and was weeping bitterly. "What's the matter?" he asked, roughly.

"They've turned me out o' doors, for father's gone, I don't know where, and mother—mother's dead,—and oh, I'm so cold and hungry, and I'm so afraid!" she cried, looking about, fearfully.

"Well, what shall I do with you, young 'un?"

The child stopped sobbing, and looking up to him with an imploring face said, with innocent confidence, "P'raps you'll take me with you."

It did not enter Brown's head to disbelieve her story.

"Take you with me," he repeated, with a grim smile, for he saw the ghastly humor of the thing,— "take you with me? Why, I haven't got a bunk for myself to-night."

The child had been bred in that state of society where hunted-down Brown was but an every-day object to her. He seemed a stranger in Edgerly, and what wonder, therefore, that he was without a lodging?

"I know of a house where they'll take you in," she said eagerly; "that is, if you can pay," she added, with some misgivings. Brown nodded. "It's right here in the street,—near the wharf; and—and—p'raps you'll tell 'em to take me in, too, and—and p'raps you'll give me a bit of bread."

"Go ahead," said Brown, and he followed his ragged guide. He was reckless, this breaker of laws, and as a gambler stakes his all on one throw of the dice, so he staked life and liberty on this small vagrant, with a feeling of superstition that his "luck" could not forsake him, for had he not befriended one nearly as wretched as himself?

The child led the way to a tumble-down wooden house. The landlady, a middle-aged virago, was just having a dispute with a slightly intoxicated lodger, which she postponed to attend to business. The delicate matter of references not being alluded to, the stranger, in consideration of a certain modest sum, was allowed to take possession of a dingy six-by-ten-feet shop, with a small room back of it, which its discouraged last occupant had forsaken.

"Two doors and a window," said Brown, peering curiously about in the miserable room. "One door leads into the shop, the other into the entry, and the window," he said, throwing it open and putting his head out, "into an alley—so!" Then he seated himself on the ragged bed, and, dangling his legs, stared into the pinched, haggard face of the child, who stood watching him very patiently. "And what may your name be, young' un?" he asked.

"Popsy," she said, and returned his stare.

"You're pretty well alone in the world?"

"Yes," she whispered.

"So am I, so am I. We might," he added, as if thinking aloud,—"we might hang on to each other, for the present at least, might n't we?"

"I bet we might!" Popsy answered energetically, with a world of gratitude in her old young eyes.

"Well, then, call me uncle; Nunc, you might say, for short. Now, Popsy?"

"Well, Nunc?"

"Fetch a pint of milk and a loaf of bread."

Popsy disappeared, and Brown lay back on the bed and laughed. The idea of his playing the part of protector was too funny; it struck him so forcibly that he forgot his own precarious position in amusement at the comic side of the transaction.

Such was the advent of Brown, who hiding by day prowled about at night in search of means to escape from Edgerly town and the Edgerly laws he had broken. Yet the man could not be the man he was without having his little joke. In his leisure moments, so very plentiful, he traced the words " Brown's Retreat " on a pine board, and, trusting to the name of Brown as a disguise, nailed it over the shop window one night, where it surprised Edgerly the next morning, to the intense delight of its owner, who nearly choked with suppressed laughter when an unsuspecting policeman, in passing, read the sign and grinned.

That policeman had a nice sense of humor, but it was as nothing compared to Brown's.

III.

BUT Justice did not sleep. Indeed she put her hand into her respectable pocket and offered two hundred and fifty dollars reward for the apprehension of the fugitive Brown, which stimulated quite a number of loafers to find him out.

November turned into the bitterest, coldest December. Approaching Christmas hardly disturbed this part of Edgerly by any undue gladness; though Brown's Retreat made a sacrifice to the season in the shape of a few twigs of holly and an evergreen-tree.

Popsy had developed fine shop-keeping talents, with a shrewd eye open for cash customers. This calculating eye, in looking over the street one December morning, lighted on a stranger in an attire several degrees better than that usually worn by the gentlemen about, with something military in his slouched hat and dyed mustache.

This personage, with his hands in his trousers pockets, stared at the sign of Brown's Retreat, and said "Hallo!" with a dim sense of amusement. Then he looked in at the door, and said "Hallo?" interrogatively. Without waiting for an answer, he leaned his elbow gracefully on the counter, and re-marked to Popsy,—

"Brown's a great one to joke, ain't he?" and he stared about at the dismal place. "Calling this a re-treat is a joke! You belong to Brown, don't you?" he abruptly asked Popsy, who stood by in open mouthed consternation.

"If you please," she said, with a little curtsy,— "if you please, sir, Brown's my sick uncle, and mustn't be disturbed."

"Mustn't he? Well, we'll just see!"

"No, you shan't!" cried Popsy, and thrust herself between the stranger and the back room.

"Why, you ferocious little savage! what harm would it do him?" he cried, retreating, nevertheless, while he stroked his dyed mustache and laughed a weak laugh, which would have been still weaker could he have seen through the door, where Brown sat on the bed with a loaded revolver in his hand, ready with an unexpected welcome.

"He's sick, and you mustn't go in," Popsy said hastily, fearing, child though she was, that she had made a blunder, even in her quick defence of him; for she knew his story, and that he was waiting for a favorable moment to escape on one of the schooners down at the wharf,—a transaction by no means strange to Popsy.

The mysterious stranger, as if in his turn to allay her suspicion, or her alarm, looked over the wares on the counter, and at last purchased a clay pipe, and then sauntered out of the shop, followed by the child's eager gaze and by a couple of cautious eyes that looked stealthily out of the inner door after the retreating figure, and made such a mental note of it, that that inquisitive person would not have been safe from Brown beneath any disguise. "The devil's in that sneaking cuss!" he muttered, as he drew his head in again. "Popsy."

"What's it, Nunc?" the child asked, putting her shrewd face in at the door.

"If that chap comes loafing round here again, you do this; do you understand?" So Popsy coughed obediently, as Brown directed. "It's getting as hot as h—ll round here. I'll have to cut, or they'll pin me again," he muttered.

"Nunc," said Popsy, still lingering, "there was another man here this morning what asked to see you; and I said you was sick, and he said he was a doctor. I said you wouldn't see no doctor; then he said he was a friend o' yourn, and he'd come round again."

There was a look of veiled fear in the man's eyes, and he clenched his brawny hands, and felt as if the game he was playing was coming to a delicate point.

The zigzag street was indeed becoming unsafe quarters. The neighborhood was accustomed to harbor suspicious characters, and after a first nod of surprise, forgot all about them. But the mysterious Brown, who was never seen, who rented a shop where there was little to sell, became the subject of conversation. The police was after him too; but it was not the police that looked in at the store and bought clay pipes. The police was scouring the country far and wide in search of the criminal, but it had not occurred to that able body to examine the region under its very nose; that duty was being performed by self-constituted spies, who had recourse to the police only at the last moment, fearing it might claim the reward. The culprit, knowing the tricks of the trade, instantly recognized his visitors' errand, and muttered a curse upon them. The man was not so delicate in his sentiments—not being a noble convict—as to doubt the honor or purity of their profession; he merely questioned their right to be stepping into the shoes of those whose duty it was to arrest him in the way of business.

"Curse them for sneaking dogs! Why can't they leave a fellow alone!" he thought, with a despair at heart that nearly made him give in, beaten.

Nevertheless, that night he once more groped his way stealthily out of the house, through a back door that led into an alleyway, darker for a cloudy night and dirtier than usual for a spell of thawing. Into this dirt and darkness Brown disappeared.

The neighborhood about Brown's Retreat, if not very honest or respectable, had a touching confidence in other people's honesty and respectability; for it always slept with its doors wide open in summer and on the latch in winter, the delicate formality of a bell being quite unknown. At midnight, or a little later, the faint light of a tallow candle woke Popsy from her slumbers on a miscellaneous heap of old clothes and a patchwork quilt, to the fact that an unknown man was bending over her. A sailor he seemed; a strong looking man, with a face smoothly shaven but for a short, cleanly cut mustache,

Being only a child, Popsy was for a moment filled with unspeakable terror at the sudden awakening, the light, and the strange man. Then there flashed into her mind, the danger of the man who had be-friended her.

Without moving her eyes from the stranger's face, she slipped to her feet, and stood at the door of Brown's room, as if to defend it. Not a word she said, but stood there shivering and trembling, with one small hand on the door-knob and a pleading look in her faithful eyes that made his own dim ; that made him turn away for an instant, and then ask in a husky voice, " Don't you know me, Popsy ? " Popsy started at the tones. " Well, this beats all ! Don't you know your Nunc ? " cried the man. " I swear, youngster, either you're asleep or I'm another man. What, don't you know me, Popsy ? " he repeated and held out his arms to her.

" Yes, you are Nunc ! " the child cried, throwing her arms about his neck, " and yet you are not."

The man was, indeed, well disguised. Since Popsy had known him his face had become rough and dark by a beard of some weeks' growth. Soap and water and a comb, had helped the transformation. The trim sailor's dress, rough as it was, formed such a

2

contrast to the wretched clothes he had picked up piece-meal.

With better clothes something of that disgraced, hunted-down look in his eyes had disappeared ; so that as far as his outer man was concerned Brown might again have been classed as a respectable member of society.

" And yet you are not Nunc," the child repeated, not quite comprehending his disguise.

Brown said nothing, but lifting her in his arms carried her into the back room and locked the door. Placing the candle on the rough table, he seated himself and took the child on his knee.

"Look here, Popsy," he began, with some embarrassment, "you know I'm hiding from the—from the "—

" Perlice."

"Well, yes, to be sure. And the fact is, to make a long story short, those two chaps who've been a-prowling round here are making the place too hot for me ; and, Popsy," he said, with a certain tenderness in his voice one would hardly have expected from so rough a man,—"Popsy, I've got to leave you, though I said I wouldn't ; and it does seem hard and mean, now, doesn't it, young 'un ? "

"Oh, Nunc, Nunc ! " the child sobbed.

"There, there ! " Brown said, rocking her to and fro like a sick baby. " Now, listen to what I've done. You don't know Jim ? Jim's a good one and has stood by me like a rock, darn him ! Now Jim's got me a berth along with him on the Mary Ann, bound for the East Indies. The skipper's glad of a steady hand, and asks no questions this time o' year. There'll come a woman for you to-morrow, Popsy, who'll take ye along with her. She's Jim's sister, and," speaking almost in a whisper, "once she was to have been my wife,—my wife. But I went to the dogs—God forgive me !—and she's only Jim's sister now. Be mindful of her, Popsy ; be true and good like her, and some day you'll grow up to be a good woman, just as she is,—Heaven bless her ! " Brown buried his face in his hands for a moment.

" I will, I will, Nunc ! " the child answered piteously. " But when are you coming back ? "

" Never," said Brown, accustomed to staring hard facts in the face,—never. But when you're a woman grown,—a good woman, mind, like *her*,—perhaps then you'll come out to me—But what's the matter, young 'un ? " as Popsy, slipping from his knee, with head bent forward, listened intently.

" Nunc, don't you hear something ? " she whispered, terror-stricken.

Instantly Brown was deadly still, listening with that keen suspense which only a man feels whose liberty and life are at the mercy of a sound.

There was the noise as of a delicate tampering with the metal about the knob of the inner door which Brown had locked,—a noise which would have been unheard in the day-time, but which the dead midnight caught.

There was only time to act. With the quickness of a man to whom self-possession in danger has become a second nature, he sprang to the low window, tore it open, and without another word or look, leaped out into the midnight darkness, and ran, ran for dear life, with the horror at heart of perhaps running into the very hands of his pursuers.

The child, with quick instinct, shut the betraying window, and then, with the hot tears welling up into her eyes, shrank back into a dim corner, and waited till the door opened, and by the flash of a lantern and the flaring light of the candle, she saw three men enter, one of whom carried a revolver in his hand. This last man was a policeman, and he stepped in with a certain business-like air which was in fine contrast to the lagging steps of the men behind him, in whom the child instantly recognized the nautical loafer of the morning, and the individual who had said he was a doctor and a friend.

"Where's Brown?" and the policeman peered about, his lantern in one hand and the revolver in the other.

"This is Brown's Retreat with a vengeance," said the nautical gentleman, while the friendly individual growled out some strong language about meddling fools.

Without a knowledge of what would happen, with the glitter of the ugly looking pistol in her eyes, but with a world of gratitude in her heart, poor Popsy crept out of her corner, and said humbly and pleadingly, " Please, sir, I'm Brown!"

.   .   .   .

Of course they tried to ferret him out, but the humorous rogue did actually escape on the Mary Ann, bound for the East Indies, with the briskest kind of a breeze to push her along.

I had a feeling of sympathy with Brown all the time, for he had a vein of humor in him ; and a vein of humor is an excellent point in a man, even if two hundred and fifty dollars are offered as a reward for his capture as a common thief.

He was, to be sure, a bit fool-hardy, in his appreciation of a joke, for in his leisure he nailed up another deal-board with "Brown's Retreat" upon it at the head of his bunk, to the curiosity of the seamen. Only one understood the delicate innuendo, and that was the good Samaritan, Jim.

As his country's prisons were never again honored by his presence, as nothing was heard of his death, as mysterious presents are continually reaching Popsy, who has grown to be a true and noble-hearted girl just as Jim's sister was before her, it is pleasant to think that the wretched criminal found some spot on earth where be prospered ; where he could have his little joke without being locked up ; where preachers say what they mean, and human nature is to be trusted.

The name of Brown is not uncommon. Should you know a middle aged man of that name, with a misty past and a taste for a joke, you might ask him if he ever heard of Brown's Retreat.

I.

DEACON NYMPHUS PROUTY, being tempted by Satan, succumbed. His fellow-deacons, on hearing of it, were surprised that Heaven did not strike him dead then and there. At present, however, he had just been in Satan's claws, and he was returning home to Timlik, travel-stained and tired.

It was a rather hilly road, and as the Deacon looked down from the summit he saw in the valley below the sharp point of a church steeple, at sight of which he paused, and, resting on his stick, chuckled sinfully.

"I've ben a professin' Christian more'n fifty years," he thought, wagging his old head, "an' I guess the Lord won't give me over for one little backslide. The ways of sin air pleasant,—I might a'most say that they air pleasanter than the ways o' righteousness." Here he shook his head at the steeple. . "Lor', Lor'," he exclaimed in sudden alarm; "the Devil's very nigh on to you, Nymphus!"

The shadows were creeping like ghosts out of the fringe of woodland on one side of the road. On the other, high on a ragged bank, stood a tumble-down house of two rooms, whose gray, decaying sides were half hidden by a disorderly tangle of grape-vines. The rank grass grew to the sunken threshold, where by the open door sat a cat which looked at the old man with wicked, indifferent eyes.

Of all the dreary places it was the dreariest.

A slim, tall girl, with a sallow face and unsmiling gray eyes, came to the door, upset the cat, and in turn moodily watched the Deacon trudging nearer. One bright star trembled in the East, and in the sparse farm houses the lights began to twinkle like an echo of sight from the stars above. The clamorous chirp of the crickets beat the air, emphasizing the stillness. Then there broke through the silence the quick, unsteady clangor of a thin-toned bell.

The Deacon glanced at the girl in the door-way.

" Be you goin' to meetin', Odelia," he asked, standing still.

She nodded. " P'r'aps you don't know that I ain't ben 'round here since mornin' ? "

" Haven't you ? "

" I guess ef I wanted to, I could tell you somethin' that 'd kinder s'rprise you, Odelia Blynn."

" Well ? "

" You come 'long down here."

She came unwillingly down the footpath trodden through the grass, while the cat followed her with elevated tail. The Deacon grasped her wrist and putting up one horny hand as a wall, whispered, " I've ben to the circus, Odelia Blynn."

For a moment she stared at him, then slowly a faint smile crept over her unsmiling face.

" I've ben a professin' Christian more'n fifty years," the Deacon continued, " and the Devil ain't had no hold on me at all, for I ain't gev him no chance. But I says to myself ' 'Tain't no glory to the Lord, Nymphus, ef you don't never backslide, cos' you keep outer the ways of sin. So you jest git into 'em, an' then see what Satan 'll do !' an' so I did, and it's six miles there and six miles back, an' I'm kinder shaky in my legs."

" Deacon Prouty, what did you see ? " There was

such a feverish light in Odelia's eyes, her lank, lithe body quivered in the faded print gown she wore, so that even the Deacon was startled.

"I never see you like this before, Odelia."

"Tell me!" she cried, and she shook the aged man.

"That ain't the way to git information out of me," he retorted, and turned away.

"I'm sorry—there!" she cried impatiently. "Now sit down and tell."

The Deacon relented, for he yearned for sympathy; so they sat down on a flat rock by the road and Odelia listened to the Deacon's story.

"Music and lights, and folks, and women smiling and riding on horses, and dancing," she repeated slowly as he concluded.

"The women-folks was that bewtiful," he added, with a grin.

Odelia did not heed him. She started to her feet in a frenzy of defiance. "Wouldn't I just like to belong to a circus! Don't I just wish I could run away, and be like one of them women that ride on horses and laugh and dance and hear music and see sights!"

"Lord hev mercy on you, you're out of your senses," the Deacon remonstrated, and then added with pleasing frankness, "Besides you really ain't good lookin' enough for that. Them women-folks they was plump an' smiling, an' they had red cheeks and sech bright eyes. Now you know you're nothin' but a yellow slip of a critter and you looks mostly cross an' no ways bewtiful that I can see. So you'd best stay here, for them ways ain't your ways."

The momentary excitement had passed and Odelia hung her head, and the light faded out of her eyes.

"It ain't right of the Lord to make some women like them and some like me."

The Deacon coughed in expostulation just as the second meeting-bell rang.

"Guess you'd best keep goin' to meetin' pretty reg'lar, Odelia, you take easy to the ways o' sin; you'd best go and git supported."

"I'm going," she answered moodily, and climbed the narrow path to the house to fetch her hood, and then went down the road to the church in the hollow.

II.

LIFE was not long enough to call it properly Timberlake, so it was called "Timlik," with a nasal twang.

The Timberlake lay in the heart of the valley, and on summer evenings when the low, pine-covered hills stood clear against a red-gold sky, then the Timberlake was transformed into a sheet of molten gold, while, amid the rushes, reeds and grasses along its banks, the bull-frogs uttered their solitary note, like the rough stroke of a bow across a bass-fiddle.

Poverty and thrift were characteristic of Timlik, which found its only relaxation in the whitewashed meeting-house with the pointed steeple.

Behind the church stood a weather-beaten shed where the farmers hitched their horses of a Sunday, and here the poor beasts shivered through the bitter winter weather. Timlik was easy about its horses, and so they were an asthmatic breed, lean in the flanks, rough of hide and of short life.

A varied array of vehicles loomed up in the dusk as Odelia approached, and a familiar hymn, dragging its weary length, greeted her as she entered the vestry. It was a low-studded room, lighted by dull kerosene lamps, and the whitewashed walls were decorated with mottoes of a godly nature, that hung askew.

The minister sat on the low platform, facing his people ; he was a young man with a hectic flush on his cheeks, and he looked tired,—but that was characteristic of the congregation. Odelia was surprised to see a stranger beside the minister, for strangers were very rare.

She sat down on a bench, and for the first time she was hardly conscious of either the hymn or the prayer. She was at war with herself, and she looked up with a conscience-stricken, flushed face when the minister said wearily : "We have among us a great sinner." Would he command her to rise and confess her wickedness?

"Let us pray for him," he added. A series of energetic groans betrayed the sinner behind her, and when Odelia ventured to look back, she discovered Deacon Prouty mopping his face with a red and yellow handkerchief.

"I'm a great sinner," he moaned, rocking to and fro. " I've ben to the Devil jest about straight."

"The Lord hev mercy on you, Nymphus," cried a sympathizing worshiper.

"Deacon Prouty, we will hear you later on," interposed the minister. "At present we are to listen to the Rev. Mr. Tourtelot, missionary to the Kalkamazu Islands, who hopes to interest you in the cause."

It is not our purpose to give Mr. Tourtelot's address. He had a certain rough, picturesque eloquence unknown to Timlik. He rejoiced in his work, and there was something contagious in the enthusiasm with which he demanded aid and workers. "We want men and women who will give their lives to the cause, who will go to that far-off world and carry the gospel of Christ Jesus to the unregenerate, who are living and dying and lost, ignorant of the blessed tidings of Salvation. Do your duty, Christian men and women, or live with the anguish of duties unfulfilled."

Timlik dispersed in a glow of ardor, and the Deacons remained to inquire into the backsliding of their erring brother. They were five gaunt and bony men, with long beards and smoothly shaven upper lips. Their hair they wore rather long and their broadcloth garments were gray in the seams; an air of acute solemnity struck a chill to the soul of Nymphus Prouty. He also regretted that Deacon Fell seemed to be the ruling spirit, for he had sold an ancient mare to that brother only a few days before, which was not all that Deacon Fell's fondest hopes had painted.

"He's a-goin' for me jest on that account," the aged man reflected, "but it ain't being a good Christian."

The minister opened the proceedings with another prayer in which he confided the erring sinner to the Lord, who would punish him as He should see fit, to which the brethren assented with groans more forcible than polite.

Then the minister looked solemnly at him. "Brother Prouty, we have heard awful accounts of you. You're on your way to hell! How dare you, an old man on the very brink of the grave?"

"Some one's ben a-tellin' stories about me," said the culprit, and his eyes rested on Deacon Fell. He was an emaciated individual, and his gray beard was tinged with tobacco juice, while a straggling halo of yellow-gray hair escaped from underneath the brown wig which he had inherited from his grandfather.

"Guess I know who's ben tellin'," and the Deacon blew a blast on his bandanna handkerchief.

"Wal', it was me, brother Nymphus," Deacon Fell retorted. "But an' old man who sells a spavined mare one week an' goes to the circus " (an awful groan corroborated this statement) "the next, guess it's about time to snatch him as a brand from the burning."

A grin illuminated Deacon Prouty's face, and he rocked to and fro in noiseless glee.

"Lord hev mercy on his sinful soul, he ain't a mite sorry."

"I move," added a righteous man with unrighteous curiosity, "that he tell us what he saw at the—place of sin."

A murmur of approbation hailed this suggestion. They stared at him, and the young minister's face was more than usually flushed.

"I've ben an' seen the Devil's works," the sinner began, boastfully. "I've ben walkin' right in the jaws of hell."

"That you hev, Nymphus, that you hev."

"An' its a bewtiful place." There was a dramatic pause and the minister sighed.

"I'm an old man, more'n seventy years old, an' I've walked in the paths o' righteousness all my days," (there was a doubting sniff from Deacon Fell which the ancient man ignored,) "an' jest when I'm ripe for glory, Satan comes 'long an', says he, no, Nymphus, not yet, for, says he, there's a circus at East Timlik. And, brethren, my soul's ben a-hankerin' for a circus or some such worldly sight, these fifty years or more. An' I jest giv' in to Satan at half past six this morning. So I walks to East Timlik six miles, an' six miles back, a pretty good stretch for an old man's legs."

"What did you see, Deacon?" a brother asked, with some impatience.

"I see lots o' wild beasts," the Deacon began, with a sense of his new importance. "There was a lion a-roarin' fit to split, and there was a sarpint jest the pattern of Mis' Pinsey's best Sunday-go-to-meetin' calliker. There was a tiger that kind'er ups when he sees me, so I pokes him with my stick. There was a elephant a-dancin' tew music—O Lor' there was lots!" Here the old gentleman paused.

"Is that all, Nymphus?"

"No, 'tain't quite all, brother Fell. I see men-folks a-standin' on their heads an' a-ridin' on hosses, an' a-playin' on instrewments." Here he paused again.

"Deacon Prouty, did you see anything else?" the young minister asked.

"I see," the Deacon replied in a hollow voice, "I see women-folks, too." The assembly groaned.

"I see women-folks, too," the ancient sinner repeated, "an' they was mighty han'some lookin'."

The assembly groaned again.

The minister cleared his throat. "Well?" he said.

"I seen them ride hosses a-standin' on their heads an' on their tails, an' smilin' all 'round. They jumped through paper hoops a-burnin', an' all tew music. An' their cheeks was that red, an' their eyes was a-sparklin', an' they'd on sech clothes. I never see sech clothes before in all my born days! White they was, an' a-glitterin' behind an' a-glitterin' before, an'—wal',' here he paused bashfully. "They wa'n't special long either ways."

Another groan greeted this description, and the minister broke in, harshly.

"That's enough, Nymphus Prouty, you've been into the fire of hell."

"I ain't a man for talkin'," the sinner remarked as he spread his coat-tails and sat down. "I will say that I've ben led away by Satan, but," he grinned defiance, "gracious, I ain't sorry. I'm a pretty old man an' whatever you do agen me 'twon't be for long."

So was Timlik disgraced. It had boasted of superior sanctity to the neighboring villages and now it

was under an eclipse. So it came to pass that Tim·
lik was on the lookout for symptoms of exalted piety
which should cause the stain of Deacon Prouty's
backsliding to be forgotten.

III.

MRS. BLYNN was of no account in Timlik. This
poor opinion began when Joshua Blynn brought
her home as a bride, a small, washed-out slip of a girl
with a conciliatory giggle, which displayed her pink
gums. Timlik resented the giggle, and being itself
of a sober nature, referred all Mrs. Blynn's misfortunes
to those days when she laughed too much ; and her
punishment was sufficient, for she lost her husband
and five children, and was turned out of her farm, after
it had gone to rack and ruin.

Now she was a withered old woman with faded
eyes, and white hair like a thin layer of cotton wool,
and even the ghost of the old smile had vanished.
She earned a pittance braiding rough straw hats, such
as are worn by farmers, and, as people did not speak
to her much, she muttered to herself a good deal, and
stared into the dim woods over the way, where the
white birches had a wind-blown tilt towards the road,
as if they were listening.

From early spring until late autumn she sat by the
open door working monotonously. It is difficult to
conquer the popular opinion that you are of no account, especially in a small place, and Mrs. Blynn re-
signed herself to the inevitable, early in her career.
Even Odelia long ago agreed with Timlik, with a bitter resentment against her mother. Though they
were miserably poor, the unwritten laws of Timlik declared certain methods of earning a living to be un-

genteel, and to hire out as a servant was the crown and summit of humiliation.

So Odelia, having exhausted the village school, employed the rest of the time in doing nothing in particular. Timlik was of the opinion that Odelia was "mighty proud," and it was considered greatly to her credit—why, no one knew.

"Things ain't ben as they'd oughter with Odelia, her mother bein' of no account," was the general verdict on her career.

So Odelia did nothing, but she went to all the church meetings, and this had been her life, to the day when she heard about the circus and listened to the missionary from Kalkamazu. She left the meeting in a state of mental dizziness. Imagination was not a faculty much cultivated in Timlik, and there was to her a pain in the birth-throe of unsuspected fancies. The familiar road was hateful, and the low hills, melting into the darkness, suffocated her. So she reached home, and opened the door into the dark room and lighted the lamp that stood on the table covered with a meagre supper. It was a sad place, and the dull green walls seemed to absorb and make sickly the light. Bits of plaster had dropped out of the low ceiling, and the ragged mats on the bare floor were a perpetual trap for the unwary. In a rocking chair by the stove sat Mrs. Blynn. On her way to fetch a mug of water out of the supply-pail, Odelia paused and looked at her mother, whose head was thrown back while her hands hung lifelessly by her side.

"Mother!" the sharp impatient young voice startled the sleeper, and she awoke in a daze.

"What's the matter," she asked, struggling with sleep.

"I was frightened! You looked as if—as if you

were dead," Odelia replied, with frightened resentment.

"An' you was really frightened 'bout me, Delia?"

The girl nodded, and sat down and ate her bread and butter in silence.

"Did you taste the honey, Delia? I bought it for you. I had a few cents saved and I thought you'd like it."

"Yes, it's nice," she replied, absently, while her mother began to wash the few dishes, quite as a matter of course.

"An' so you was frightened for me, Delia," she repeated, reverting to this unaccustomed touch of feeling. Then she sat down in her old place and took up her work. "It's a hard life for you, child. Sometimes I think it 'ud be better for you if I was dead and gone, and then I think I'm better'n none."

The clock over the stove ticked noisily in the silence.

"I don't know what you'll do when I'm gone, Delia, 'cept go out to service, on'y you're so dreadful proud."

Odelia looked at her mother a moment, and then she spoke in a low voice:

"I want to go away as a missionary, mother."

"Delia, you're not goin' to leave me, you're not goin' to leave me, child!" and the old woman dragged herself forward, and laid her hand on the girl's knees. "I've lost all in this cruel world, don't you leave me, too, Delia."

"I shall go mad if I stay here, mother. There's nothing for me to do. I'm wasting my life away. To-night I found out my duty: it's to go out into the world and to bring the Gospel to heathen men and women. The missionary said to-night that they wanted workers in the field who'd give their lives to the cause. And as I came home I felt, all of a sudden, that Jesus wants me out there, and so I must go at his call!" The old woman rubbed her hands together and at last spoke. "Wait till I'm dead, Odelia, wait till I'm dead," and she threw herself forward and broke into sobs.

IV.

TIMLIK always stood in an attitude of condescending approval to self sacrifice. It was in a spirit of stunned wonder that it heard of Odelia Blynn's intention to go out as missionary to the Kalkamazu Islands, those islands which could only be reached by way of Cape Horn. The natives were degraded and savage, wild beasts and earthquakes abounded, and mail facilities were limited to letters once a year.

Timlik rejoiced over these facts, and Odelia rose to an extraordinary height of popularity; even Mrs. Blynn's being of no account was temporarily forgotten.

Deacon Fell came himself to inquire into the matter one winter day, and for the first time in twenty years he again crossed the threshold. Mrs. Blynn looked up in an apathetic way as the Deacon's sharp red nose was thrust in at the open door. A shaft of sunlight lay across the bare floor and the cat basked in its rays, and Odelia stood at the window with an eloquent protest in her slim, flat back.

She turned, and both women stared at the Deacon, who calmly sat down, opened a singular garment of a moth eaten buffalo hide, and proceeded to uncoil several yards of comforter from his neck. Then with one hand on each knee and his sharp face bent

forward, he said, "Wal', Odelia, air you truly a-goin'
off missionarying to the heathen?   Now, do tell."

Mrs. Blynn paused in her work as Odelia answered,
shortly, "I want to go, I'm dying to."

"Then why don't you?" asked the Deacon.

"Mother won't let me."

Deacon Fell drew himself up and his eyebrows
rose in righteous astonishment.

"Do you mean to say, ma'am, that you air standin'
in the way of your gal's salvation?"

"She's a-goin' to wait till I'm dead."

The Deacon stared at her, and Odelia's eyes filled
with angry tears.

"The minister wrote to the Board of Foreign Missions, and they said that I was to go to the Islands
as soon as they'd hear of others going the same way.
And now, when I thought it settled, mother won't
let me go."

"Wait till I'm dead, Delia,—you're dreadful im
patient."

"Dead!" the Deacon cried in virtuous indignation,
"it's jest them no account folks that live forever."

It was a remark in the nature of a soliloquy and
perhaps he did not intend Mrs. Blynn to hear.   She
paused in her work and looked at him.

"Do you know what you air doin'," he asked,
frowning," you're keepin' Odelia from doin' her duty."

"Am I?"

Then Odelia turned upon them, her sallow face all
aglow.

"That's the way she goes on, and I can't stand
it!   Why won't she let me do my duty?   You'll
make a wicked woman of me yet, mother," and without another word she ran out of the house.

The Deacon felt it was time for a serious word.

"Mis' Blynn," he begun, not unkindly, "you jest
be a reasonable woman and let her go.   Ef the Lord

has set her that work to do, it ain't for you to keep her here. It'll be an awful disappointment for Timlik ef she don't go. Timlik's heart is jest set on it and we mean to do the han'some thing by her. Now what'll become of her if you air took? She'll have to go out to service, an' you know yourself she's proud, dreadful proud."

"An' ain't she got no work to do here?"

The Deacon resented the interruption.

"No," he retorted.

The old woman rose slowly and pointed to the door. "You hard man," she said, "leave this house. When you come to die one day, all alone in the great, wide world, an' your children far away, think of me, Deacon Fell, think of me."

"Gracious sakes," the Deacon began pettishly, but there was something in that poor old face he could not resist, and he slunk out of the house, dragging a yard or two of dingy comforter behind him.

V.

IN the meantime Timlik rejoiced over Odelia Blynn. The farmers' wives sent her presents and invited her to tea. Afterwards the neighbors dropped in, the best room with the "two ply" was thrown open, and here Odelia told all she knew about Kalkamazu, for the Board of Foreign Missions had sent her a box full of books on the subject. So great was her importance that she was borrowed by the neighboring churches to tell the story of her future duties, and the only disappointment was that she did not speak the Kalkamazu language.

And yet the old woman of no account remained obdurate. "When I'm dead she can go," she replied to all entreaties.

In those days the ladies of Timlik came often to the little house to soften Mrs. Blynn. They were gaunt, sallow women, with sunken cheeks and painfully perfect false teeth, and they coaxed and taunted her with high, shrill voices, to which she opposed an obstinate silence, braiding her hats and chewing. All the ladies chewed some favorite substance. One enthusiastic friend did one day warn Odelia that her mother was becoming mighty queer and light-headed like, and she wouldn't be surprised if she didn't last. "Then," said the good lady, tipping her calico sunbonnet forward, for the spring sun was rather warm, "then there'll be no one to keep you from doin' your duty by them poor, heathen critters, Odelia," and so departed.

The girl stood at the door, shading her eyes with her hand, when the minister came towards her from the village. It was a sunny spring day, with a chill in the air, the clouds chased across the steel-blue sky and the Timberlake in the distance was covered with white caps. A soft green mist lay on the woodlands as the promise of coming summer, and a brook among the trees across the way, tumbled and frolicked down its pebbly bed, with a fresh, sweet cadence.

"Walk up the hill with me, Odelia, I wish to speak to you," the minister called to her.

She went towards him and waited for him to speak, for he coughed, and his breath came short and fast.

"First, Odelia, the people want to see you in the vestry to-night ; they have a surprise in store for you."

After all, she was young and she longed for what is the birthright of youth, and so her heart beat fast and a vivid blush crept up to her face at the thought. But something more serious was to follow.

"I have also had a letter from the Board and you must decide within a day if you will go to Kalkamazu. It seems that a missionary and his family are to sail next week and they will be glad to take you along, but, as there is another applicant for the place, you see that you must make up your mind. Of course they ask you first, as you were the first to apply. Good-bye, Odelia, don't fail at the vestry to-night."

Odelia went on as if in a dream, conscious of only one thing: she must decide. Her whole soul was on fire with visions of heroic purpose and self sacrifice, and she loathed her commonplace life, with its emptiness and its poverty. "It is my only chance and if I lose it. I shall have to be a servant," she thought, in bitter revolt.

How far she had gone she did not know, when some one called to her. "Where be you goin', Odelia Blynn?" and as she turned, a shrill, unnatural voice shrieked, "To the devil, to the devil."

At the words her heart nearly stopped beating. It was a narrow, lonely path through a pine forest, in which, on a small clearing, stood a cottage of a couple of rooms, and before the threshold, wrapped in an old buffalo robe, sat Deacon Prouty, while in a tin cage, swinging from the branch of a tree, hung a parrot with a scarlet tail and a cruel beak.

This was the Deacon's home. At present he was under the severe displeasure of the church, which he bore with feelings regulated by rheumatism. If that was bad, the Deacon considered it wise to be submissive, but if he felt well, then he didn't mean to be bossed by any one. To-day the ancient man felt pretty smart and quite independent of religion.

"Was it he who spoke," Odelia asked, pointing to the parrot.

"Yes, an' wa'n't it 'propriate? I bought him in East Timlik for company. But he does swear awful. Wa'n't it 'propriate!" he repeated, blinking at the girl.

"I don't know what you mean."

"Lor', there ain't no folks here who'll tell you the truth, you poor critter! You think you're goin' to do your duty by them unbelieving heathens? Lor' sakes, you're goin' straight to the devil. Your duty is to home with your mother! You just leave heathen preachin' to other folks an' you stay here an' do for her. I ain't spoke to you since the day you wanted to go circusin'. I didn't tell on you or I guess they'd a-talked to you pretty smart. So I was s'rprised when I hear on you a-goin' to bring religion to them heathen sinners. Lor', Odelia, guess I know you! You're jest dyin' to git away from this place, that's all. There ain't no religion 'bout you or you'd stay an' do your duty to home."

Odelia stood before him as if rooted to the spot. "Them folks is a drivin' of you on; they don't care nothin' what becomes of you or your mother. Gracious, it's wickeder than the circus."

"Don't, don't, I won't hear you, you wicked man," she cried at last, struggling for breath, and without another word she disappeared down the path she had come.

"Where be you goin', Odelia?" the Deacon piped after her, regretting that he had driven away a chance visitor, but no one answered.

The blasphemous parrot plumed himself and bit the bars of his cage and looked amazingly like the Deacon. Then he whistled a hideous tune, to which the old sinner in the buffalo robe kept time with his head, with great zest and enjoyment.

VI.

THE early spring evening had crept on when Odelia returned home. It was too early for the lamps to be lighted in the scattered cottages, and it was too dark for serious work.

The ploughs lay idle in the long furrows of the fields, a few farm laborers trudged along the road homeward, and occasionally a characteristic Timlik steed harnessed to a loose country wagon, jolted past.

There was no sign of life about the little house as Odelia approached, and her own unrest made the silence seem more oppressive. The girl looked about her in vague surprise as she opened the door.

"You've ben late comin' home, Delia," said her mother.

"How nice you've fixed yourself up, haven't you, mother."

There was an expectant air of festivity in the poor place. The stove was newly blacked and the ragged mats had disappeared, and the supper stood on the table in the best holiday china on the best tablecloth. All trace of work was put aside as never before.

"How real nice you look, mother," Odelia repeated.

"I've finished my work," she answered, looking down at the idle hands in her lap.

"Why, mother, you've got on your wedding-dress," Odelia said, with a start.

"Yes, yes, my wedding-dress," and Mrs. Blynn smoothed it down gently. "I've ben very happy in it, Delia. I should like to have it on when I go, 'cos your father liked it. He might'n know me if 'twa'n't for that, for I'm a broken an' changed old woman."

"Don't speak so!" Odelia cried, with quick resentment; "it's putting on that old thing makes you."

"I ain't wore it since the year we was married," she went on, nevertheless. "I was nice enough lookin' then, an' Joshua liked it. Two shillings a yard, I paid for it, an' mother said I was crazy to put all that money in it for a day's wear,—but Joshua liked it," and she gazed down with faint pride at the antiquated gown, with its faded pink roses.

Suddenly she looked up and met Odelia's troubled eyes. "The minister's ben here an' gone, an' he spoke to me."

"And you'll let me go, mother," Odelia longed to cry, but something forced her to be silent.

"I told him what I told you all along. Now sit down an' hev your supper."

But Odelia could not eat, and every mouthful seemed to choke her. "She's coaxing me to stay," she thought, and pushed her plate away. "They want to see me at the Vestry to-night," she said at last, rising, "and guess I'd better go now."

At the door she turned at the faint sound of her name and a quivering, broken sob.

"Odelia!"

She went back to her mother's chair and looked silently down at her.

"Odelia, child, let me kiss you before you go." Involuntarily she knelt down and the white, trembling lips touched her cheek.

"I loved you more'n you thought I did; I jest couldn't live without you, child. There, go now."

The door closed and the soft spring breeze rustled faintly through the ghostly birches that leaned forward, listening, forever listening.

VII.

A SMALL boy with a red head was on the lookout for Odelia when she reached the church. It was a great day for Timlik, and the small boy welcomed her with shouts of rejoicing. Deacon Fell followed her in and gave her a considerate poke forward as she looked about bewildered. But the minister came towards her through the crowd and led her to the surprise, which was of a bulky nature and temporarily hidden under a cloth.

Then he held her trembling, cold hands and made a little speech. "The people of Timlik wish you to know how they rejoice in your devotion to the call of duty. They wish to show you that they appreciate your heroism in giving your life for a noble purpose. They desire to hold a place in your heart when you are far away, and they expect to be very proud of you, Odelia Blynn. In testimony of their love and esteem they beg you to accept this slight remembrance, with the hope that in the far distant land its tones may bring you comfort."

So speaking the minister whisked the cover from the surprise, which stood confessed in all its glory: it was a melodeon. The trifling circumstance that Odelia could not play did not concern Timlik, nor that as luggage it might be expensive transportation to Kalkamazu. Timlik had done itself credit and it groaned approval. Deacon Fell rubbed his hands for joy, for it was he who had bought the surprise in East Timlik and received a handsome commission.

As for Odelia, she bowed her head over the melodeon and wept for joy and ·pride. "You are too good," she sobbed, "and you know I mayn't perhaps go after all, for mother ain't willing."

"The Lord'll work a miracle for you, Odelia," said a sympathizing neighbor, "an' p'rhaps He'll move the obstacle out of your path."

"Anyhow, Odelia, you let us know to-morrow, sure," the minister added in conclusion.

Timlik was not foolishly gallant, so after supper all round the folks dispersed, and though it was quite late, no one felt that Odelia could not go home alone. She went swiftly up the familiar road. She had never before been so happy or so excited.

Suddenly a voice seemed to say, "Suppose she

won't let you go, even now?" "The Lord will work a miracle," she cried. "But if not?"

A flood of angry thoughts surged through her brain. "God forgive me," she exclaimed in sudden terror.

A ray of light streamed towards her through a crack in the green paper curtain. "Mother's up, still," she thought in some surprise, "or she's left the light burning for me." That, however, she had never done before.

"Perhaps mother's sick."

Her heart beat fast as she slowly opened the door; the clock ticked as usual, the lamp burned on the table and, the idea of being frightened!—there sat her mother asleep in her usual place. Yes, asleep. Her head rested in her hand and both were supported by the high back and the arm of the chair.

"Mother," Odelia called, but the quiet figure did not stir.

"Mother!" she repeated sharply and touched her shoulder. "I want to tell you about the pleasant evening, mother."

She looked at her one long, awful moment, and then with a sudden, terrible cry she sank down on the floor by her side.

"Mother, mother, speak to me, mother."

From between the worn dead hand and the worn dead cheek slipped an old glove, a man's glove. It fell and touched the girl's head as it lay in her mother's lap, and she started and shuddered at the light touch. "It was father's," she said, and shivered as with intense cold.

The cat slipped in at the open door and chased a slim flask about the floor, and at the sound Odelia awoke out of her stupor, and, as it dashed against her, mechanically she picked it up. It had contained laudanum such as is used by country folks for a variety of ills.

"The Lord will work a miracle and He'll remove the obstacle out of your path."

"I killed her!" Odelia cried.

.   .   .   .

At last, with wonderful strength, she lifted the slender figure and carried it to the bed in the other room, and laid the glove once more under the still face. She drove the cat out of the house, closed the door and went down to the village for help.

The doctor and minister came back with her.

"She took an overdose of laudanum," the doctor said, and then added with some hesitation, "I fear she's been in the habit of taking it for some time past."

As the minister was leaving he paused on the threshold. The faint streak of coming dawn broke in the east, and the stars were fading out of the sky. A song-sparrow thrilled the silence with a carol of joy, and in the distance an early cock crowed loud and long.

"Odelia," said the minister, "now you'll be ready to start next week, for there's nothing to prevent your doing your duty," he added, kindly.

"Duty," she repeated. Her lips were parched as if with fever. "That wasn't my duty. It ain't such as me ought to go."

He looked at her in surprise; he did not understand.

"Tell them I can't," she cried, in a passion of renunciation.

"You are doing wrong, Odelia."

He watched the struggle in her down-bent face. Then she spoke.

"It ain't wrong, it's right."

"How will you earn your living now that your mother's gone?" he asked, with cold disapproval.

She turned from him. Her voice was hard but there were tears in her eyes.

" I shall go out to service," she said.

Odelia closed the door and the minister walked down the road lost in thought, and in the east broke forth the glory of the morning.

THE HEART STORY OF MISS JACK.

I.

ONLY the rich and great ever went to the Pennock Shoals. There were a few cottages on the island where the more exclusive lived in fashionable and expensive discomfort; the rest were content with its single hotel.

Nobody ever did anything at the Pennock Shoals, but everybody was immensely respectable. Indeed, the Pennock amusement was to discover if any one failed to reach this supreme standard of respectability.

In this desirable summer resort Mrs. Pendexter owned a cottage. Rumor cruelly declared that this had helped to make the lamented Mr. Pendexter possible as a husband.

Mr. Beresford, strolling from the Pennock hotel across the lawn to Mrs. Pendexter's desirable cottage, saw before him, as he had seen for three weeks past, a queer little house perched on a rock, a flower-garden, that flaunted its gold and scarlet against the blue sky, and below, beyond the rocks of the island, the great sea, and in the distance white sails mirroring the sunlight.

Mr. Beresford was hardly conscious of all this beauty, but he would have felt its absence. The first time he had called on Mrs. Pendexter he was greeted, on entering the room, by a solitary occupant two feet high, with a small fat body squeezed in a red jersey; impertinence was betrayed in his turned-up nose, and cunning in his black eyes.

"What's 'oo here for?" this apparition demanded.

"I came to see your mother, my little man," young Beresford replied engagingly, trying to lay a friendly hand on the imp.

"I ain't a little man, I'se a boy. You go home; she don't like you; she said so to Jacky. I heard her, —I did," and young Adolphus Pendexter danced a dance of joy.

"O you bad boy!" a gentle, feminine voice cried; but the white hand that grasped the jersey from behind was firm, and Adolphus was carried out in disgrace.

"He tells the most dreadful lies," Mrs. Pendexter remarked composedly, sinking into her chair; "he's a Pendexter all over."

Mr. Beresford stroked his dark mustache, and pondered in some perplexity on the infant Pendexter, as he approached the cottage.

Mr. Robert Beresford had a certain charm for which he was not responsible,—it was inborn. He would look intently in your eyes, if you were a woman, and somehow you were sure you were all the world to him; at the same time you became suddenly conscious of any short-comings in your gown. If you were a man Mr. Beresford met you on the equality of common sense, and you respected him.

He went on his smiling, conquering way through the world till he met Mrs. Pendexter. For once his weapons failed him, and in his new earnestness Mr. Beresford even ceased to smile.

He had once solemnly vowed never to fall in love, at least never to marry a widow, especially a widow with a child. When he could so far separate his love for the fair sex in general to concentrate it on one individual in particular, it was always for a theoretical "young thing," whose mental and moral education he meant to complete. With human inconsistency he had not only fallen in love with a widow, but a widow with a dreadful child. Far from being a young thing, whose education was to be his care, she really made him, Robert Beresford, feel like a raw school-boy.

The afternoon sun swept through the low windows of Mrs. Pendexter's cottage, and came in, like Mr. Beresford, across the veranda.

The veranda was curtained by a tangle of delicate vines, that swayed in the sea-breeze, sweeping across the summer garden, with its blaze of flowers, and beyond their beauty lay the endless stretch of sea, glittering in the sun.   It also fell aross Mr. Virginius Chick.   Mr. Virginius Chick was an ancient ruin, whom Beresford hardly counted, for he seemed to bask, in a grandfatherly way, in Mrs. Pendexter's light.   Mr. Chick would never see seventy-five again ; he looked like a perambulating champagne bottle ; he had a wheeze, a red face, narrow forehead, and triple chin, and he was the embodiment of money. The sunlight fell across Mrs. Pendexter, a picture of summer elegance and languor, in a cloudy white gown, that rippled and fell about her, and at sight of this creation of white lace and coquettish knots of ribbon, Mr. Beresford started visibly.

Mrs. Pendexter was aware of the start, and a pink flush touched her delicate face.   There was an eager eloquence in Beresford's look, quite out of place in the presence of Mr. Chick.   To this glance Mrs. Pendexter opposed two dovelike eyes, full of innocence and entreaty, and so warded off a scene which would have been highly objectionable ; for Mr. Virginius Chick sat on the corner of the sofa, with a scarlet face, an agitated and asthmatic wheeze, and jealous eyes that were hardly grandfatherly.

Mrs. Pendexter did not carry her heart on her sleeve; indeed, it was rumored that the departed Pendexter had doubted the existence of this necessary organ. Yet he had no reason to complain, as Mrs. Pendexter mourned for him in garments that reflected great credit on his memory, and the greatest on her taste. Perhaps it was the exquisite decorum with which Mrs. Pendexter mourned for Mr. Pendexter that, for a moment, chilled Bob Beresford.

The very day before this one he had said to her, as she stood, a slender figure, clad in the gloomiest of crape, in her garden, amid the glory of nasturtiums, marigolds, and poppies that clung about her, "If you cared so little for him, why will you persist in wearing that dismal black and those ghastly long veils?"

"It is becoming; besides, it is my only fortress of defence," she answered, with some amusement. "I know five men who are only waiting to see me in colors, to honor me with a declaration. I am simply warding them off."

"May I ask if you do me the honor of counting me among them?" Mr. Beresford demanded, with amazing *sang-froid*.

"Do you really think me guilty of such presumption?" and she turned to pass up the narrow path.

"Stay," he cried, with forced composure. "If I ever see you wear a dress of another color than black, it will be a sign of capitulation to some one?"

For a moment she was silent, standing with her graceful head down-bent over the great bunch of poppies she held, quite aware of the charming picture she made; then she looked up: "I shall have been conquered," she answered with a smile, as she passed into the house.

Mr. Beresford, standing beside Mrs. Pendexter's chair, thought of that scene of yesterday, as his eager eyes rested on her white laces and embroideries. He hardly looked torn by hope and fear and jealousy, as he stood before her, hat in hand ; and yet he was so.

Perhaps Mrs. Pendexter recognized an emotion in his intent gaze that needed a safety-valve. " I think," she said, dexterously applying the valve, "I think that as Miss Jack cannot have been baked in the Pennock Ovens, she must have been drowned there. Mr. Beresford, pray go and see, and please bring her back alive. Miss Jack is the first governess "—and Mrs. Pendexter turned to Mr. Chick with this explanation—"who has staid with Adolphus more than a week. Johnny took Adolphus and Miss Jack out rowing this noon, and they left her in the Ovens to cool, and forgot all about her."

" So you insist on making a hero of me ? " Beresford asked, lingering.

" I can do many things," Mrs. Pendexter answered, with a fine smile, " but I am not capable of that."

Mr. Beresford turned away with a feeling of impotent passion that wrecked on her repose. She was about his own age, and yet she was vastly older. He rebelled against her, protested against her, and was unaffectedly miserable unless he sat in a certain wicker chair, in that charming room, watching her delicate face, and even willing (Heaven help him !) to make a truce for her sake with young Adolphus, who at the age of five seemed to possess a fund of infantile wickedness sufficient for fifty.

Beresford was hardly blind, and he called himself a confounded fool for being so at the mercy of a woman. Yet, as he stepped into Mrs. Pendexter's flower-garden, he knew that all his happiness was bound up in the mystery of a snow-white gown.

Instead of receiving an explanation he was sent to the Pennock Ovens to rescue Miss Jack. Miss Jack! What did he care for Miss Jack?

At the thought he stumbled against another individual who did not care for Miss Jack. It was Adolphus, rolling in the gravel.

The infant made a hideous face at Beresford, turned a somersault, leaped to his feet, and, placing himself in a sparring attitude towards the visitor, cried, with undisguised joy: "Jack's drowned! Johnny 'n me left her in the cave a-purpose."

Yes, poor Beresford would even take this imp into the bargain, if a certain woman would only—

He tried to pass, with a smile on his face, expressive of artificial pleasure at sight of young Adolphus, when he heard the same shrill voice shriek after him:—

"Chick says you want to be my pa; you sha'n't be my pa! you sha'n't!"

"Confound Chick's impertinence!" Beresford thought, in a white rage; yet what could he say? He did not stop to argue with Adolphus. Perhaps his retreat was ignominious. "It may yet be my privilege," he reflected, with grim satisfaction, "to thrash the Pendexter character out of that boy."

Five minutes later Mrs. Pendexter, who had trailed her laces into the garden, could see the strong, steady stroke of his oars as Beresford rowed away from the wharf to the "Ovens." The "Pennock Ovens" were two caves, cut off from the island at high tide; at low tide they were pleasant loitering-places; but they were dangerous when the water rose in their depths with a sweep and roar that were deafening.

Mrs. Pendexter followed the boat with absent eyes, and she lifted them in a meditative way to Mr. Chick, who had followed her.

"Youth," Mr. Chick remarked, as if in answer to

some unasked question, and lifting his white eyebrows high on his scarlet forehead,—"youth is desirable, but it is fleeting; more fleeting," he added,
impressively, "than"—"money." Mrs. Pendexter
finished the sentence with a gracious smile, and
stooped to pick a pansy for Mr. Chick's buttonhole.

II.

THE truth is that Bob Beresford really did save
Miss Jack's life. Miss Jack had retreated into
the cave before the Alantic Ocean, and was perched
on a rock over which the water was already dashing
and surging, when Bob swam in,—it was the only way
in which he could reach her.

Miss Jack prided herself on her presence of mind,
so she did not faint till Bob, having rescued her, and
lifted her into his boat, she could do so and not be
in the way.

Mr. Beresford was far from feeling like a hero;
he had, indeed, an uneasy sense that between them
they cut a ridiculous figure. Being occupied with
rowing he could only look helplessly at Miss Jack's
forlorn figure in the bottom of the boat. He had a
not very poetic vision of a black alpaca gown, that
shed a stream of water over a scant balmoral skirt,
and two congress gaiters. Miss Jack's black hat
had slipped to the back of her head, and a tiny
stream of blackened water was trickling down her
face. It was either this reviving fluid or Mr. Beresford's absently intent gaze that acted as restorer, for
life seemed suddenly to come back to her, and, with
a gasp, Miss Jack sat bolt upright.

She glanced up and down and sideways, and then
she looked at Mr. Beresford. At sight of his intent,
handsome face, Miss Jack drew her alpaca skirt

over her congress gaiters and blushed ; it was her first acknowledgment of feminine weakness.

"You have saved my life, sir," she said with surprising stiffness ; but there was a curious trembling in her hands as they smoothed her drenched skirts.

"It really was nothing," Mr. Beresford hastened to reply, filled with a vague alarm that this young person might bore him with gratitude. "I only hope that you will not take cold. Here we are at the wharf. Take care, Miss Jack. Let me help you up the steps. By George ! the inhabitants have turned out *en masse.*"

Sure enough the little wharf was full of gayly dressed people, who made way for the dripping hero and heroine to pass, and, while they stared at them to their hearts' content, made audible and uncomplimentary remarks. Popular curiosity but not popular enthusiasm was aroused ; the heroine was only Miss Jack, young Adolphus's governess, and young Adolphus took it very ill indeed, that she had not chosen to be drowned. Even Beresford felt how different it would have been had he had the inexpressible bliss of rescuing Mrs. Pendexter from a watery grave. He would not have walked silently beside her, only intent to get her off his hands. Ah, no !

They reached Mrs. Pendexter's flower-garden and Beresford opened the gate.

"I am obliged to you, sir," Miss Jack began, with a gasp, looking with painful shyness into his politely attentive face.

"I—I am sorry that you got so wet only for me," she continued, with humility. "I am afraid that your clothes are quite ruined ;" and she looked disconsolately at Mr. Beresford's dripping garments. "Would you let me "—

"What ?" Beresford demanded with chilling courtesy.

"Oh, dear me! nothing!" Miss Jack cried in terror, clutched her bedraggled skirts, and fled into the house.

What indeed had she rashly wished to offer this elegant man?

"I couldn't afford to buy him a new suit of clothes," she confessed to herself (Miss Jack was from Maine, and painfully conscientious), "but I did want to offer to have them cleansed. I didn't dare, though."

.   .   .   .

Mrs. Pendexter had a surface geniality, which was skin deep. That peculiar virtue came out in full strength as Miss Jack, that same evening, combed out, as usual, Mrs. Pendexter's wavy brown hair.

Mrs. Pendexter examined in the mirror before her, with silent amusement, the two figures reflected. Her own rounded form, half hidden, half revealed by the laces and embroideries of her loose wrapper, while the dusky hair falling over her shoulders shadowed her lovely face. In curious contrast this to the awkward and angular figure behind her.

For the first time in her twenty-eight years of life Miss Jack was so weak as to be absent-minded. Miss Jack was not an object of pity,—far from it,—she was a person who carried about with her a private pedestal, upon which she stood, not to be worshiped, but to see over people's heads. To-day she had ascended this height to judge of Mr. Beresford, and failed. For the first time Miss Jack looked up to some one.

It would have petrified Mrs. Pendexter to know that Miss Jack, whom she scorned as an ill-dressed woman, should stand towards her in an attitude of criticism as harsh as the ancient Puritan employed towards the dreaded Scarlet Woman.

Miss Jack came from Maine, as we have said, and

there was, as it were, an icy precipitate in her atmosphere, oddly in harmony with her angular move-
ments, the puritanic rigidity of her mind, and her
sallow face, from which the rather sparse sandy hair
was drawn back with uncompromising harshness.

Miss Jack was not without an aim in life; she
hoped some day to be sent to a far-off country, there
to teach those religious precepts inculcated in the
stern white meetinghouse of her native village, where
once in a while a religious frenzy shook the people
out of the vegetating quiet of their lives. If the
subject of marriage had ever entered Miss Jack's
mind it was not in connection with love, but simply
as a greater convenience in the missionary enterprise.
Love she considered as a kind of insanity, while
feminine graces were the invention of one in whom
she firmly believed.

"What are you thinking of, Miss Jack?" Mrs.
Pendexter demanded, suddenly, looking at the reflected face.

Miss Jack started, gave a sharp pull at Mrs. Pendexter's hair, dropped the ivory brush, and remained
silent.

What if that frivolous woman could look into her
soul! She shuddered as one who has been detected
in some crime, remembering those thoughts, and a
traitorous glow swept across her face. In her sinful
mind she had lived over once more the scenes of
the afternoon. Once more she, Miss Jack, felt herself upborne through the surging water by the strong
arms of a man, and against her heart she again felt
the beating of his. All this as she stood impassible
behind Mrs. Pendexter's chair.

"Miss Jack, have you ever been in love?" her tor-
mentor asked.

"No," Miss Jack whispered more than said, in a
daze of astonishment at herself. Yesterday she

would have resented so impertinent a question, would
have mounted her pedestal and discoursed, yea, even
unto Mrs. Pendexter.

"You have had quite a romance to-day," that lady
said, rising, and turning her surface geniality in a
cool glow on Miss Jack. "Romances often have a
pleasant ending," she concluded, and smiled Miss
Jack out of the room with a queer smile.

"To think that piece of wood is a woman. It
must be very convenient to have no feeling," Mrs.
Pendexter pondered, as one overburdened with too
much. She paused to listen, for the house door below was softly opened. It was only Miss Jack, who
had stepped on the deserted veranda. The moonlight lay across the sea over which she had rowed
that afternoon; and Miss Jack, rowing once more
over the sea in her thoughts, sighed wearily. It
marked an era in her life.

What had Mrs. Pendexter meant by romance and
love? They were not for her. And yet, why not?
she asked herself, with something like resentment
against Fate. Was she not a woman? Had she not
a heart to love? She was a better woman than that
frivolous creature upstairs. She was more intelli-
gent; and yet—

She looked down with some scorn at the scant
folds of her ill-fitting gown. That happiness should
hang on the fit of a gown!

"If I were as well dressed as Mrs. Pendexter I
could make him like me," she concluded, with feminine injustice. Because she saw through Mrs. Pendexter's wiles and falsities, Miss Jack only gave her
credit for fine gowns. Miss Jack went upstairs, and
by the light of a candle she examined her scanty
wardrobe; and that night—Heaven save her weakness!—Miss Jack sacrificed her conscience to vanity,
and put her scanty front locks in curl-papers.

III.

EVERY morning Miss Jack and Adolphus battled with the alphabet and the nine figures. From these daily scenes of warfare Miss Jack retired with an unbecoming flush on her tired face, while the button of her linen collar invariably worked round to her right ear in these educational struggles.

The morning after her rescue Adolphus looked up at her with a glance which made Miss Jack tremble.

"What's those?" he demanded peremptorily, pointing to a couple of paper bunches on Miss Jack's forehead.

"It's—it's nothing!" and Miss Jack surreptitiously removed the curl-papers.

"How funny you look!" young Adolphus then remarked, frankly.

Something that blurred her gaze rose to Miss Jack's eyes, and she coughed to clear her throat.

What if Mr. Beresford should think she looked funny! Listening to the thrilling narrative of A B C, she tried to picture to herself what change combing out would make in her appearance.

That afternoon Miss Jack came down in Mrs. Pendexter's parlor with an odd, sparse fuzz about her face, and at her throat was pinned an awkward knot of ribbon, that seemed to make her a trifle plainer than before.

Mr. Chick sat in his usual corner, wheezing. Mrs. Pendexter, in another white gown, the very summit and crown of expensive simplicity, raised her eyebrows with languid surprise at Miss Jack's transformation.

"Pray sit down, Miss Jack," she said, stifling a yawn, and tired to death of Mr. Chick's society.

Miss Jack, who had never been so honored before,

sat stiffly down on the stiffest chair in the room, which stood by the open door, and, half hidden by a screen, she added her silence to that other silence to such good purpose that Mr. Virginius Chick rose to his gouty feet and took his departure.

Mrs. Pendexter settled herself more easily in her low chair, and became interested in a book whose binding was in harmony with her dress. Presently the garden-gate swung open, and some one strolled up the garden-walk, crossed the veranda, and stood in the doorway. It was Mr. Beresford. He looked around the screen and became aware of Miss Jack.

"You, Miss Jack? How do you do?"

A delicious thrill crept up Miss Jack's spine, and her heart beat very fast. He absolutely looked down into her face as he looked in the faces of other women. For even she, Miss Jack, knew his ways! Perhaps, she thought wildly, perhaps she did look nice after all, and the little fuzz and the little bow were not without success.

"Now he will go," she thought, with all her soul in her eyes and a trembling of her pale lips. "He will go to that other woman, who is but a form for fineries and who has neither heart nor soul."

So thought Miss Jack while Beresford still spoke to her,—spoke to her with wonderful earnestness, laying aside the artificial homage that characterized his manner to women. But in her pain and joy she did not hear a word he uttered.

Still Mr. Beresford did not go. She heard instead the delicate rustle of a gown, there was the faintest suggestion of passing violets, and Mrs. Pendexter had left the room. Miss Jack was alone with the man who, like a modern god, had awakened in her soul the woman.

She sat before him with her thin hands clasped

cruelly, and with down-bent face.   No, she could not trust herself to gaze into those deep, gray eyes.

"Do you know, Miss Jack, how I have watched you?" Beresford broke the silence.

"No."   Miss Jack's lips formed the word, but her voice failed her.

Watched her?   What could he mean?   What possible interest could he have in watching her?

. Mr. Beresford drew a chair up, and sitting down, looked quietly into her face.

"You have a quality which is not so common with women as men suppose; you have such lovely patience, Miss Jack."

"Patience!" she repeated, and raised her eyes to his, perplexed.

"I have sat here so often with Mrs. Pendexter, and admired your unwearied kindness to her boy, spoiled and ill-behaved as he is."

"I love children, sir; it is no virtue in me."

"The man you marry will be very fortunate," Mr. Beresford continued, gravely; "such sweet patience in a wife is the highest virtue; it is strength in misfortune."

"I shall never marry," Miss Jack replied, with a catch in her breath, looking at him with troubled eyes.   "I fear you are laughing at me, sir."

"Laughing at you!"

He was so evidently hurt that she hastened to say to him, with lips that would tremble:—

"You say such very kind things to all ladies,—I —I could not help noticing."

"So you have been watching me in turn, Miss Jack!" he said, smiling.   Then he rose, and Miss Jack's heart beat with coming pain: now he would certainly leave her.

She looked wistfully into the garden, where two humming-birds were playing hide-and-seek in the very hearts of the flowers, and the sun shone as never the sun shone before.

"Will you come into the garden with me?" Mr. Beresford asked. "It seems a sin to stay in the house this beautiful summer day."

A look of such delight swept over her face that Mr. Beresford smiled in answer.

"Do you know how lovely you can look?" he asked, in frank wonder. "You will pardon me for saying so, but surely it is not the most beautiful women who reach the perfection of beauty."

This to her, Miss Jack! What could he mean?

Taking her hat she followed him into the garden, and watched him breathlessly as he stooped and gathered a great handful of forget-me-nots, blue as the sky above them. He was to her the embodiment of manly strength and beauty. He had come into her barren life as the sun shines through prison-bars, and she was grateful.

Perhaps he read her soul in her eyes; it was not hard, for the soul was a very simple one.

"Miss Jack, will you take these flowers, and wear them for my sake?"

She took them awkwardly enough, and tried to fasten them in her gown as she had seen Mrs. Pendexter do.

"I am so very awkward," she said, wistfully, as some of the flowers fell to the ground in her struggles. "Mrs. Pendexter is so—so graceful."

"You are one person and Mrs. Pendexter is another. I would not wish you to be like Mrs. Pendexter," he said, gently.

"Why not?" she asked in surprise.

"Is the beauty of the rose greater than the beauty of the violet?"

What did he mean? Was she dreaming? Who was the violet?

She looked across the sea, and a sudden feeling came over her that it would be good to lie down among the flowers now, with his voice in her ear, to fall asleep and never to wake again. She had never thought life a burden before, but she felt that now without him the very sun would shine no more.

A humming-bird swirled and whirled about her, and its gold-green plumage glistened royally in the sun. With a flutter he flew against the flowers on her breast and rested there a moment, she was so still.

"The very birds love you," Beresford said, watching her.

"Please say no more kind things to me," she cried, with so passionate a protest in her voice that the humming-bird flew away, and the forget-me-nots rose and fell with the quick beating of her heart.

"I am not like other women," she cried; "I am poor and plain. What is there in me to make you so kind? Your kindness is cruel."

For the first time she looked into his face full and frank.

"You are a man who plays with women's hearts"—

What was it her lips dared to say?

"Only with hearts that are offered to me without the asking," he said, simply. "You," he added, with a frankness which would have been cruel but for its earnestness,—"you are a plain woman; you have nothing of that which heretofore has attracted me, and yet you do attract me. I do not mean to say fine words to you. What I say I cannot help saying. You attract me — the woman in you is stronger than the man in me."

She looked up at him with a smile which once more seemed to make her beautiful.

He stooped and took a spray of the forget-me-nots on her breast and held it in his hand.

"Yesterday I found you," he said, his eager gaze holding hers. "I rowed you across the sea, and we were alone together. To-day I found your soul, and I want to be alone with you again on the sea. Will you come with me?"

"Yes," she whispered, as if in a dream, and followed him across the lawn to the rowboat moored at the wharf. All the world was a world of enchantment to her, and in it they two were alone together. Steadily he bore her across the deep, deep water, and in the distance she could hear the idle flapping of sails and the cry of sea-gulls.

The glory of a summer day was over the enchanted island they had left, and on the sea lay the brooding quiet of the afternoon.

The splash of the oars, that caught the light of the sun on their glistening blades, alone broke the stillness between them, as she watched him with bated breath — so happy! God knows, so unspeakably happy! and not daring to look in his eyes, that watched her, she knew, with a tender, wondering look, as one who finds unknowingly a jewel of great price.

"I have found you," he said, a little huskily, bending forward. He laid down the oars, and the boat drifted with the tide. "I have found you, beloved, and I will keep you. Come to me!"

He held out his hands to her and drew her towards him, and for one divine moment her head lay on his breast.

Oh, the glory of that summer day! The cruel glory,—the cruel happiness! "I love you! love you! love you!" he cried.

IV.

AS sure as that she was living the words had been spoken: they rang in her ears.

What had happened to her? Miss Jack looked about her dazed. She was still sitting in her corner by the screen and the open door, but she was quite alone.

A passionate voice—his voice—said again, "I love you." To whom?

Miss Jack rose to her feet, and held out two trembling hands, as a blind person would. There was an odor of violets in the air that made her faint, and in her usual corner sat Mrs. Pendexter, and beside her Mr. Beresford, half kneeling, looked into her averted face with imploring eyes.

"You know that I love you blindly, foolishly," he cried. "You know that I love you as you would wish a man to love. My love for you takes away my very manhood"—

"Mr. Beresford, you have evidently forgotten that Miss Jack is behind the screen. She is probably listening."

"What do I care for Miss Jack! The whole world may listen to what I have to say."

"Pardon me, Mr. Beresford, I would rather not."

"You certainly do not speak like a woman who is in love," Beresford said, bitterly.

"I am not," Mrs. Pendexter remarked, with exceeding frankness.

Miss Jack drew a tremulous breath and cowered behind the screen. For the salvation of her soul, she could not have left the room.

"I had some hope," Beresford said, with an entreaty which was pitiable,—"I had some hope when I saw your black gown changed to this ;" and he touched her dress as only a man who loves touches the garment of his beloved.

"So had five others. I told you so. You make the sixth. And—perhaps I might just as well tell you,"—Mrs. Pendexter hesitated.

"Well ?" he asked, rising.

"I have already given my promise."

"You said that you were not in love." He spoke through his set teeth, and looked down at the woman he loved.

"I am not," Mrs. Pendexter began, but rose with uncommon swiftness at the sound of ponderous feet shuffling across the veranda. Mr. Virginius Chick came into the room, jealous, suspicious, and scowling. Mrs. Pendexter looked into his face with a very faint smile.

"My dear, Mr. Beresford has just come to bid me good-by. I was about to tell him that the next time he would see me I should be your wife."

Mr. Beresford was so dazed when he left the room that he nearly ran against a thin, black person on the piazza.

"Pardon me ! Oh, is it you, Miss Jack ? Good-by ! I'm going."

"Going, Mr. Beresford ? Good-by."

A dismal and long-drawn howl swept through the air.

"Miss Jack, where are you ? Why don't you see to Adolphus ?" Mrs. Pendexter cried, with her languid voice pitched to an uncommonly high key.

Miss Jack turned down the garden-walk with a curious, pinched look in her thin face, as if all youth and hope had vanished out of her life.

"I guess I must have dozed off and dreamed," Miss Jack thought drearily, "God help me !"

So she came back to reality again in the shape of Adolphus Pendexter, who was battling with a grim cat, upon whose stately back he was trying to ride. The cat hissed, the infant Pendexter howled, and Miss Jack took up the burdens of life again.

"FATHER."

I.

JACK WARDLOW stood before the entrance of the Hotel Metropole, in Geneva, and examined the prospect.

He was a man above the middle size, his shoulders well back, with a promise of strength, and the rather negligently artistic cut of his clothes was tempered by good taste. Above everything, he had an amiable, smiling face, which left his friends in doubt whether he could ever hope to live up to it.

He was a painter by profession; belonging to that tribe of young American artists in Paris who paint from a French recipe. In general he was not dissatisfied with existence, though now he confessed to being a trifle bored. A sharp wind swept across the lake, and, with an impatient shiver, Wardlow lighted a cigarette and looked down the street, with its tall, gray houses, till his eyes rested on a vehicle, which clattered toward him and pulled up with a jerk at the entrance of the hotel.

The head waiter so far unbent as to meet half way the individual who shot out of the carriage.

The stranger was a short, thick-set man, and when he took off his slouchy hat he mopped his head—apparently as a matter of habit—with a red handkerchief.

Pulling a plebeian traveling shawl about his shoulders, he fixed the head waiter with shrewd gray eyes, and demanded, "Any museum in this town?"

The head waiter, betrayed into truth by the unexpectedness of the question, mournfully said, "No."

"Thank God!" the other exclaimed, stumping back to the carriage.

"Nothin' to see," he murmured. "This is just the place for me! A regular one-hoss town. Come out, mother. Don't forget anything, Rose."

The free Swiss mountaineer who drove the cab, and who was only conspicuous for independent dirt, rolled off his box and stared at mother while she was extricated from the vehicle by the head waiter.

"Father," mother began, struggling for breath.

"Bethia, just the place for us," father cried, stalking on ahead, free as air, while mother followed, much bewildered. It was the head waiter's succumbing to youth and beauty which prevented the last of the party—who blushed as red as the long red cloak she wore—from depositing the whole collection of small luggage on the sidewalk, out of sheer weariness. Followed by the approving head waiter, she was about to pass Wardlow, still loitering by the door, when an imperative voice briefly called out: "Rose —body."

With a blush and a shy raising of her brown eyes to Wardlow, she returned to the chariot, and, in passable French, begged the Swiss mountaineer to be careful how he handled a long and mysterious box which formed a portion of their eccentric-looking baggage.

"Rose—body! how very remarkable," Wardlow mused, as the wearer of the scarlet cloak disappeared. "If they are traveling about with the body of a deceased—good heavens, impossible! Certainly they don't believe in mourning; I should say not. Scarlet, with a line of black fur about the hood. Curious traveling costume. On the whole, I rather like it. I'll go in and reconnoiter."

In the hall he discovered "father" leaning against a pillar, and staring with much surprise at a huge printed placard against the wall.

He still wore his traveling shawl, the old felt hat was on his head, and the red bandanna was in full play; he seemed to be an object of mingled scorn and perplexity to the soul of the proud head waiter.

At the sound of footsteps, father turned and gazed at Wardlow with a shrewd smile.

"So you're a Yankee? Should have known it even if I hadn't been told.

"Very flattering, I am sure," Wardlow murmured.

"The head waiter told me. I'm a great one for finding out things. What may your name be?"

Wardlow looked at his countryman helplessly, then handed him his card. Father extracted a pair of steel-bowed spectacles from a shabby case, and proceeded to study the scanty information.

"Mr. John Winthrop Wardlow, Boston. I suppose some of your folks came over in the Mayflower?" he demanded, with a grin.

"I really don't know. If they did, I wish they had staid in England. May I ask whom I have the pleasure of addressing?"

Without a waste of words father took him confidentially by the arm and pointed to the following printed notices against the wall :—

"Bains chaud—1 franc 50 centimes. Bains froid —1 franc. Bains de vapeur—2 francs."

"Excuse me, but I don't understand," Wardlow confessed, after reading this statement of facts.

"A very curious circumstance, quite a coincidence," father said. "I don't read French, myself, but I suppose that is their way of spelling it. I spell mine with an 'e.'"

"Spell yours with an 'e,'" Jack repeated, in perplexity.

"My name is Baines. Baines with an 'e.' Thomas
G. Baines, Pittsburgh, Pa. All I ask you is, why did
they put it up there?"

Jack struggled for self-command. "It means
baths," he explained.

"You don't say so?"

He looked suspiciously at his neighbor, then turned
about, muttering, "Baths — bains — baths — don't
know about that! Seems to me,"—here he stopped
short as the mysterious box, standing on end, came
within range of his irritated vision.

It was a kind of pine coffin-shaped structure, with
"Thomas G. Baines, Pittsburgh, Pa.," stenciled on
one side, and, near by, the caution, "Glass. This side
up, with care."

"On his head!" was all father exclaimed, as he
sternly contemplated the pine monument.

"Shall I—" the head waiter began.

"Yes," father interrupted with a growl, "take it
up to Miss Baines's room. Leaving him down here!"
he growled, following the porters who bore the mysterious burden upstairs.

Wardlow watched them till he saw the last of Mr.
Baines's short gray trousers disappear up the marble
stairs, and, for a moment, he was lost in reflections.
"If it is a body, it is disposed of in a very business-
like way. But why should Miss Baines have to give
the body house-room? And if it isn't a body, what
is it? By George, I mean to know," Wardlow exclaimed, and followed in father's wake.

He looked up and down the first broad corridor,
and, sure enough, by an open door stood Miss Baines,
apparently in considerable distress.

To her appeared Wardlow, suggesting assistance
with smiling eyes, that took in Miss Baines, and, be-

yond Miss Baines, the mysterious pine box deposited in the very center of the room.

"Can I be of any assistance? You seem in trouble. I met your father downstairs. I am an American, like yourself," Jack began, and stopped, slightly embarrassed.

Miss Baines looked at him with brown eyes quite devoid of coquetry.

"I would like to get rid of that, and I can't," Miss Baines said, with a deep sigh. "We've had him with us for three months, and father is so afraid he may be lost."

"Three months? He—who—what?" Jack asked, bewildered.

"It is Thotmes the Second. Father bought him, for he intends to start a museum of antiquities in Pittsburgh. We've brought him all the way from Egypt. He is a mummy."

For a moment they looked at each other, then Wardlow laughed, but his amusement found no response in Miss Baines's perplexed face.

"You know," she continued, with unaffected sadness, "I cannot forget that he really is a body, poor thing! though he is a mummy. I can hardly sleep when he is in the room. I'm so sorry that he's not nicely buried. I'm always thinking of his poor wife and children; how dreadfully they'd feel if they knew that father means to take him to Pittsburgh."

"But, Miss Baines, you mustn't forget how many thousand years ago he died."

"It's of no use," she replied, with mournful certainty; "they are somewhere where they can see, and I know just how they feel."

"Poor old chap!" Jack exclaimed, filled with sudden commiseration for Thotmes II.

"Miss Baines, you don't know me," he said, "but I can assure you I am honest, and I give you my word of honor not to run away with Thotmes. Suppose I have him carried across to my room and there he can stay comfortably while you remain in Geneva. He won't be stolen and he won't spoil your dreams, or indeed mine. I am afraid I'm not so tender as you are."

"It is very kind of you. Perhaps father wouldn't miss him for a few days; but," Rose added, with a sigh, "father always has him placed in my room to cure me of superstition and make me independent. I mostly see to the trunks as well. It is for my good, you know."

"Hang father!" Jack thought. "Tell me, will you trust him to me?" he continued, aloud.

"Indeed, I will!" Before she could say another word Jack was downstairs, and in five minutes more Thotmes II. was transferred to Wardlow's room. Sitting tête-à-tête with the deceased monarch, he studied the stenciling.

"I'm booked for Geneva as long as father stays," he reflected. "Poor Thotmes, what a curious destiny yours—the crown of Egypt and the dust of Pittsburgh! To think that you haven't even the pleasure of knowing how sorry she is for you. If anything could comfort a fellow under such circumstances, that would in spite of—father."

II.

IT was Mr. Baines's boast never, under any circumstances, to do anything like any one else.

He had been torn from his Pittsburgh tannery by a severe and sudden illness. On recovering, and in the same attire in which he went to his business of a morning, he embarked for Europe, and there regained his health and those peculiarities which distinguished him.

"Father," in traveling-shawl and bandanna handkerchief, led his family through Europe, Africa and Asia. He planted his sturdy legs on Arabian soil and ate cold camel in the desert. He insisted on mother's keeping house in Jerusalem, and, turning up in Egypt, he became the victim of a mania called "Baines's Museum of Antiquities," for which he collected a variety of expensive trash, which followed in his train as if European collectors had one eye, and that was enviously fixed on his treasures.

With unerring instinct Mr. Baines always went to the hot places in the heat, and to the cold places in the cold.

It was owing to accident that he did not reach Switzerland in the depth of winter; the truth is, he needed a breathing spell to collect his ideas. Europe troubled him; there was too much to see in a small space. He thought of Thotmes II. and a few other trifles he had bought, yet, somehow, he felt, try as he would, he could not compete with the "Loovers" and the "Pity Palaces." But here was Geneva without the shadow of a museum, and Geneva was as old as the hills, while Pittsburgh's museum was started and stowed away in—Jack Wardlow's room.

To him Mr. Baines explained his plans.

He acknowledged the superior merits of masculine society by deserting mother and Rose for Wardlow. Mother did not care, but it was hard for Rose, as Mrs. Baines hated walking and objected to driving; so the poor child had nothing to do but to look out of the window, sighing a little as she watched father stump through the park over the way, beside the gallant man who had such a pleasant smile, and who three days before had saved her from Thotmes II.

It was not till the second day after their arrival

that Wardlow, going upstairs, met Miss Baines descending.

"I have had no chance to tell you how well I
sleep," she said, smiling shyly.

"And I sleep no worse. I have just left your
father—he does not even suspect. I hope you believe he is quite safe—Thotmes, I mean."

"Indeed, I do."

"Miss Baines, there is such a pretty walk by the
lake,—do let me show you!"

Miss Baines consented, but, somehow, fate was
against them in the shape of father. They found him
at the hotel entrance, expatiating to the head waiter
on the low and thievish dispositions of all Europeans,
and the superior intelligence and wealth of Americans.
All this in a distinct, nasal voice, with much waving
of a pair of vigorous arms.

"Going out, are you?" he asked, as Wardlow and
Rose passed him. "I guess I'll go too." And he
took such possession of Jack, that Rose had to walk
behind them in the narrow paths, and having accidentally interfered with the free play of father's feet,
was commanded to return to the hotel and see to
mother.

"But, Mr. Baines, the walk will do her good," Jack
remonstrated.

"Don't you worry, she's got health enough. Besides, I ain't for having my women-folks round all the
time."

Rose went back without a word, but for the first
time in her nineteen years of existence, something in
her heart rebelled against father.

The next afternoon Wardlow eluded father and
looked about for a glimpse of a red cloak.

The great drawing-room stood open and Wardlow
strolled in; sure enough, he saw the object of his
search seated on a scarlet "pouf," reading to mother,

with a tired flush on her bent-down face. Mrs. Baines was surreptitiously napping, with a look of profound wisdom.

Rose gave a startled glance over her shoulder, and blushed as Wardlow came towards her.

"I was so disappointed not to have that walk yesterday," he began, in a stage whisper. "I looked for you this morning, but your father would take me out."

"I was very sorry," Rose murmured, with a sigh; "but I mustn't speak now, or mother will wake up. She always wakes up if I stop reading."

"But, if she is asleep," Jack remonstrated.

"Please don't. I would like to talk, but I mustn't."

"May I sit down and listen? It would be such a pleasure, such a—a privilege."

"You mayn't think so,—it's a sermon on Justification by Faith or Works, and it worries mother a good deal, for she isn't sure—There, I knew she'd wake if I stopped."

"Don't lose a minute, Miss Baines, go on reading —she may go to sleep again," Jack urged.

But mother's eyes were open and she looked wildly about.

"You don't read as distinctly as you used to, Rose, or perhaps I don't hear as well. I didn't even hear you come in, Mr. Wardlow. Sometimes I think justification is by one way, and sometimes by the other. He is considered very learned—I wish he were clearer. I really think that I know as much about it now as I did before," which was very likely, as Mrs. Baines had been fast asleep all the time.

III.

WARDLOW climbed the narrowest of zigzag streets that wound up hill like a corkscrew. It led him to a mouldy square, paved with cobble-stones and made more dim by a row of linden trees that backed up against a weather-beaten church.

The yellow leaves were beginning to fall, and a young person in a red cloak was absently collecting them with the end of a huge cotton umbrella, till they lay in withered heaps at her feet.

Wardlow, with an involuntary exclamation, looked up and down the square as if reconnoitering, and in three strides he was beside her.

"Why, Miss Baines, you here all alone?"

Miss Baines appeared to check a desire to run away; but she only looked past him, and then down at the umbrella, and at last her eyes rested on the familiar shawl over her arm.

"I have lost father," she said, and was silent.

"By Jove, a happy accident," Jack thought. "As luck—I mean ill luck—will have it," he said aloud, "I cannot find him. I was to meet him here to go to the Dubois watch factory."

"He gave me his shawl and umbrella to hold, and then he went away. I suppose he meant me to wait for him. He has been gone some time."

"Would—would you be willing to take a walk now, Miss Baines?"

"Oh, I must not."

"You know we have tried eight times, but your father would go in your stead. It isn't that I don't appreciate him, he is a very remarkable man, but it —it isn't quite the same thing, is it?"

"Father is so afraid of missing something," Miss Baines murmured.

"Hang him! I wish he would!" Wardlow thought, savagely.

"He said yesterday," she added with a sigh, "that he has seen all he wants to of Geneva."

They were silent a moment, when from the open door of the church swept out the deep, full tones of the organ.

"Perhaps," Wardlow ventured, "if you will not take a walk, you will at least come into the church and sit down. Your father will be sure to look in— he expects me also, you know. You must be tired; let me take the shawl."

It was a gray old church, with a stone pavement, much worn; rough straw chairs were piled up against the pillars, and a point of red light burned before the deserted high altar. In a rambling gallery, at the back, the organist played in desultory fashion, and the only other living creature about was an ancient chore-woman, who was sweeping the floor. A few patches of scarlet and gold lay on the worn pavement, where the daylight fell through a painted window, and there was still a faint odor of incense in the air.

Wardlow placed a couple of chairs in the shadow of a pillar, and for a moment they sat there without speaking.

"So your father has seen all he wants of Geneva?" Wardlow broke the silence.

"It doesn't take him long; he goes to work so practically. I don't know where the time has gone. You know we've been here nearly two weeks."

"And so in a day or two you will be gone, and— shall we ever see each other again?" he asked, leaning forward.

Her eyes fell before his earnest look.

"I hope so," she whispered, at last.

"Hope so?"

"What more can I say?" she asked, taking a deep breath.

They were quite in twilight, and the music swept softly past them.

"If—if we should ever meet again, you wouldn't be sorry, would you?"

The dark eyes met his with shy reproach.

"I'm going to Cologne in two or three weeks; there is to be some kind of a great time there, well worth seeing, and if I could induce your father to go there, perhaps—perhaps we might meet again."

"Indeed, I should like to see you again, Mr. Wardlow.   You have been very kind to—us."

Again there was a momentary silence, which Jack broke:

"Let me put the shawl under your feet; you will be chilled."   So, doubling up father's sacred shawl, he knelt and placed it there with infinite care; then, still kneeling he looked up into her face.   "I have known you just two weeks, Miss Baines—but to me they have been an eternity for—O Rose, my darling, if you only knew how I love you."

"Mr. Wardlow!"

"See, dear, I can be patient—I will wait forever for your love "—

"Mr. Wardlow, you would never think well of a woman so lightly won," and the hand in his firm clasp struggled faintly.

"Had I known you forever, my darling, I "—

"Mr. Wardlow, I beg of you, rise—there is father."

"Confound him," muttered Jack.

Sure enough, there was father, hat in hand, peering through the darkness, and mightily triumphant.

"Found you at last!   Guess where I've been!   In the steeple—all the way up."

"See how dusty you are, dear!   Stand still a moment and let me brush you."

Rose began to dust father, when of a sudden she gave a nervous laugh. "O father, just see!"

Mr. Baines could not see, for the accident had happened to the tail of his linen duster, upon which was marked in outline stenciling, "Thomas G. Baines, Pittsburgh, Pa."

With Jack's help father emerged from this garment and examined the disaster.

"I sat on it. It'll never come out. I know, I made the ink. I thought the stencil-plate was dry when I laid it down. That's what I went up the steeple for," he explained to Wardlow.

"To sit on a stencil plate?"

"Gracious, no! I've stenciled it upon the steeple as high as I could reach," father continued, with a knowing wink. "I always do it. There ain't no place in Europe, Asia, or Africa where you don't see that name. It's on Solomon's Temple in Jerusalem, and on the top of the highest pyramid."

"When I undertook this tower (tour) it came to me like a flash to do it. Some folks use lead pencils, others jack-knives; but when I do a thing, I do it thorough, so I brought my stencil-plate along. It saves time, and this blacking just eats into the stone. I mean to come back some day and do the places all over again, just to see how the ink wears."

"You don't say so!" Jack murmured.

"There's nothing like being wide awake. I want all the folks who go everywhere to know that there is some one from Pittsburgh, Pa., who's as spry as the best of 'em. Now let's go home."

He led the way through the iron gate and looked casually over his shoulder at Rose.

"Guess you'll be glad to get out of here, daughter. We're going to-morrow. I've bought three watches and two clocks, so I calculate we'll be set up for life as far as time-pieces go.　By the way, where's my shawl?"

"I forgot it.　It was left in the church, father."

Rose ran back, picked it up and, turning, stood face to face with Wardlow, who had followed her.

"I love you, and Rose, my darling, I'll be patient and some day you will learn to love me."

She looked into his face as if to speak; but, as if the words would not come, she darted past him into the dim square, where the withered leaves were whirl‑ing in a sudden gust of wind.

IV.

AFTER hundreds of years the Cathedral of Cologne was at last completed.　The final stone, to rest on the apex of the spire, swayed aloft, waiting for the great day when it should be lowered with all due pomp and ceremony, and when, in the presence of kings and princes, amid the booming of cannons and the ringing of bells, the mighty edifice should be de‑clared finished.

A few days previous to the great event, the curious —that is, those who were steady of legs and not too short of wind—were at liberty to climb to the highest pinnacle, up some seven hundred steps.　Winding in and out of the scaffolding they could reach the point where the last stone swayed over the still un‑finished tower.　This altitude was never again to be reached by the most persistent tourist, for, after the 16th of October, the scaffolding was to be removed, and the two spires were to be seen free from that net‑work of beams, with which they had been surrounded, apparently since time immemorial.

In the old part of the city, not far from the Rhine, where the ancient houses have each a different gable, where there are no sidewalks, but a good deal of gutter between the cobble-stones, there stood an antiquarian shop, called "The Golden Bell." It was a curious, tumble-down place, opening directly on the street, and from the musty warerooms on the ground floor, to the gable roof, five stories overhead, it was crammed with all sorts of antiquarian odds and ends. There was, besides, an art gallery in an L beyond, where the most famous of the old masters were represented, apparently in a state of dotage.

The gem of the collection—in size, at least—was a trifle by Rubens, which represented, in an area twelve feet square, a remarkably well developed old patriarch receiving a volume from a couple of angels, whose draperies needed washing. That this production was authentic, was attested by a "barn-door" torn in the skirt of the patriarch's garment.

Two men stood in front of it, while the third, a Frenchman, ostensibly examined the pictures on another wall. Of the two, one was the shopkeeper. The other was Jack Wardlow.

Wardlow examined the patriarch with undisguised enjoyment.

"Rubens—ah, yes," he murmured. "A little thing done for an album ; probably never meant for exhibition. He may have been right. It shows that the Great may have moments of—well—imbecility. Next."

Wardlow moved to the next picture, and, at a quickly suppressed exclamation, the shopkeeper cocked up his head and the Frenchman glanced over his shoulder.

"Velasquez," the shopkeeper grunted in explanation, "thirty-six inches by twenty-five. Fifteen hundred mark ; same price as that one, which is very cheap, very cheap ; it's so big ;" and he nodded at the *soi-disant* Rubens.

Wardlow, with his hands clasped behind his back,
studied the Velasquez, with his soul in his gaze. A
woman looked down upon him from the canvas with
dark, brooding eyes that had a strange, golden glimmer in their depths. A mass of bronze hair crowned
the low forehead and level brows, while a robe of
some lustrous gold brocade, left bare neck and throat,
that all but throbbed with life and passion.

"I see the picture is signed," Wardlow said, at last,
to break the silence.

"They are all signed," the man of trade remarked,
injured.

"Of course the signature is a forgery," Wardlow
mused; "yet I'll stake my knowledge, my whole future, that these shrewd knaves have cheated themselves. It is a Velasquez. If I only had money
enough! But, hang it, I'm cleaned out."

He turned away and stared at the patriarch, when,
suddenly, he threw back his head and laughed.

"By Jove, I have it—father! He shall buy it.
It's worth $100,000 at least. All is fair in love; why
not do him a good turn? Father is naturally ill
disposed to artists; would be more sympathetic if I
were a gentleman pork-packer from Chicago. Now
if I help him to as neat a bargain as he ever made,
at what will the old gentleman's gratitude stop?
Nothing. The waiter at their hotel said they would
be sure to be in this afternoon. To see her again
after three whole weeks!"

He turned to the shopkeeper: "Look here, I shall
come back to-morrow with a friend, to whom I wish
to show these two pictures," and diplomatically he
included the patriarch. "He or I may buy one or
both."

No sooner was he gone than the Frenchman saun
tered up and although he barely glanced at the
Rubens, he remained lost in deep thought before
Wardlow's fair woman.

V.

"THE young Mees is in, certainly."

This from the obliging waiter of the "Dom-hof" on the Cathedral Square, to Wardlow, that afternoon.

"The young 'Mees' will do," Jack confided to himself as he knocked at the door.

She stood by the window watching the turmoil in the square below; at sight of him her lips quivered a little.

"You see I—I—have turned up again," Wardlow replied, struggling with a slight huskiness of voice.

"Do I look very murderous, Miss Baines?"

"Why, Mr. Wardlow?"

"I have been solely occupied in killing time. Three weeks ago it was two weeks, now it is five weeks. Five weeks is a very long time. How can I ever win you? If I could only kill a lot of dragons or fight a few chaps, as they used to! But now there is nothing to kill but time, and that is the hardest of all. Forgive me," he cried; "if you only knew how long these weeks have been; how you have pulled me here by my heart-strings."

She was so sure of him now, that she could look into his eager face with a smile and a doubting shake of her head, hypocrite that she was.

"What have you done with Thotmes, Mr. Wardlow?"

"Poor old sinner, he has been my only consolation; your legacy, you know, when I found that, by some accident, he had been left behind."

"We were so afraid you might forget us—"

"Forget you, O Miss Baines!"

"Us, I said, Mr. Wardlow. Ah, there is father.

6

I thought I heard him coming upstairs. "Father, you remember Mr. Wardlow?"

"So, you're here again."

"I haven't been here before," Jack replied, with a sense of injustice, as he shook the horny paw held out to him.

"Curious, but you always seem to be 'round. Got the body safe?"

"Body? Yes, to be sure, yes, quite safe. I'll send it to you."

"No hurry. Glad to be rid of it for a time. By the way, you did us a good turn to tell us to come here for this powwow. I've hired three seats near the Emperor of Germany for the show down there," nodding in the direction of the square, where elaborate grand stands were being constructed before the entrance of the Cathedral. "I've engaged a window to see the procession, and done nothing but look at kings and queens,—and most of 'em aren't much to see, either. There's a little king expected at the depot in an hour, the head waiter tells me. I'm going; will you come along?"

Jack, meditating an assault on father, said he was at his disposal, and watched Mr. Baines, in a genial glow, back into the familiar shawl, which Rose held ready for him.

The two men walked on in silence for some time, during which Jack endeavored to accommodate his long strides to the eccentric gait of his companion.

"Mr. Baines," he said, at last, "would you like to do a stroke of business?"

Father pricked up his ears like an ancient warhorse.

"I know of a picture which you can buy for $375, which is worth one hundred thousand at least."

"You are joking!" and Mr. Baines stood stockstill in the crowded street.

"Upon my honor, no."

"Why don't you buy it yourself?"

"I am an artist, and—well, I haven't enough ready money," Jack said, annoyed at his forced confession. "I'm on my way back to Paris to earn more."

"You are honest, at least. But how came you to discover this treasure?"

"Because I know pictures," Jack replied. "I found it in an antiquarian junk-shop where no one goes except to be cheated, so people fight shy of it. I have found one or two good things there in my time, for I only buy that of which I can judge."

"But why let me get all the benefit of this luck?"

"Because," Jack began, in some embarrassment, "because I'd like to put you under obligations, for I"—and he looked earnestly into father's face—"for I long to be under a life-long obligation to you, sir."

"Hum!" father said, reflectively, and for the life of him, Wardlow couldn't make out if Mr. Baines understood him or not.

V.

FATHER declared himself at Jack's disposal the next afternoon, at 4 o'clock, and the young man was to call for him at the hotel. Not to keep the reader in suspense as to the catastrophe, when 4 o'clock and Wardlow arrived, no Mr. Baines was to be found in or out of the "Domhof." At 5 o'clock, Jack, in consternation, drove to the "Golden Bell," hoping that father might have strayed in there. At 6 o'clock mother was crying, and Rose, with a very pale face, was trying to comfort her. At 7 o'clock the host of the "Domhof" declared that the police ought to be apprised, as in the present crowded state of the city, something might have happened.

At 8 o'clock the Chief of Police and all the police departments, were notified of the disappearance of an elderly American gentleman.

In their sitting-room mother was silently crying in a corner, while Rose, in her cloak and hat, stood before Wardlow, who held her hands in his.

"For your mother's sake keep up your courage," Wardlow implored. "God knows I would give my life to be of service to you—forgive me! But you must stay here."

As she still stood before him in a daze of trouble, he unclasped the long, red cloak.

"My poor child," he said, with infinite tenderness, and at the words she turned away, and kneeling beside her mother, she hid her face in the poor lady's lap and cried as if her heart would break.

.   .   .   .

As for father, not to keep the anxious reader in further suspense, he was neither dead, wounded, nor robbed ; he was simply an involuntary prisoner some 500 feet above ground, with as superb an opportunity of studying Gothic architecture—for which he did not care a rap—as mortal ever had.

In the solitude and silence of the scaffolding about the great towers of the Cathedral of Cologne, as near as a human being will ever again reach its highest pinnacle, Mr. Baines was imprisoned, with only the moonlight shining through the wooden network to keep him company. He could hear the confused hum of the city, lying below with twinkling lights, the clang of the church bells, while, beneath him, the "Kaiser" bell boomed out the hours in a fashion that made the sacrilegious intruder shake in his boots. On the other side, the Rhine flowed silently on its way to the "Sieben Gebirge," a river of moonlight, broken only where the boats floated down the tide.

Father was not poetic ; he ignored both the moon

and the scenery. He hugged himself in his shawl and shivered, when a cold blast of wind played hide and seek in the scaffolding, and jocosely threatened to knock him over.

With futile rage he looked down at the "Domhof" in the square, and wondered how mother and Rose would account for his absence.

Mr. Baines was the victim of misplaced ambition, and it had cost him dear. That afternoon he stole away to perform at leisure the ascent of the cathedral. He was neither actuated by curiosity nor a weak taste for the beautiful. Mr. Baines had heard that in a day or two the scaffolding was to be removed, upon which a bold plan occurred to him. Had it been connected with a lead pencil all might have been well, but as it had to do with a bottle of blacking and a stencil-plate, it proved his destruction.

To begin with, father was not as much impressed by Wardlow's story of the picture, as he should have been ; neither did he calculate for the length of time it would take him to make the ascent. When he reached the summit he found only a couple of workmen clearing up the débris that had fallen from the surmounting cross, for sight-seers there were none.

Fortune, apparently, favored him, for one of the workmen shouldered a box of stone chips, nodded to his companion, and disappeared down the only flight of steps which led to the platform on which they were standing. The chance was fine for father, and retreating behind a beam he extracted from his pocket an ink bottle, a brush, and a stencil-plate, and then peeped out to seize his opportunity.

From below the " Kaiser " bell boomed 5, but Mr. Baines did not care, for he was watching the remaining man, who, in turn, examined the pure gray stone of the farther spire, with undisguised pride. Quick as a flash, father darted from his place of concealment to the other, and, in a moment more, "Thomas G. Baines, Pittsburgh, Pa.," was immortalized on the great south tower of the Cathedral of Cologne.

It was father's misfortune that to reach the steps he was obliged to pass the workman. With great discretion Mr. Baines again extinguished himself behind the beam, but, as ill luck would have it, from the contemplation of one tower the stone-cutter proceeded to the other, and the next moment he stood face to face with the jet-black information—rather down hill—that Thomas G. Baines was of Pittsburgh, Pa.

"Himmel—donner-wetter—kreuz-sakrament!" he roared.

Father smiled, but he felt that this was no time to appear.

After a moment of consternation the stone-cutter fetched his tool-chest, and vainly tried to scrape off the black with his chisel.

"He doesn't know how it eats in," father chuckled, and, seized with compassion for such wasted energy, he disclosed himself.

"Don't, don't, it won't do any good," he remonstrated, as if the man could understand. He glared at father, pointed to the inscription, then at him.

Father nodded. "Yes, that's me, Thomas G. Baines, Pittsburgh, Pa., and you may scratch till you're blue and you'll never get it off."

With a volley of ugly German words the stone-cutter shook his fist in father's face, grasped his tool-chest, and in an instant disappeared down the steps.

"Most remarkable fellow," father declared, quite bewildered. "What's the use getting so mad about it? 'Tain't his house. Glad he's gone. Guess I'll go in a few minutes."

There, father was mistaken, for after descending

some 200 steps in and out of the scaffolding, when he
at last reached the heavy iron door that leads into
the body of the church, and down to terra firma, he
found that door to be securely locked.   He banged
away at it for half an hour, till he was forced to the
pleasing conclusion that he was destined to spend the
night on top of the Cathedral of Cologne.

. VI.

THAT memorable night Wardlow did not go to
bed.   He sat in the office of the " Domhof " and
answered the summons of forty-five policemen, who
came in turn for him to identify Mr. Baines in the
persons of forty-five vagrants in every stage of intoxi-
cation and general lowness.

About 7 o'clock the next morning—a chilly morning with a gray haze in the air—he came back from a
visit to a distant police station, pondering as to Mr.
Baines's probable fate.

To be honest, and as Jack was not in love with
father, it must be confessed that he was filled with
natural indignation that the old gentleman should
have disappeared before he had settled about the
Velasquez.

" Just my luck," he exclaimed, and, as he climbed
the three or four steps into the " Domhof," he looked
over his shoulder towards the cathedral, which lay at
right angles to the hotel.

" My God ! " he shouted, stared, then with one leap
was down the street, and the next moment he grasped
by the shoulders an individual arrayed in a familiar
shawl and wearing a hat much crushed.   At Wardlow's touch a face expressive of cold misery, and eyes
that flashed fire and fury, met his.

" In God's name, where have you been, sir ? "

"Been? Ugh! You wait till I've had my breakfast."

"Your wife and daughter are nearly distracted with grief on your account."

"Women folks—fools," father returned.

Wardlow followed Mr. Baines, with a secret grief that he should have turned up so undamaged.

"We've had the whole police force out after you, sir."

"What kind of a ninny do you take me for?" father cried, exploding.

Jack commanded himself.

"At least, sir, you will let some one prepare your wife and daughter for the happy event."

"Guess I'll see to that myself," father replied, and trotted upstairs.

You see, father not having had any anxiety on his own account, was not disposed to countenance such weakness in others, neither was the last night spent in such a lively fashion as to uphold him in the supperless, breakfastless, and chilly condition in which he found himself.

That morning the stone-cutter who had locked him out, came to his airy prison and talked to him in such a threatening way—though Mr. Baines didn't understand him—that father could hardly realize the transformation caused by two broad gold pieces which he instinctively slipped in the horny palm of that "son of toil."

From that moment, by some magic not unconnected with gold pieces, the honest laborer grew calmer, and escorting father down to the entrance, took leave of him with a grip of friendship and pleasure.

VII.

MOTHER did not die of joy, neither did Rose. "O Thomas, Thomas, I thought you were dead," Mrs. Baines sobbed, clinging to him.

"But I ain't, and I want my breakfast," Mr. Baines replied, as he struggled out of her grasp.

That was all. After breakfast, when he had filled the void within him and was thawing, then Rose said, with a blush creeping up to her dusky hair, "Father, Mr. Wardlow—"

"I don't want to hear about him," he interrupted.

"Father," Rose continued, leaning over the table, "we are under the greatest obligations to Mr. Wardlow. If it had not been for him, I don't know what we should have done last night."

"What's he got to bother about me for? I ain't an infant in arms. I wish he'd mind his own business!"

"I never thought you could be so cruel, father," Rose cried, indignantly.

"Look here, daughter, what d'you mean by that?" Mr. Baines asked in amazement.

"You are unfeeling, for you won't let mother and me show how glad we are to see you. You make nothing of all that mother has been through, and you weren't even civil to Mr. Wardlow who was up all night long, trying to find you. You are under great obligations to him and you'll always be! All I wanted you to do was to thank him."

"Obligations!" father shouted, starting to his feet. "I won't be under obligations to any man. Guess I know what'll make us quits. See if I don't. What did he say the name was? Idiotic name for a shop. Oh, yes—Golden Bell. I'm going out. Obligations, indeed."

Father slammed the door behind him, and in a moment, they saw him drive off in a cab with a seedy individual who did duty in the hotel as an interpreter.

Father never did anything by halves, and the way he made a bee-line for the picture-gallery of the "Golden Bell" quite refreshed its owner.

He was rather staggered on being confronted by the patriarch, which, the shopkeeper explained to the interpreter, was one of the two paintings the gentleman had admired, the other, a smaller picture, having been sold to a Frenchman. Mr. Baines felt that he was receiving a good deal for his money, and so, without more ado, he purchased the trifle.

An hour after a covered furniture van, drawn by a couple of dray horses, rumbled up to the front entrance of the "Domhof." Beside the driver father sat in democratic independence, his face beaming with smiles ; for he was at heart a generous soul, and as he was, according to Jack's statement, about to oblige him $100,000 worth, he looked not unconscious of superior virtue. He also rejoiced to think that very soon he would be able to wash his hands, so to speak, of this gigantic work of art and leave its future disposal to another.

Cautiously father climbed down from his perch and ran against Wardlow, who was hanging about the "Domhof" in a very low state of mind, and who observed Mr. Baines's arrival in speechless amazement. Father's dominant desire was to get rid of him, for he felt that the sidewalk was an inappropriate place for a presentation speech. Ignoring Wardlow's coldness, he said: "Won't you go upstairs? I think daughter wishes to speak to you." Rose's indignation against father had not subsided, and as she held out both her hands to Jack standing before her, she looked into his face with tears in her eyes, and said, with a gratitude which included father's, "How can

I ever thank you enough for your goodness to us, Mr. Wardlow?"

"Don't try to—you make me feel ashamed. Miss Baines—Rose—my darling—do you not know that I would die for you!"

He held her hands and looked into her downcast face, and at his eager gaze she looked up at last, and it seemed as if you could hear their foolish hearts beat in the silence as she whispered, "I—I would rather you'd live for me—Jack."

Just as he held her in his arms and kissed her, as if he never meant to part from her again, the door opened, after a perfect chaos of scuffling, to which they had been oblivious, and father burst in with a genial smile, which froze on his face at the scene before him.

"I'd prepared a little surprise for you, Mr. Wardlow, but you've given me one which beats it hollow. How dare you, sir! Why, I don't know you."

"You can inquire about me, sir," Jack said, boldly, "then if you find my record unsatisfactory, I will give up your daughter."

Before father could recover from his amazement, Rose threw her arms about his neck and rubbed her coaxing cheek against his.

"We will be patient, father, and not unreasonable. You know you were not rich when you fell in love with mother."

For a moment father succumbed, but the allusion to mother brought him to himself.

"Good Lor', yes, mother. She's waiting in the bedroom with our surprise." So speaking, he trotted to a side door and flung it wide open. Sure enough it disclosed mother sitting before the patriarch, frameless. for so majestic were his proportions that hardly any door would let him pass. Mother was staring at the *soi-disant* Rubens in consternation.

"This," said father, with a backward wave of his hand to the picture, and in a tone of deep reproach to Jack, whose amazement lacked all the ingredients of joy, "this mother and me wish to give you as a remembrance, for Rose says we are under obligations to you—"

"Not I, Thomas, not I," mother interrupted, refusing her share of father's little surprise.

"Please don't give it to me! Do pray be under obligations," Jack cried, in undisguised alarm.

"You know you said it was worth a hundred thousand dollars."

"That picture! That isn't worth a copper—it is the vilest daub I've seen for many a day. The picture I meant was a small one—"

"That is sold," father groaned.

"You see, father, you still are under obligations to him," Rose ventured to say, patting his hard old fist.

"I suppose if I'd give way to you, the obligation would be on the other side?"

"Yes, father, dear."

"Well, I'll see. What I want to know is, what shall I do with that," and he turned to the patriarch with a scowl.

It was then that Wardlow laid the foundation to father's future favor. "Present it to the Pittsburgh Museum—it is quite an art gallery in itself," he suggested.

"Gracious, yes," father exclaimed, with an involuntary sigh of relief. "I had quite forgotten the Baines collection."

"There is Thotmes, you know, father," Rose added.

"Really, my darling, I hate to part with Thotmes," Jack murmured. "It was he who first—"

"Oh, but, Jack, dear, you can't have everything."

.   .   .   .

Of course they were married, so it is no use to

disguise this singular fact. Five months from that October day, Mr. and Mrs. John Winthrop Wardlow, permanently established in Paris, strolled down the main gallery of paintings in the Louvre. Mother, gorgeous in black velvet, followed them, greatly admiring her son-in-law, while beside her trotted father, with an unmistakable indigestion of the "old masters."

Wardlow was proceeding leisurely, explaining this and that to his wife, proudly conscious of admiring glances thrown in her direction, when of a sudden he not only stopped as if he had turned to stone, but he grew deathly pale as he stared at a picture on the wall, in a gorgeous new frame, upon which was engraved in distinct black letters: "Velasquez, 1599–1660."

"Jack, dear Jack, what has happened?"

"Our picture, Rose! A real Velasquez, as I knew. Worth thousands. To have all but had it, and to lose it, and then to find it here! It is too horrible."

"But, Jack, dear, father lost it as well."

"Bring him up. I want him to suffer a little."

Father and mother were stranded on a red velvet bench and father was staring at the generous skylights overhead, while mother dozed.

"Mr. Baines," Jack said, with much emotion, as father came up to him, followed by mother and Rose. "This, Mr. Baines, is a real Velasquez, and it is the picture you did *not* buy in Cologne."

Father, wholly unmoved, closed a calculating eye and remarked, "I should say that the other one is four times as big."

"A very bold looking person," mother added, with much disfavor.

"You call that an 'old master,'" father continued scornfully, "why it might have been painted yesterday. As for the young woman, she looks so natural she might be mother."

"Go 'long, Thomas, how can you!" mother exclaimed, quite shocked.

"Only a figure of speech, mother. Now that picture I sent to Pittsburgh—anybody down there'd know it for an 'old master,' because it was so almighty dirty. Besides it was so big with the new frame I ordered for it, that they had to build an L to the picture gallery a-purpose. Now if I'd sent that," and father pointed his forefinger at the masterpiece of Velasquez, "they could have hung it anywhere. Besides, Pittsburgh is particular; they'd never go to see her—there's nothing surprisin' about her! But take an 'old master' like that Rubens I sent 'em, there's nothing like it on earth. That race of men died when Rubens died," and father shook his head in deep meditation.

"They were giants in those days. If you can call to mind the patriarch's arms—not a young man, but what muscles, Jack."

THE STORY OF AGEE SANG LONG.

FOR a whole month I listened in agony to the tinkle of the front-door bell, and when footsteps
shuffled up and down stairs and then out, I leaned
back in my chair and laughed mirthlessly at my own
disappointment. I was a young doctor waiting for
my first patient.

Such was my despair, because the neighborhood to
a man refused to be cured at my hands, that at last I
ceased to keep up appearances even with my old
landlady, Mrs. Macgruder. At first she was unmis-
takably overawed by my writing-desk, a very handsome skeleton, a couple of skulls, and a few hearts
and livers in spirits, which I kept on a shelf in my
office. However, I had not been her lodger one week
when she took an early opportunity to tell me that
she thought I was very young.

Regarding me, as she did, as a medical infant, I
longed to have her become horribly ill with a compli-
cation of disorders till then unknown to science,
whereupon I, like a nineteenth-century knight-errant,
would come to the rescue, save her, and earn her
eternal gratitude. It is needless to say that she continued in good health.

Mrs. Macgruder dropped into my office at all hours,
and on a certain late November afternoon she came
in with an untimely feather duster, which she held
over her head in an Oriental fashion, while she subsided into my office chair, one fat hand spread over

her fat person. From this shelter she favored me with sketches of the Macgruders, interspersed with sops of comfort.

"I've been a-talking about you, sir. If you was my own I couldn't think more of you. My heart's that soft I'd let you poison my best friend. It was only last night Sally Macgruder's first cousin said as he'd be certain to have you, sir, if he was took ill. Next week he's going to Texas to settle. But, Lor'! he may break his neck twenty times afore that."

"Mrs. Macgruder, I am sorry that I can't enjoy your society any longer," I said, with dignity, "but I have a—a consultation."

"Dear me!" Mrs. Macgruder said, with a parting stab, "and you so young!"

She vanished, and I stared hopelessly out of the dingy window. Fifty years ago the street was solidly respectable; to-day it is quite ungenteel. A few dying trees before the old houses, displayed upon their sides cards proclaiming lodgings to let and table board, at starvation prices. The bit of ground railed in before each house, was fruitful now in broken bottles and bones. Here organ-grinders were welcome, and the inhabitants were generous to monkeys; itinerant street bands played here with redoubled vigor, for they were at home, and the garrets loved them. I settled in this modest location thinking that this, indeed, might be called the foot of the ladder.

Twilight crept on, dull and gray, and the narrow street was deserted. It was so still that I could faintly hear the tooting of the street band, frozen into a garret, and it was growing so dark that the skeleton in the corner, modestly wrapped himself in a shadow. Suddenly the door-bell rang, and for the first time in four weeks, I paid no attention to its tinkle, and turned about half scared, as some one knocked at my door, which opened, and a figure crossed the threshold. I thought it was a child wrapped in its mother's poor shawl, and I could not see her face at first for the hood about her head.   The child dropped a series of curtsys, and then I noticed that she carried a great bundle in her arms.

"Agee Sang Long, sa'," said a thin, quavering voice, as a small hand pushed the hood aside, and I was startled to find the child to be a tiny Chinese woman, whose set and careworn face showed her to be at least sixty years old.

For a moment I could only stare at the queer, yellow, flat countenance, with its snub-nose, and a mouth like a pale slit between a long upper lip and a short chin.   Coarse black hair fell across her bright black eyes, full not so much of intelligence, as of a pathetic remonstrance.

"And what can I do for you, Agee Sang Long? Are you ill?"

"I no ill, but he be.   He a' my companee, my on'y frien', and he be so si'.   I bring him to you, docto', fo' to makee well."   Whereupon she softly undid the bundle and discovered, wrapped in a warm shawl, a melancholy specimen of a cat.   "I hab monee, docto'; I can payee ri' off.   You makee he well," she ventured, wistfully, as I took the poor beast in my arms.

It was humiliating to find that my first patient was a cat, but after a month's waiting even a cat was welcome.   The poor thing was suffering from slow poison.   I explained it learnedly, while Agee bobbed a curtsy, and held one limp paw in her yellow hand. I administered a hopeless antidote, and then they prepared to go, the patient wrapped in his shawl, and cuddling up to that heathen breast.

"He' be a dolla', sa'," said Agee Sang Long. "Me ha' monee to payee you."

The blood rushed to my face.   I couldn't take a fee for a cat.

7

"No, Agee, it's all right," I exclaimed, as if fees were no object. "I'll come round to-morrow and see the patient." I wished to cast dust in the eyes of Mrs. Macgruder.

I watched her down the street, and my blood boiled as some ragamuffins tore after her, shouting "Rat! rat!" As I turned away I saw something glisten on my desk. It was a silver dollar that Agee Sang Long had left.

The next day I hunted up No. 2 Paris Court, where my only patient lived. Paris Court consisted of six shabby houses, in the rear of front yards full of remains. I groped my way through a decaying arbor to reach No. 2. I never saw houses look so ill at ease. They had once been respectable, if not opulent. This had been a suburb with fresh air, and a brook had trickled past; it was a dirty puddle now. Chestnut trees once shaded the porches, and over the fences, white and purple lilacs had blossomed in spring. One day a suspicion crossed the houses that the town was creeping dangerously near, and a few months after, they found themselves imprisoned by rows of dirty brick dwellings that shut out the sunlight and air. At first they clung to gentility, but when the trees died, and the bushes withered for want of air, and the lilacs were parched with the heat and dust, and when the pretty fence itself broke down under neglect, then they gave up pretending, and, like gentility when it at last gives up appearances, broke down worse than their neighbors.

I stood in the dull, musty entry, and shouted, "Agee Sang Long!" and I was about to repeat it, when queer sounds, proceeding from a door opening near by, struck my ear. I knocked, and as no one answered, I turned the door-knob and entered a poor little room, with the light of day creeping feebly through two small windows that were cross-barred by gnarled and stalky remains of ancient grape-vines on tumbling trellises. Everything but two great wash-tubs was very diminutive, and, as I hastily noticed, scrupulously clean. But there was only one thing I distinctly saw. In the middle of the bare floor, on a wooden cricket, stood a small, rude, pine box, and in it, surrounded by wintergreen, and about his neck a new ribbon, lay my patient of yesterday. Beside it crouched Agee Sang Long, her head against the box, sobbing bitterly, and on a chair at its foot, stood a music-box, which cheerfully and monotonously rattled out "The Beautiful Blue Danube" waltz.

"Agee ! why, Agee Sang Long !"

At the touch of my hand she looked up with frightened eyes and a haggard face.

"Oh, docto', he die—he die ! Him all frien' I hab," she sobbed. "Dey pizen him, and I hab no frien' mo'."

Then she rose, with something of Oriental composure and politeness, and put her own grief momentarily aside to attend to me.

"It is only a cat, Agee," I suggested, awkwardly. "There are plenty of cats in the world ; you will find pets enough."

She looked at me with patient wonder, and a spasm crossed her ugly face.

"Wha' diee, diee. I lub no cat mo'."

All this time the air was rent with "The Beautiful Blue Danube."

"Who poisoned your cat ? " I asked.

"De peopl' in de house. Dey ha' me 'cos I Chinee. Dey wan' me turn ou' ob de house."

She said this with unflinching composure. She hardly pitied herself ; it was all fatality.

"Do they ill-treat you ? " I asked, indignantly.

"De man of de house he drinkee, and when he drinkee, he ha' all Chinee. Dey try to pizen I. Dey pizen he." She turned back and patted her dead friend.

I looked at her aghast. All this persecution against a harmless, lonely creature, in this nineteenth century, as if, by the grace of God, we were in the Dark Ages!

" Are you all alone in the world? "

" Yes." Not in pity at all; simply as a fact—a fatality.

" Look here, Agee," I said, as I left the room, "if these wretches annoy you in any way, come to me, and I will see that it is stopped."

As I turned into Paris Court, I was so indignant that, for a moment, I forgot my own pressing cares. It was a very cold evening, and the sharp wind swept up all small objects and whirled them round the corners. I was going at a swinging pace, buried in wrath, when something came puffing up behind me and pressed against my legs with piteous whines. I looked down, and found it was a dog. Such a dog! Never in my life had I seen so pitiful a cur. Thin and lank, spindle-legged, and so emaciated that his ribs were all outside, and covered with a pink-white hide ; he was a perfect albino of a dog. In race he was a terribly diluted bull-dog, and one pink eye gazed trustfully at me out of a black surrounding, the only bit of color upon his ungainly person. He shivered and whined and waved an emaciated tail, and, when I went on, he followed me as close as if he were an ancient retainer. I felt that he reflected discredit upon me, and I vainly endeavored, by suggesting rats, to lure him into byways.

When I reached Mrs. Macgruder's, I sneaked into the house, and left him whining and shivering on the steps. I took off my overcoat in my office, and, stirring the fire, sat down in its blaze. Unfortunately I heard that wretched dog howl outside, till at last I could bear it no longer, so I opened the door and let him in. He required no pressing invitation, but sat contentedly in the humblest place by the fire, and gazed at me with blinking eyes, his jaws open, and his tongue finely displayed. If ever I saw a dog smile, that was the dog, and he beat the floor with his tail in a way I knew was meant to be complimentary and grateful.

I don't know why I thought of Agee Sang Long as I gazed into his melancholy eyes, but I felt instinctively that these two belonged together. So the next morning, after a breakfast such as he never dreamed of in all his wildest dog-dreams, I took him to my Chinese friend. She looked at us without surprise, and accepted him, when offered by me, as another bit of fatality.

"He'll be company for you, Agee," I urged, "and I shouldn't be surprised if he were a good watch-dog." This I remarked doubtfully, the ancient retainer having brought no reference as to character. Nor was his pedigree, as exhibited in his countenance, reassuring; but, somehow, he looked trustworthy, and instantly proved to be a dog of no prejudice, by cuddling up to Agee and holding out a paw, until the little woman took it in one of her hard-worked hands.

"Goo' doggee," she said, and looked gratefully into his pink eyes.

Whether it was instinct or a trick, we never knew, but he was only happy when he could cuddle up to some one who would hold his paw. At night, when Agee's work was done—she scrubbed, washed and ironed, and did chores for a living—she locked the door, and then she and her dog sat by the fire, side by side, he with an affectionate paw in her left hand, while her right held, upside down, the breviary she could not read.

Beside them on a chair, so close that none of its

delicious strains could be lost, the music-box ground out "The Beautiful Blue Danube," Agee listening reverently.   This music-box was her joy.   After years of toil she had saved twenty dollars, and, not without deep reflection, she spent ten in a burial lot—for she longed to rest peacefully in death, she who in life had been so tossed about—and the rest she invested in this precious music-box.   It is unnecessary to say that she was cheated, for it is the privilege of civilization to get the better of heathens.   However, she listened to "The Beautiful Blue Danube" and "Coming thro' the Rye" with profound joy, heathendom and Christendom battling in her breast sometimes, when she yearned to consider the music-box as something divine.   But Christendom conquered, for she was a Christian.

Years and years ago she had been converted, and every Sunday morning she trotted to the cathedral with her prayer-book, that she could not read, clasped to her Chinese breast, and as surely as the martyrs of old, she suffered persecution on the way.   The people frightened her, but particularly the children, and she only felt safe and at peace kneeling on the stone floor, with her head bowed on her breast, and her yellow hands folded humbly.   Then it seemed to her as if she were not so very different from the people about.   To be sure, they would edge away, and sometimes, in the interval of prayer, a hard Irish face glared contemptuously at her, but she expected no better.   There was peace here in the light of the gleaming candles on the high altar, and the sunlight falling through the beautiful gold and scarlet windows, out of which people with kind, divine faces looked down upon their poor sister, not clad in scarlet and gold and azure, but ugly and forsaken, and yet not so far removed from them, as God sees men, their deeds and suffering.

Forty years before, a Salem sea-captain had brought her from China as nurse to his little child, and somehow she stranded on civilization, and never returned to her Celestial Kingdom.   She was utterly alone in the world, not a woman of her race in any place around, and society was banded against her.   The ladies of Irish extraction, who took in washing and scrubbed, persecuted her for daring to do the same. They did her all the mischief they could, and succeeded in all but killing her.   Ill-smelling powders were thrown into her room, gunpowder was put in her coal, and water on her firewood ; her cat was poisoned, and a sick sparrow she saved from wind and weather, was freed from its cage and flew away.   She did not complain, she did not think of revenge, and— oh, for the narrow-mindedness of such a wretched Chinese !—she saved the life of her worst little persecutor.

It seemed as if Agee Sang Long turned the tide of my ill-luck, for, from that day, patients began to drop in slowly, and so it was a week or two before I saw her again.   She was such a frail creature, full of rheumatism, and she had a heart trouble which I felt was serious.

It was a glorious December afternoon when I stepped briskly into Paris Court, to inquire after Agee and our mutual friend, to whom she had given the extraordinary name of Mowa.   I felt that life was worth living.   I had had a run of two patients ; one of whom, I distinctly remember, was a considerate coal-heaver, whose skull was temporarily damaged by a brother in trade.

I stepped into Paris Court, just concluding that the world was a beautiful and satisfactory place, when a creature crossed the sunshine like a ragged shadow, and stood in my path—a woman like a nighthawk, a bird of ill omen.   A pale, sullen face, framed by rough red hair, half hidden by a rusty shawl, looked into mine.   She was a ruin of cheap finery, and some good looks, and she was young.   As I opened the gate of No. 2, this woman came up behind me.

"Are you going in there?" she asked, and hesitated.

I turned, and her worn eyes held mine.

"Yes.   Can I do anything for you?"

"For me?   Yes."   Then she added with unexpected violence: "No, you can do nothing.   God couldn't help me."

I turned from her.

"Wait," she cried.   "There's a Chinese woman down there—lives there.   You know her?   Is she kind or is she cruel?"

"She is a good woman," I replied, surprised, "and she is very kind."

"She ought to be bad; the world is bad to her," the girl muttered.

"She is better than many a Christian.   What do you want of her?" I asked, peremptorily.

"If she were no better!" the woman exclaimed, with a mirthless laugh; and without answering my question, but with a strange, searching look out of those worn eyes that had seen awful things, she turned and shuffled away, a blot on the sunshine.

I opened Agee's door, deep in thought, when, to my amazement, I heard a baby's voice.

"Why, Agee Sang Long!" I cried.   For there she sat on her accustomed cricket near the stove, and she held a baby in her arms.   Mowa sat before her, thrusting an unheeded paw nearly into her face, and devoured by jealousy, and, as usual, the music-box was spinning out "The Beautiful Blue Danube."   As I looked at the baby I thought I had never seen so patient a little creature before.   It was a baby with a past, and it had known trouble.   Though it was en-

veloped in an ancient shawl of Agee's, it was unmis-
takably a beggar. But it was appreciative, and liked
music, for it smiled at the music-box with a strange,
Sphinx-like expression in its clear eyes. But the
most extraordinary sight was Agee herself, for she
was laughing, and it was the first time I saw her ex-
press an emotion of mirth. There was no merriment
in her eyes, but her mouth was widely distended, ex-
hibiting gums and tongue and teeth to full advantage.

No sooner did she see me than she struggled to her
feet, the baby nearly capsizing her.

"Him mine!" she cried in triumph. "Him lef'
at de doo' las' nigh'. Lookee, docto'; him nice
babee."

She put him in my arms as if she were conferring
a favor, then gazed joyously at us both, while the
neglected Mowa rubbed against me, with a pathetic
desire to be noticed. I looked into the poor baby's
eyes, and vaguely thought, "I have seen those eyes
before." Then, of a sudden, it all flashed across me,
and I saw again the woman whose worn eyes, full of
a bad past, had held mine. Now I understood.

"Shall you send him to the Orphans' Home,
Agee?" I asked.

"Me keepee babee," she answered, with some reproach. "Me workee for babee. Me hab monee.
Me makee a gen'leman ob babee."

The future gentleman becoming restless with me,
he stretched out two soft arms to be taken by Agee.
Never shall I forget the joy and pride with which
she received him.

"Him my babee!" she cried, enraptured, hugging
him tight. For the first time in forty years a human
creature showed her love; a creature weaker than
herself clung to her for protection, and the mother
instinct, that nature gives even to a poor Chinese,
made her strong and happy.

When I left them, Agee was again sitting on her cricket, rocking the baby to sleep, and singing to it some unearthly song, of Chinese origin probably. Mowa's head had found a resting-place on her lap, and he kept time with his tail. Ah! she was a different person now, Agee Sang Long. She had an object in life.

How hard she worked to make both ends meet. She denied herself everything to buy warm clothing for the baby, and she gave Mowa a bite when she was very hungry herself. Her rheumatism was bad, and she had queer pains inside, she told me; but that could not mar her great content.

She, who had always been so lonely and deserted, noticed that now, when she left the house, a wild, wan creature would appear suddenly and dog her steps. Agee imagined that this person desired to speak to her, so she lingered on her way to give her a chance; but the other only retreated in haste, her poor rags fluttering in the chill air.

"She be a unfotnit lady," Agee said, with much delicacy, describing her to me.

It was Christmas-time, and Agee Sang Long, being a person of family now, determined to celebrate the day. She worked harder than ever, supposing that were possible, and though the rheumatism was very bad, it could not subdue her. On Christmas eve, after she had washed all day, she came home through the heavily falling snow, and proceeded to scrub her own floor until it shone. She washed the baby, and then she turned Mowa into a monument of soap-and-water wretchedness. Having arrayed herself in her poor best, she made the baby fine, tied him into a chair for safety, then turned him temporarily around, with his back to the Christmas surprise in store.

Mowa whined and was restless. He sniffed at the

window and growled at the door, but Agee did not notice him.

ị   At last her surprise was complete. She clapped her hands and laughed ; then limped to the baby, caught him in her arms, gave him a great hug as a Christmas present for herself, and turned him about so that the whole glory burst at once upon his blinking eyes.

The baby crowed with joy, and Mowa barked. Agee Sang Long laughed until the tears stood in her black eyes and rolled down her furrowed face. Such a Christmas tree ! It stood in a flower-pot, and was nearly two feet high, and nine little candles made it a scene of extraordinary brilliancy. And that wasn't all. On one branch hung a collar for Mowa, and on the other a rattle and a rubber elephant for the baby, while three gingerbread men leaned unsteadily and sadly against the branches, as if they rather suspected what fate had in store for them.

Mowa, much protesting, was decorated with the new collar, the baby swung the rattle and clutched the elephant, and the music-box played " The Beautiful Blue Danube." Then Agee sat down on her cricket with the baby in her arms, while Mowa, in front of her, looked fondly into her yellow face, and then they proceeded to eat the gingerbread men, each after his own fashion.

Mowa stopped in his feast to turn to the window and growl. Discovering that the source of gingerbread had run dry, he ran toward the door and growled, then trotted back to Agee, looked at her, wagged his tail, and ran back toward the door. There he sat down on his haunches, with a look upon his mongrel countenance which plainly declared that he had no opinion of the human kind.

There was a hesitating knock at the door, unheeded except by Mowa ; then the door opened, and a woman crossed the threshold—a terrible woman, like a blight and a curse. Her rags were powdered with snow, and she shook with cold, but she only looked at the child in Agee's arms. It was a wild, hungry, jealous gaze, and she turned to Agee with but half-suppressed violence in her pale face.

"I am cold; let me come in," she said, harshly.

The candles on the tree flickered and blew out in the gust of icy wind sweeping across the threshold; the lamp on the chimney smoked and burned dark, the dog sniffed uneasily at the stranger, and even the baby turned away from her with instinctive fear.

A white rage filled the woman's face as the little Chinese patted the frightened child and tried to restore his equanimity by a sight of the elephant. His sobs grew fainter and fainter, and so she put him on the floor, where he lay doubled up. trying to find comfort in his toes. Then she went towards the woman, who still stood by the open door.

"Come in and ge' warm, you poo' ooman," she said, kindly, and touched her ragged shawl.

The woman shrank away with aversion, but she came in the room, nevertheless.

"I no do you harm," Agee Sang Long said, sadly, feeling the aversion to which she was accustomed.

The woman sank down on a chair by the stove, and stared at the child.

"Le' me dry yoo shawl," Agee ventured, humbly.

"Leave me alone," the other interrupted, shaking her rough head, from which the shawl had fallen.

"Sal I gib 'oo a cup of tea?" Agee persisted. "Ity warmee 'oo."

The woman turned on her in a frenzy. "Leave me alone, you rat; I hate you."

Agee Sang Long shrunk back, more in dismay than terror. She looked at the woman with deprecating reproach, then stooped and took the baby in her arms, as if to assure herself of some human love. Mowa, the faithful, crept close to her and held out his paw; and so the three stood together in the shadow of the extinguished Christmas tree, and gazed wistfully at their enemy.

Some strong feeling was evidently at work in the woman. "Let me take the child," she cried, with sudden passion.

"He be 'f'aid," Agee Sang Long implored, clasping the little one tighter to her breast.

"'Fraid of his mother!" the woman shrieked, threw herself upon the poor creature, and tried to tear the child out of her grasp.

"Don', goo' ooman; he's so li'le babee; he 'f'aid," Agee urged, trying to shelter the poor thing.

"You wretch! you heathen wretch!" the woman screamed. "Dare to keep him from me!" And the next instant she had him in her arms, and hugged and kissed him with half-mad passion. "I can't live without him. I gave him up because we were starving," she cried, wildly. "And so I left him at your door. But they told me here in the house, that you were teaching him your dirty Chinese ways. But you sha'n't have him," she cried, spurning with her foot Agee Sang Long, who kneeling before her, clasped the ragged skirts with piteous hands.

"Leave him to me, dea' unfotnit lady," she cried, the tears streaming down her face. "Lib wid me an' I workee for 'oo till I diee. But leave him. Him all I ha' in dis wi' worl'."

"I'd rather he'd die with me."

She turned, and the baby in her arms struggled out of the shawl and held out his arms to his Agee Sang Long. As if that culminated the creature's fury, she snatched the child back, and, with a cruel blow, flung Agee Sang Long to the floor, and vanished into the night.

A couple of hours later I came down Paris Court, for I had promised Agee to look at her tree, but I was belated. As I turned into the court, the snow beating against my face, a dog bounded up to me, whining. It was Mowa. "Why, old boy, what is it?" I asked, trying to pat his blunt head. But he escaped, ran forward, looked back to see if I was coming, and never stopped until I stood in the doorway of the familiar room.

In the middle of the floor I saw, by the light of the dim lamp, an undistinguishable heap that filled me with sudden terror and pain, though I knew that it was only a poor Chinese. I knelt down and lifted her unconscious head, then laid the frail little figure on the bed. It was so hard to bring her back to life, and I almost despaired, when suddenly her eyes opened, and she looked across my shoulder at the open door, where a wretched woman stood with a baby in her arms. I recognized both, and I understood.

A flicker of joy crossed Agee's face as she saw the baby. Without a word I rose, took the child from its mother, and placed its soft cheek against Agee's.

I turned to the woman. "Behave yourself, or leave the room," I said, sternly, "for you are in the presence of death."

"I am sorry now," she muttered, uneasily. "I did her wrong.—You see I've come back. I didn't think I hurt you so bad when you fell."

"Did she hurt you, Agee?" I asked, gently. I saw that the poor forsaken creature was dying of the heart-disease that I feared, but evidently it had been brought on by some great shock.

"Oh, no, no!" Agee Sang Long murmured, and laid her face against the baby's, and touched its soft cheek with her lips. "She do me goo', for she his mudder, poo' unfotnit lady."

She became dimly conscious that a faithful paw was stretched up to her ; she groped toward it with one weak hand, then, turning toward the baby with a contented smile, she fell asleep, to awaken in a land where men are equal before God.

JOHN STERLING'S COURTSHIP.

I.

I AM John Sterling. I was first mate on the *Sally Tompkins* and Joe Snow was second mate, when we were scouring the Atlantic for mackerel, it being mackerel season.

Joe Snow and I had shipped on the *Sally Tompkins* for the first time ; and this was the first time we'd met, though, on comparing notes, we found that he hailed from Oversea and I from East Oversea, about two miles of dreary sand stretch apart, on Cape Cod. We also found that his bunk was just over mine in the *Sally Tompkins;* by the same token I soon discovered that he had nailed a woman's picture just in sight of his bright black eyes, when he'd wake of a morning.

In all honesty and truth this made me feel precious lonely, for I had nothing to look at except the sagging of the mattress over me, for young Joe had a good solid weight, though he was as spry as a squirrel.

I made believe not to notice her at first, and I kinder shut my eyes in passing, being rather tall, for I said to myself, "He ain't the man as 'd want his sweetheart stared at by every fellow, and he can't help her being jest there."

However, I did catch sight of her once, and it was the sweetest face in all God's world, with eyes so kind and a mouth so tender, that it made my heart ache,

(112)

though I liked young Joe none the less for the woman
who loved him.

One day there came up a gale that made the *Sally
Tompkins* curtsy to an extent that was a credit to
her manners, and, in the midst, down came young Joe's
beauty, and young Joe after, much against his will.
I picked her up in a twinkling and held her out to
him. "My sister," says he, by way of introduction,
and dusts her as a man only dusts the picture of his
sister.   It was kind and fond, you know, but it wanted
something.

God forgive me, but I was glad!   I stood quite lost
in a suppressed joy, when luckily the *Sally Tompkins*
gives a lurch, and I decide to postpone consideration
of young Joe's sister.

"So that's your sister?" I asked the next time we
had a minute to talk.   This time I looked at her
straight in the face.

"Yes, that's Sis.   She's an angel," says he coolly,
as if it was a matter of course.

"What's her name?" said I, clearing my throat a
bit, for it would get husky like.

"Oh, Olive."

"Does—does she live in Oversea?"

"Yes."

"Perhaps some day I'll see her," I went on, dreadful rash.

Then says this young Joe, perfectly thoughtless,
"I hope she'll see you, for I want her to know the
kindest, dearest fellow in the world."

Then he laid his hand on my shoulder, and, somehow, I said to myself, looking into his smiling eyes,
"If the sister is anything like the brother, and if she
don't like you, then I shall be sorry for you, John
Sterling."

From that time, the ice being broken between us,
young Joe talked a good deal about his sister.

8

"There's only one fellow in the world good enough for her," he said at last, his eyes flashing. Then he laughed, showing all his handsome white teeth. "I'm going aft, old fellow," and he leaped up the gangway. "I don't like to be below when the waves play high jinks with *Sally*. Come 'long!"

I didn't come for a minute, for his thoughtless words had made me sore.

"So there's some one chosen," I thought, and my heart was like a lump of lead. Then said I to myself: "Don't be a moon-calf, John Sterling! A pretty girl like that don't wait for your coming."

I climbed up the gangway as steadily as the wild tumbling and tossing of the *Sally Tompkins* would let me, for we had struck about as ugly a bit of weather as I'd seen for many a day. A dull leaden sky lay over the sea, and the spray and the waves came dashing and swishing over the deck, and the *Sally* rose and fell in the trough of the sea, as if every moment was to be her last.

Said I to myself just then, "What ain't taut and fast on this ship I don't give a copper for, and a man 'd better look to his footing aboard this craft," when I heard a cry that wrung my heart, for I knew the voice.

"Man overboard!" came in a shout of horror, for it seemed death—certain death. Then followed a trampling of feet, a wild confusion of voices, just heard through the storm and the flapping of sails, as the schooner came up to the wind. I was at the ship's side in a bound, and saw in the gray dim distance, a speck that a moment before was a face that had smiled into mine. Her life and his and mine I lived in a flashing second, and then, though they tried to hold me, I was overboard, and before I could think, the *Sally Tompkins* was tossing far away from me, and I was struggling with the waves.

Heaven be praised, by a miracle—for God was

good—I reached him in that terrible sea, as he was sinking.

They launched a lifeboat, at the risk of their lives, and saved us. It is strange that, of the two, I should have been the one to be unconscious and light-headed. From the moment we were saved I knew nothing, till I looked up one day and saw young Joe bending over me, with tears in his eyes, while the *Sally Tompkins* glided along as smooth as you please.

"So you're really saved, young Joe?" said I.

"And so're you," he cried. "God bless you, you brave man!"

"Don't," I murmured; for I was very weak, and could bear but little.

Now, curiously enough, the first thing I saw as I turned, was *her* picture nailed just in sight of me. I used to lie there hours at a time, wondering why it was there, watching it and dreaming about it in a helpless way.

But I was very weak, and of no more use aboard than a land-lubber in a squall, and when we came in reasonable sight of land, and the low green shores melted into gray sand and blue sea, I said to the skipper that he'd best land me along with his mackerel, and p'r'aps I could find at East Oversea what I hadn't yet found on that tidy bit of timber, the *Sally Tompkins*, namely, health.

"Young Joe," said I, as I was leaving—"I'm going to East Oversea."

"East Oversea is two miles to the east'ard of Oversea," he remarked, with much cheerfulness.

"You said you had a grandfather and a great-aunt living there," I said, a-leading him on.

"Grandfather Snow and Great-aunt Jerusha—yes."

"Shall I give 'em your love?" said I. "I may happen in at Oversea some day."

"No," said he, with a grin far from respectful.

"He's seen right through you, John Sterling," I
thought, and turned away, all scarlet.

"Look here, old boy," he says, and gives my shoulder a hearty grip; "there ain't much love lost 'tween
grandfather and Aunt Jerusha and me. So don't go
outer your reasonable way to tell such a whopper.
But you can go and see Sis, and if you tell her you're
John Sterling, I guess that'll do. And all I got to
tell you, old boy," says he, as if I was a land-lubber-
boy goin' on a first journey (he was awful bold) "is,
there's only one fellow good enough for her in this
world, and don't you be so blamed bashful."

I sighted him again as I stood on the wharf, while
he leaned over the *Sally Tompkins*, smiling at me and
at all the world, like the rising sun.

I thought over what he said, and couldn't exactly
understand his meaning, except that another man 'd
been luckier than I. As for bashfulness, why, it
wasn't in his place—no, 'twasn't—to talk of bashfulness. "It 'ud be money in your pocket, young Joe,
if you'd be a bit more so yourself," thinks I, dreadful sore, and swung round and steered toward East
Oversea."

II.

THERE were four Overseas, and in the dark they
were so much alike you couldn't have told one
from the other.

To be sure, East Oversea had a railroad station,
but that was so far from making it a center of traffic
that the single horse attached to the mildewed vehicle in the shadow of the modest station, had worn four
permanent holes in the ground waiting for customers
that never came.

A single grass-grown road formed the one street,
and the United States mail rarely consisted of more

than one letter, which was a satire on the leather bag with a patent lock which national generosity furnished for Oversea correspondence.

The train rumbled leisurely to the East Oversea station—even the trains ceased to be in a hurry near the Overseas—and, to the amazement of the station-master, a passenger alighted.

The station-master was supported in his duties by a couple of antiquated fishermen and the owner of the mildewed chariot. All four were chewing tobacco, and three were whittling sticks, as the passenger approached.

"Lor,' ef that ain't John Sterling!" they said, with one accord; then, turning to each other, remarked, dispassionately, "Ain't he pale, though?"

The owner of the chariot did not bid for custom, for it was an unwritten law of East Oversea, that for a native Oversean to return home in its stately peril, was to put on "airs." That was left for the unwary stranger, who shot in through the front, for the sufficient reason that a previous owner had permanently nailed up the doors because the latches had ceased to catch.

The animal that drew this vehicle pricked up his ears in a vain hope that a customer would release him from bondage, but he sank into apathy at sight of John, for he knew his man.

"Anna Maria ain't grown any fatter since I've been gone, has she?" John said, bestowing a friendly thump on the animal's protruding ribs.

Now this was not to be denied; so John was silent, and looked kindly at Anna Maria. He had grave, pleasant blue eyes, and when he could so far be false to his national melancholy as to smile, it was like the sun rising on a sad landscape.

"And how's mother?" he asked the assembled company, gathering up his carpet-bag.

"Pretty middlin'," they remarked, still in chorus.

"Guess I'll go and see her," John suggested, as if it were a new and startling departure.

"Perhaps you'd better," the chorus answered, approvingly ; and so John went.

John's mother had the best house in East Oversea. It stood on a proud sand bank, and was surrounded by a row of weeping willows. From the back one could see the Atlantic roll in as near as the Oversea bar, and from the front there was the view of the street, and at night could be counted the patient lights of seven lighthouses and the life-saving station. The smooth, treacherous beach lay like a silver line edging the shore, quite unbroken save where the mouldering beams of a wreck struggled out of the engulfing sand.

The people of Oversea were of a silent, moralizing turn, presenting to jokes a stolid front, but enjoying greatly the sad things of life.

John, quite overtopping the willows, entered his mother's house by the kitchen door, and was greeted by the pleasing smell of frying doughnuts, that had a certain general resemblance to Mrs. Sterling herself, for, like them, she was fat and round and pleasing. It is perhaps only just to say that such a departure from Oversea characteristics was due to the good lady's not being the real native-born Oversea article.

Mrs. Sterling, being so amazed at the unexpected sight of John, and her thoughts being also engaged with the doughnuts, she several times endangered his life by trying to prod him with the frying fork. John sat down in the wooden rocking-chair and answered all questions methodically, while he stroked the cat that had leaped on his knees, and watched his bustling mother, and then looked out at the sea glittering in the sunshine, framed by the scarlet geraniums that bloomed on the window-sill.

"Mother," he said, at last, "no woman ever looks so pretty as when she's doing her woman's work."

"Now, John, what put that in your head?" she asked, in great perplexity. "I've heard such things said before, John; and 'twas always the unmarried kind as said it."

John grew red to his short, straight hair, and was silent.

"A man as is unmarried," Mrs. Sterling continued, gracefully rescuing several beautifully brown dough-nuts from the spluttering fat, "an' if he's seen a girl he likes, sets her in his mind a-dustin', a-cookin', an' a-scrubbin', jest as he sees her, bless his innocent heart! in her Sunday clothes."

"I wasn't thinking of anybody but you, mother," John said hurriedly, and stroked the cat's outraged fur the wrong way. "There was a young fellow aboard the *Sally Tompkins* from Oversea—young Joe Snow—do you know his people, mother?" and John couldn't help the healthy glow that half betrayed him.

Mrs. Sterling, with her arms akimbo, rejoiced at a fruitful topic of conversation, and went into a long and detailed account of the Snow family, taking in by the way, biographies of the various side branches, and was in a fair way of bringing up with Noah's ark in her reminiscences, when John came to his own rescue. Not a word of Olive all this time.

"Do you know Grandfather Snow, and Great-aunt Jerusha?" he asked, artfully.

"No; only I heard they're about the tryingest old folks—"

"And—and—" John began, in great agitation.

"What, John?"

"Nothing, mother. I guess I'll take a walk before

tea. Guess I'll jest go to Oversea. Got any errand in Oversea, mother?"

"Lord 'a mussy, John! why, you've only jest come!" his mother cried, and shook her head. Did I ever have an errand in Oversea—now did I? In Oversea, of all places!"

"Well, then I won't go," John declared, and sat down with an abruptness which was equally unexpected.

"John," his mother said, anxiously, as she went up to him and patted his head, "you're sure you haven't had a bit of a sunstroke, John, dear?"

III.

BUT John did go to Oversea. He had a way ot disappearing out of the house, and though he always steered east, north, or south, somehow he always landed in Oversea—which lay west—and that with a surprised expression, as if he hadn't expected it at all.

It took him a long time and cost desperate efforts before he summoned up courage to penetrate to the heart of Oversea, which was the town-pump. One day, after a dozen fruitless trudgings over two miles of grass-grown highway, with a sea-breeze stirring the modest weeds and flowers along the path, and the blackberry vines clinging to the gray sand, he reached the blue pump once more, and debated in his modest heart how to find Olive.

Oversea was a place from which young men fled with enthusiasm, and its population consisted entirely of very old folks and very little folks. Samples of the latter were playing about the blue pump, and, with the engaging playfulness of infancy, were squirting water over each other.

Now it is certainly true that a naturally bashful

man will meet, well, anything dreadful, rather than run the gauntlet of irresponsible infancy.

With one accord they solemnly stared at him ; for a masculine stranger was an event in Oversea. They were a sandy-haired, bony little race, with colorless, shrewd eyes, and were preparing very young to follow in the melancholy characteristics of their parents.

Standing about the pump, they made audible and unflattering remarks as to his personal appearance. John smiled on them with a slight exaggeration of friendliness, perhaps, in his efforts to break the ice, when an urchin in cotton breeches, bare feet, and no hat, remarking, in a melancholy way, "What be you a-grinnin' at, stranger?" being himself impervious to the lighter emotions, so completely routed John, that he fled, and never took breath again till East Oversea was reached.

Oversea always had a Joel Snow, just as it had a pump and a meeting-house. The Snows were a slow, methodical race, and they generally died with great regularity at the age of threescore and ten. When the masculine Snows couldn't fish, they kept the one little shop, which contained everything that the modest heart of Oversea desired. A crazy bell rang as the shop door was opened, and, there being one low step downward, the unwary always shot into the presence of the then Joel Snow, till one day, by an astonishing convulsion of nature, they shot into the presence of Olive instead.

Though Oversea was most decidedly blind to beauty, it had a dim consciousness that it liked to trade with Olive. She would turn her bright, smiling face on a querulous old woman as if the fate of the world were involved in a cent's worth "o' somethin'." She had a cheery word for the old fishermen who sat about the pump evenings, and in the gloaming told of the storms they had seen, and the wrecks, and that, after all, 'twasn't young folks as knew what danger was.

Oversea was so full of old people that, perhaps, Olive's young face might have grown old in the contemplation of so many wrinkles, if it hadn't been for the children. To be sure, there was young Joe, her brother, but he was always away; so there was only herself to tend the little shop and wait on the old grandfather and great-aunt. Grandfather was ninety and great-aunt was ninety-two. In winter they sat on either side of the kitchen stove, and in summer in the shop, for a glimpse of "life." They were like two aged winter apples with wrinkled pink cheeks. They were stone-deaf, and horribly jealous of Olive, and always prepared to do battle with the unknown who was to come "a-courtin'."

From the altitude of ninety all others were so young, that there wasn't an aged man in the village whom they hadn't nearly turned out-of-doors, suspecting unhallowed designs on Olive. They made the house hot for young Joe and for young Joe's occasional friends who came to Oversea and, without exception, fell in love with Olive. Tokens of this hopeless passion always took the shape of molasses candy, bought of Olive in the morning, and presented to her in the evening, as a Paris novelty, on the kitchen veranda. Here hopeless love chewed it alone, while the old folks in the kitchen glared out furiously, and Olive knitted, smiling in a motherly way.

One day she had a letter from Joe which set her to dreaming, for youth will have its rights. The letter said: "When you see John Sterling in Oversea, be good to him, for he saved my life at the risk of his own; he is just the bravest, best fellow in the world;" and a lot more, written with boyish gratitude and enthusiasm.

So Olive dreamed a little for the first time in her

young life, and longed to see Joe's hero, never thinking that the bravest of men had not been able to
muster courage enough to penetrate farther than the
town-pump.

One late afternoon the old people sat beside the
kitchen stove, dozing. They had a way of roaring at
each other—in supposed whispers—and in the way of
conversation they had roared themselves speechless.
A heavy stride, heavy with an artificial boldness, came
down the veranda, and then a heavy hand knocked
modestly at the door. As no one answered, the intruder, after the fashion of Oversea, turned the door-
knob, and, unexpectedly to himself, bolted in.

Two very old people were dozing on either side of
the stove. Aunt Jerusha's cap had slipped to one
side, giving her a rakish appearance, while Grandfather Snow's spectacles, pushed high on his forehead,
looked as if they were keeping watch. Grandfather
was snoring deeply, while Aunt Jerusha kept up an
accompaniment of little shrill gasps.

For a moment John Sterling stood speechless—it
was John—when, by some unaccountable accident,
the old people awoke and stared at him with little
eyes full of wrath.

"Sister Jerusha," the old man roared, in a supposed
whisper, "he's come a-courtin'."

"I want to see Miss Olive," John shouted, blushing violently at having to roar out his dearest wish.

"Ain't he got a sly face?" said Miss Jerusha.

"Ef you don't go away, I'll set the dog on you,"
grandfather shrieked.

"Go away! go away!" Miss Jerusha added, waving her hands at him. "Don't come a-courtin' here."

"You don't think I've come a-courtin' you?" John
remarked, in great disgust. Aunt Jerusha didn't
hear, so she nodded vigorously. "I'll be hanged,"
John murmured to himself, "if I know when these

women-folks's vanity ends.   Well, I ain't comin'
a-courtin'," he roared through his hands, as if he were
in high gale at sea.

"Wa'al, so you ain't comin' a-courtin'?" the old
man piped in; and John nodded.   "An' who be ye,
anyhow?"

"I'm John Sterling."

"Can't hear."

"John Sterling."

"Can't you open your jaws?"

"John Sterling."

"Wa'al, John Sterling, glad to see you; but ef
that's all you've got to say, guess we won't mind your
going." ·

"I came to see your grand-daughter."

"Courtin'?" Miss Jerusha interposed, acidly.

"Oh, she ain't much to see," grandfather an
swered; "and what's the use o' wastin' time?   She
don't care for what ain't dreadful young or dreadful old.   Besides, she ain't in."

"Oh, well, then," said John, with a deep sigh, and
shut the kitchen door on the two old people, who
roared and chuckled and winked their little eyes at
each other.   John turned down the road in a stunned
condition from disappointment and much shouting.

If he had come courting indeed!

A great glow swept up from his foolish old heart
at the bare thought.   "I mustn't forget that there's
only one man in the world good enough for her," he
thought, bitterly.

The sun was just setting, and half of its golden
disk had sunk into a golden sea.   The faintest,
softest breeze swept across the land, and the only
sound that broke the stillness, was the chirp of the
crickets.   A rough stone wall ran along a bit of the
road, to which the blackberry vines clung with ripening fruit, and the golden-rod swayed in its shadow.

John, buried in his reflections, looked up hastily at the sound of children's voices and shrill young laughter and his eyes became eager in their gaze.   It must be a prosaic man who forgets how his sweetheart looked when first they met.   Poor John never forgot. She was sitting on the low stone wall, and his infantile enemies were playing about her, evidently subdued.

She watched the children with smiling eyes, while she knitted busily at a big blue stocking, but the smile faded away as she looked up and saw John passing by.

Yes, passing — poor weak John !   The stocking dropped into her lap, and she followed him with wistful dark eyes.   "I'm sure that is John Sterling, but he doesn't know me," she thought, with a feeling nearly of pain.

John strode down the road in hot haste.   He pitied himself in a vague way.   He conjured up a picture of that too virtuous man who alone was worthy of her, till he clinched his fists and cried, " Confound him ! " with such vigor, that he startled a couple of cows grazing in a field beside the road, and they looked up at him with soft, reproachful eyes.

At a turn of the road he pulled up sharp, and called himself a fool, with a short and to the point expletive, and go back he would.

And go back he did, slowly, very slowly ; and when he at last reached her, he had nothing to say but, " You're Olive Snow, are you not ? "

He did not see how her dark eyes brightened at sight of him.

" And you are John Sterling, I am sure.   I was certain you would look just as you do," she said, and put her sun-browned hand in his.

He was very awkward and silent, but that, she reflected, was an eccentricity of heroism.   Certainly he dropped her hand with an alacrity far from polite, and having looked at her gravely with his deep blue eyes—such dear blue eyes, poor Olive thought—he then gazed over her head and sighed. How could Olive know how bitter he was with fate at that moment! "If I see her again I'm a darnder fool than I was jest now in passing," he thought.

He roused himself enough to answer Olive's little remarks, each preceded by a faint sigh of disappointment. John sighed also, and talked of Grandfather Snow's amiability and Aunt Jerusha's, till poor Olive's eyes were wide open with wonder. At last he looked about him in a helpless way, and then sighed again, and it being perfectly evident that if he really had something to say he couldn't say it, John went away with the pleasing feeling that he was a hopeless failure in general conversation.

When Olive came home, the whole family roared at her.

"Some one's ben here; 'twas a man," Aunt Jerusha piped up.

"He said his name 's John Sterling," grandfather continued; "but he ain't come a-courtin'," he concluded, as if to dispel any such pleasing illusion. "I asked him. Says I, 'Air ye comin' a-courtin'?' 'No,' says he, 'I ain't comin' a-courtin'.'"

Olive knew the old folks' ways, and she had always laughed at them. But to-day—oh, to-day was different! She turned to the open window and watched the golden and scarlet gleam of the lighthouses, and the scarlet and gold were blurred in the seeing.

Something like a sob came to her throat, and she fought with it and conquered. The old folks watched her greedily, but she said nothing, only she was very silent, and at last she hurried up to her room.

She understood all now, she thought, her face wet with tears. What wonder he seemed so embarrassed in his talk with her, and so relieved to go at last! He did not know the old people. He might have even misunderstood their dreadful questions, and supposed—and, at the bare idea Olive sobbed as if her heart would break—and supposed that they wished him to come courting her.

"He will never come again!" she cried at last, "he will never come again. I hope he never will," she murmured, but very hopelessly. Time had passed, and it had grown quite dark. An uncertain hobbling upstairs and a tremulous thump at the door brought her to herself, and there stood the two old people and demanded their gruel.

"You are very old, poor dears," Olive thought, conscience-stricken, and led them downstairs, and made the gruel and tucked in their napkins.

"He! he! hope he won't come courtin' again," said grandfather, in a stentorian whisper; "courtin' spiles the gruel."

IV.

NO sooner did John reach home than he felt that he had been a grievous failure. Running off at a tangent, as many a bashful man does, he yearned to go back, and to display himself in that amiable light which, if it could not work destruction in Olive's heart, would leave, perhaps, a mild flavor of regret, in spite of that other "blasted paragon," as John called him.

Until that fateful day, John's long and sinewy person had been arrayed in garments whose fashion was to him a matter of profound indifference. However, the day after John's meeting with Olive, Mrs. Sterling received a shock. In the garret stood a wardrobe containing the best garments of her deceased husband. Mrs. Sterling, climbing up to these heights, met a ghost, at sight of whom she shrieked, and would have fallen down the narrow stairs if the ghost hadn't saved her with two vigorous hands.

"Oh, John!" she sobbed, "you've got on the clothes your father wore when he came a-courtin' me, and you're as like him as two peas in a pod."

Love had done this thing—it had made John vain. He looked down at himself with innocent pride, and felt that even if he did not make an impression, his clothes must.

Perhaps some of the courage that attended that by-gone courtship still clung to the garments, for John stepped down the road at quite a brisk pace, and in no time at all he was gazing into Olive's little shop through its modest window.

Oversea was not proof against good clothes, and as fashions there were always ten or twenty years be-hindhand, John's black broadcloth, in which he felt as much at home as if he had been armed *cap-à-pie*, was regarded with much respect by the youth of Over-sea. The ladies of Oversea, in fact, forsook their household pursuits to gaze at him surreptitiously from back doors. Rumor had it that he was a summer boarder, than whom, to the simple mind of Oversea, no one could be more opulent or more foolish.

Then the crazy shop bell set up a din, and the un-known disappeared into Olive's store. The younger generation flattened its nose against the window for further information.

A veritable ghost would not have caused more con-sternation than John did. Olive, coming into the kitchen, turned quite pale, and the old folks, in their usual place by the stove, glared at him with angry eyes.

John shook two old reluctant hands, and held Olive's one blissful moment, and having fired off all his ammunition, stood helpless in the enemy's camp.

"I came to call on you," he shouted at last to grandfather.

"Don't see why; you were here yesterday," grandfather retorted, with extreme frankness.

"He's comin' a-courtin'," Aunt Jerusha shrieked. "Look at his clothes! 'Twas in jest such clothes Nephew Joel came a-courtin' Mary Jane Hyde, she who was your mother, Olive."

"Aunt Jerusha, dear aunt, do please stop!" Olive cried, piteously.

Perhaps that lively old lady had a momentary touch of humanity, for she concluded with indignant mumblings, while grandfather remarked, "Don't be a durned fool, Jerusha. What air you a-takin' on for?"

"Please go away," Dorothy implored, turning to poor John. "You see, the old people are jealous of every one who comes here."

Whether it was that the courage of the old love battles fought in these famous garments was contagious, whether it was that John felt hopeless, and having, in his opinion, nothing to lose, so dared anything, certain it is that John grew bold.

"What'll they do if you get married?" he asked.

"I marry?" Olive repeated, in surprise, turning from Aunt Jerusha, whom she had succeeded in quieting. "Why, if I ever do marry, John Sterling, it will be after those to whom I owe duty will need me no more."

"He's courtin'! he's at it again!" Aunt Jerusha burst out, with gathering venom.

"Then he's a fool for waiting—that young man o' yours," John said, bluntly.

"What do you mean?—what young man?"

"The man you're to marry," John cried, in a burst of rage and jealousy.

"I marry? Who told you so?" Olive asked.

"Who told me so?" John repeated, and sat down

on the nearest chair for reflection and support.
"Why, young Joe said—"

"Why, bless you, John Sterling, what did he say?"
a familiar voice cried, while the shop bell shook itself
mad, and a breath of the freshest sea-breeze swept
through the open door.

Sure enough, it was young Joe himself who stood
in the open door.

"Oh, Joe! dear Joe!" and Olive hid her face on
his shoulder.

"Halloo! little girl, what's the matter with you?"
and Joe patted her head, and turned with some surprise to the others. "And what's up with the old
'uns? and—in Heaven's name, John Sterling, perhaps
you'll explain?"

"He's comin' a-courtin'," Aunt Jerusha interposed,
shrilly.

"Oh, Joe! Joe! take me away," poor Olive sobbed;
then she looked up at John with a little catch in her
breath. "You'll forgive them," she murmured, "for
they are such old, old people, and they really mean
no harm," and she turned away; but John stood in
her path. "I've something to say you mayn't like to
hear," he said, gravely; "but I must speak. I love
you—oh! I love you so dearly, Olive, that this is
all a-torturing me." She stood before him with her
face hidden in her hands. "I would have come
a-courtin'," he faltered, "if—"

"If what, John?" Joe asked.

"If—if you hadn't said that there was only one
man in the world good enough for her," John answered, grimly.

"And that's true, John," young Joe said, and laid
one hand on John's shoulder, and slipped the other
about Olive's waist.

"Don't say it again!" John cried. "It's enough

for me to lose her.   I deserve better of you, young
Joe!" he exclaimed, turning upon him.

Over Olive's face, hidden on Joe's shoulder, there crept a blush that tinted her throat and neck and fair round chin.

"Olive, little girl," and Joe smiled, "what do you think of this man?"   But Olive would not look up— she could not say a word.   "Shall I speak for you, Olive?   Shall I tell him what you think of him?" Joe asked.

Olive hid her face deeper on Joe's shoulder, and sobbed a bit.

"Why, Olive," John cried, and a blissful, heavenly light dawned in his great dull head, "and wouldn't you be angry, dear, if I really came a-courtin'?" Olive peeped up from Joe's shoulder, and smiled a little and sobbed a little.   "Why, Olive, my darling, there's that other man," John cried, in great bewilderment, coming very near.

"That—that other man is you—John," Olive faltered, and though John was the bashfulest man in the world, he held her in his arms the very next moment.

"Olive," said Joe, "I'm sure you and John don't need me any longer."

John agreed with him.   He felt that he could do his own courting now.

There was nothing mean about young Joe.   "I'll tell you what I'll do.   I'll break it to the old folks for you."   He turned to them with his friendly smile. "I said I'd break it to you," he explained.

"What?" they asked, with wide-eyed expectancy.

"Olive's going to marry, and you—" he said, wickedly.

"Durn you, young Joe, have it out!" shrieked grandfather.

"—And you've been doing the courtin'!"

THE PROFESSOR OF DÖLLINGEN.

I.

THE doctor's hand came down with such a bang that the dominoes before him leaped up in consternation, and the students at the next table, who were smoking and drinking over a noisy game of cards, turned to see what the matter was. The professor's shaggy eyebrows twitched nervously over his absent-minded gray eyes and round spectacles, at this manifestation of the doctor's excitement.

"Yes," the doctor repeated, "an idea!"

"But, my friend," the professor began, slightly irritated, with a touch of superiority in his tone, "don't agitate yourself."

"I tell you," the doctor continued, with an angry glance at his unconscious neighbor—"I tell you it would be better for the world, if pen, ink and paper were confined to an elect few. It is the misery of our age that every boarding-school chit and every old pedant,"—another look—"consider themselves called upon to give the world the benefit of their minds—bah! —on one hand to fill the circulating libraries with trashy romances, and on the other hand to publish works which are but the accumulated result of years of reading, given to the world as original because the old idiot"—another look—"has forgotten where his mind ends and other men's minds begin. Ugh," the doctor exclaimed, in utter disgust.

(132)

"Hagen, now—" the professor again began im·
patiently.

"I swear," the doctor interrupted, "if I had any
control of the literature of this world, I would make
it a law that every one proposing to write a book must
come before some proper authority, and there and
then show that he has at least one good, original idea
in his work. Only one idea. I am reasonable, you
see. No matter how simple and unpretending that
idea might be, it should obtain permission for the book
to be published. I know, I know—you need not
speak," the doctor cried in a passion—"I know it is
a quixotic plan, and cannot be brought about," "or
where would you be, my learned friend?" he thought,
looking scornfully at the professor, whose face appeared curiously blurred behind the clouds of smoke
from his porcelain pipe. So thinking, with the scorn
that could not be suppressed, he buried his face in the
tankard of beer before him, to hide his emotions in
congenial bitterness.

"Of course I agree with you," and the professor
took his pipe out of his mouth, and spoke with the
impatience natural to a man who hates to be a lis-
tener.

"Oh, no, you don't; you would be a jackass if you
did," Dr. Hagen said, under his breath.

"What I wonder at is, how we got on such an irri-
tating subject."

"We were talking of your book, *The Progress of
Lucifer*," the doctor answered, with a malicious twinkle in his green eyes.

The professor drew himself up and frowned at the
doctor. "Strange!" he cried, "strange! Had we
been talking of some frivolous story, it would seem
natural; but after speaking of a work that deals with
the subtlest truths in Nature—a book that must form
an epoch in literature, upon which I have bestowed

the ripest thoughts of the ripest years ! " he concluded, greatly excited.

" Perhaps the thoughts and years are over-ripe, decaying," the doctor muttered with much contempt.

" What did you say ? "— The professor had the habit of absent-minded people, of only hearing what he chose to hear. " Recall your words, sir," he cried excitedly.

The doctor was caught, and in his confusion, his face turned three shades deeper red than his usual color, which was that fine crimson to be expected in a choleric gentleman of sixty. He was a little, stunted man, with a large head thickly covered by a crop of short, tightly-curled gray hair, that contrasted most oddly with his red face, out of which two green eyes looked defiantly into the world through a pair of gold spectacles. As for the mouth, it was a great long slit, firmly pressed together, and when open, it revealed a superb set of teeth, white, strong and cruel.

The doctor was disgusted with himself—at his unnecessary stupidity; but instead of apologizing, he half rose in his chair and sniffed the air with an injured expression.

" Sir, your manner is an insult," he cried to his enraged companion.

" Sir," the professor retorted,—"you have insulted *me.* You hate success, but you cannot control it. I will leave the world to judge of *The Progress of Lucifer ;* and as for your opinion, I hold it in the greatest contempt."

However, Nature had never intended that the professor should cope with the doctor, though he was certainly twice as tall and twice as broad as the little man. Hatred and envy he was indifferent to, so long as they did not touch his literary works, of which each in turn was his world, his all. He was a very learned man, with perhaps· a trifle too much reverence for past wisdom, and a want of toleration for new ideas. In certain circles, sacrilegious young men did call him an old fogy and a pedant, but the wicked remarks never reached his ears. Thus, when some new book of his was to be reviewed, faint-hearted critics took off their hats before the long words and ponderous sentences, and weakly bade the top-heavy stranger "God speed" into a new world.

When the professor was not absent-minded, there was a pleasant light in his gray eyes that brightened the heavy features and swept away the dazed, far-off look, like a fog before a summer's sun. But now he was trembling with wrath. With a look of assumed firmness, though his great hands shook, he grasped his faithful cotton umbrella and his well-worn, tall hat, and, with a voice choked by suppressed passion, said, as ceremoniously as he could under the circumstances, "After such language on your part I cannot again look upon you as a friend, Dr. Hagen," and marched majestically away, with his long pipe under his arm, leaving the little man dumb and amazed.

Just as he reached the door the professor paused. "Waiter!" As that light-footed functionary stood before him, the professor pulled an old, time-worn purse from the depths of his breeches-pocket. "Waiter, here are five groschens to pay for two glasses of beer for that gentleman and two for myself. You may keep the other;" and so speaking, while the gratified waiter held the door open, as if for the exit of a whole triumphal procession, the old man, in the happy consciousness of being a generous enemy and heaping coals of fire on the doctor's head, walked out into the chilly autumn air, and the door of the little inn, with its contents of smoke and beer, was shut upon him.

The professor and the doctor were not cronies. They were simply two odd men, who, not being able to find their mates, had drifted into the habit of meeting each other at the tavern of an afternoon, to smoke a pipe and drink a glass of beer over a game of dominoes. The professor was too much wrapt up in his own thoughts to be a very intimate friend for anybody, and the doctor had too bad an opinion of everybody to desire to be an intimate friend.

The doctor was a man with a ceaseless, secret pain at heart: he was an intensely ambitious man, with an ambition directed into a channel which was forever closed to him. His profession he chose from necessity, but the dream of his life had been to become a great writer: it had remained a dream. His standard was too high for his abilities, a lesser one he disdained. So, from one extreme to the other, he remained an obscure physician in a small German university town, seeing men of less talent than himself become famous, looking with keen, angry eyes behind the scenes of their daily workings; recognizing the tinsel and makeshifts and unreality, till his whole life seemed flooded with scorn and misanthropy.

"Waiter!" the doctor cried grimly, his firm, white teeth set on edge—"Waiter, did that—that—person pay for me?" he asked, pointing with his thumb over his shoulder, in the direction of the professor.

"He did, sir," the man replied.

"Then he made a mistake: I pay for both. You can keep what he gave you." So the doctor, in his turn, pulled out a scantily-filled purse and counted four groschens into the astonished waiter's hand. The doctor was a misanthrope, and gave only the exact sum, but the professor always had a penny to spare, if only for the grateful look on a man's face.

So the doctor, to his own satisfaction, balanced his enemy's coals of fire, and having relieved his feelings, took up his silver-headed cane and the round cap with a tremendous shiny visor, and strode out of doors, muttering to himself and bestowing all manner of maledictions on every object in the world, among which, after the manner of misanthropes, he was careful not to forget himself.

II.

IN the mean time the professor shambled along through the chilly air in the direction of his lodging, muttering to himself and gesticulating with his umbrella in a very angry fashion. His poor old heart beat with rage and grief to think how that—that—crocodile of a doctor had spoken of him, and, by implication, of his *Progress of Lucifer*, the work that was child and wife and life to him. Day and night, he had worked at it. Many a breaking dawn had discovered him at his writing-desk, poring over musty manuscripts, trying with half dazed brain, to understand crabbed old characters, or plunged, to all appearance beyond rescue, in philosophical speculations of the most abstruse kind.

Now he shambled along till he reached the narrow street with the chronic lack of sunlight and the old, old houses, in one of which he lived over a confectioner's shop, which was, curiously enough, a sore and constant temptation to him, for he had a passion for sweets. The confectioner, a round-faced, fat man in a white apron and a paper cap, looked with great pride on his lodger overhead, whom he called " comrade " in select and intimate circles—not owing to the professor's sweet tooth, but because he, the confectioner, considered himself something of a literary character, as he wrote all the mottoes for his candies. The good man's friendship did not end here, but often and often he invited the professor into the little back room as he passed, and treated him there to a glass of maraschino and a piece of cake, then lingered about respectfully, to catch whatever of wisdom must fall from the lips of so distinguished a man.

Now, however, so great was the professor's indignation, that neither cake nor maraschino could retard the heavy, wrathful steps with which he ascended the stairs to his solitary room.

The professors of the university of Döllingen were not very royally paid, but they had the infinite satisfaction of starving in excellent company. Our professor had a title twice as long as his purse, and he was content. He liked to have his belongings at arm's length about him, so that he could reach some dusty tome of an early morning, without getting out of bed, by just stretching one long, gaunt arm out of the bed-curtains to the book-shelves above his head.

It was a low-studded room, with two huge windows, whose diamond-shaped panes were favorite resorts for spiders and flies. In one corner, discreetly hidden by a green baize curtain, stood the bed, and in another, the great wardrobe that the professor had inherited from his mother. The walls were covered with books; books lay on the painted floor and on the chairs; they even encroached on the sacred precincts of the wardrobe; and as for the wash-stand, why, the pitcher stood in familiar proximity to that learned book of Fabricius, the *Holy, Sagacious and Learned Devil.*

But everything in the familiar room was blurred to the old man's sight. In great agitation he threw himself into the leathern arm-chair at his work-table, and buried his face in his hands. Suddenly, moved by a curious, uncontrollable impulse, he thrust aside the heap of papers and references that littered the desk, and from whose every page Satan and Lucifer and the Devil peeped forth in his heavy, irregulai handwriting.

"Fool! fool!" he cried passionately, then laid his hands upon them again with a certain tenderness, as a fond father tries to shield the child of his heart, whom some danger threatens.

But there was no peace in store for the poor professor. His head ached furiously and his hands and feet were like ice. With a shiver he started up and paced the room with hurried, irregular strides.

"I—I have taken cold," he muttered to himself, chafing his gaunt hands, and continued muttering, as he strode up and down the room.

"Damn him! damn him!" he cried at last, standing stock still and shaking his fist at an imaginary doctor. "But I defy him! I'll write a pamphlet against him: I'll—I'll unmask him, the envious wretch!" and over the professor's face there spread a triumphant smile. "I'll write a letter and say what I think of him as a doctor, and have it printed. I'll say he is decaying, over-ripe, gone to seed. Ha! ha! ha! Nothing underhand about that: he will recognize his enemy."

So in the gathering darkness he sat down at his desk, and began to scratch away on the first piece of paper that lay before him. But his fingers failed him, and he sank back, shivering and dizzy.

"I'll wait till to-morrow—to-morrow; he cannot escape me," he muttered. "And—yes, yes, I had better go to bed. How the room swims about! Ugh! I am afraid I have taken a bad cold," and the professor shivered in the chilly darkness, in which only the bed and wardrobe could be distinguished, looking grim and ghastly in their respective corners.

The professor dispensed with light at his simple toilet, for he was, above all things, a creature of habit; and in a moment more his harassed, aching old head was tossing about on the pillow, while his outward shell lay in artistic confusion on the floor.

III.

THE sun shone in at the professor's window the next morning, and, in cheery fashion, could be made to stop nowhere but at the green curtains of his bed, where it doubtless obtained admission through some forgotten hole—not an unusual thing in the belongings of the learned man—for, in a second more, the professor put his old head out to look at the unusual guest.

Simultaneously with the appearance of his head, the knob of the door was turned, dishes rattled, then the click-clack of a pair of pattens ; and the next instant there stood before the professor's gaze Hebe, with a tray containing his breakfast of coffee and bread ; Hebe with a mop under her arm ; Hebe looking domineeringly at her charge from under an enormous cap of a whitish material, which fitted with uncompromising closeness about her head, and was tied under her huge chin, by two simple tape strings.

Hebe was accustomed to her vocation, for she was included in the bill, and so she clacked about in her wooden shoes in search of a chair. As they were all covered with books, she calmly emptied the Talmud, Velez de Guevara and an old book of Wynkin de Worde, with a dozen or more biographies of the Devil, on the floor, to the mute horror of the professor ; and at last, on the rescued chair, she placed the breakfast at his side, and then, leaning on her long-handled mop, she calmly watched him.

" Ho ! " Hebe exclaimed at length.

" What is it ? " the professor asked, accustomed to this mode of address.

" Ho, but the city authority "—by which she meant a policeman—" left this an hour ago for you."   With

these words the handmaiden began a methodical examination of a dozen pockets, and at last, from a very
secret recess of her petticoat, produced an official-
looking document sealed with the three great seals
of the university of Döllingen, the whole a little the
worse for the wear of Hebe's pocket.

"Dear me! what can it be?" he exclaimed, turning it every which way.

"Perhaps if it were opened"—Hebe volunteered,
when the professor, looking up suddenly, felt that she
was slightly familiar and a little near, and with a
sharp "Take the dishes away now, Trinka"—for
Hebe's earthly name was Trinka—wounded that faithful chore-woman to the heart.

The official-looking envelope was at last opened.
"Good God! am I dreaming?" shouted the professor.

It was dated the day before from the university.
As the professor read the date he remained open-
mouthed, and at length could only gasp, "What a
coincidence!"

The document was printed, and ran thus :

"The Faculties of all the universities of Germany
have met for the purpose of deciding in what manner
to prevent the present corrupting influence on our
literature and our nation of the publication of the
vast quantity of worthless books and other printed
matter, injurious alike to intellect and morals.

"As the literature of a country is the education of
its people, the greatest minds in Germany have, for
this purpose, given their most faithful and valuable
counsel, the result of which has obtained the august
sanction of our emperor, who, for the sake of his beloved people, has commanded that which we would
only too gladly have tried as an experiment shall,
from this day, become a law."

"THE LAW.

"From this day forth, in every city there shall be established the office of censor of literature, to whom all works previous to publication must be brought for examination, that he may judge if it will be for the advancement of literature that they be printed. If there is only one good and original idea in a whole work, the book shall be published. If, however, it is found that the book contains but old ideas in new language, then it will be best that such a work be suppressed. This law shall hold good in the case of every manuscript, of whatever magnitude, which is to be printed and sold."

Underneath was written in the well-known hand-writing of the secretary of the university of Döllingen : "'Three rooms have been set apart in the town-hall for the censor of literature, who enters upon his office to-day, and may be seen between the hours of 9 A. M. and 2 P. M. by any applicant who feels convinced that his work contains the requisite qualities for success. In conclusion, it will be as well to state that those whose works are completed will be wise to apply immediately, as the censor will be overwhelmed with duties as soon as his office is more popularly understood."

"Good God!" the professer again cried, and sank into deep meditation. "What will the doctor say when he hears of this?"

He meditated profoundly, and the upshot was that, it being a mere formality for such a man as himself, and as *The Progress of Lucifer* was completed, he would comply with the advice of the writer and take *Lucifer* to the town-hall.

At the same time he would satisfy his curiosity—which was greatly aroused—by discovering who was the man who could be impartial, inhuman and wise enough to criticise every variety of polite and learned literature.

"One thing I am sure of," he muttered as he performed his ablutions—"that Hagen knew all about it yesterday, and instead of telling me outright, like an honest man, he went about hinting and sneering. But I'll be even with him yet," he exclaimed angrily; and in his passion got soap into his eyes, and so splashed and sputtered away, that the *Holy, Sagacious and Learned Devil* was more drenched than comfortable for an individual presumably used to warm regions.

It was just ten o'clock when the professor descended the stairs with *Lucifer* under his arm, and content and satisfaction beaming from his face.

"Why, bless my soul! how do you do, neighbor?" he cried, for there, on the sidewalk, stood the confectioner, brilliant in his Sunday best. "Where are you going at this time of day?" he continued, amazed.

It was neither Sunday nor a holiday, and the baker —for of course he was also a baker—should by rights have been standing behind his counter selling penny tarts.

"I am bound to the town-hall," the little man said, with much pride.

"Are you, indeed?" the professor cried, astonished. "So am I; then we will go together."

Thus the gratified baker accompanied the learned man, lingering one step behind as a sacrifice to his notions of respect.

The professor walked on engrossed in thought, while the honest confectioner racked his brains for a topic of conversation worthy of so great a man; and he was still so engaged when they crossed the market-place.

The market-place was silent and deserted this morn-.ing, except for the bronze statue of an old fighting prince, immortally portrayed in periwig and cocked hat, and mounted on a well-fed horse with a superb mane and tail.

At the door of the old, weather-beaten town-hall, with the memory of something Spanish in its time-stained angles and curves, there was a small crowd of people going in.

"Curious," the professor murmured. "I never saw so many people here.—I suppose I must leave you now," and he turned to his companion.

"I am going up to the first floor," the man answered.

"So am I, and, so it seems, are all these people," and the professor watched them file up the great stone stairs.

"Perhaps," the little baker ventured to say—"perhaps we are all bound on the same errand."

"Ha! ha! ha!" laughed the professor. He could not help it for the life of him. "Ha! ha! ha!" Connecting his *Progress of Lucifer* and that rabble! As he thought of it he laughed again.

"I myself am going for this purpose," the confectioner said humbly; and, with these words, he drew from his coat-tail pocket an exact copy of the solemn looking envelope which the professor had received that same morning.

"You? you?" cried the professor. "Do you mean to say that you cultivate literature as well as confectionery?" and he stared at his neighbor with wide-opened eyes.

"A little, a little," the other answered, not without pride. "If your honor was at the Baroness Stumpf-stein's party last week you must have noticed my work, for I wrote all the mottoes for the sugar-balls." So speaking, the little man with his right hand on his breast struck an attitude which all but said, "I am the Man!"

"Ha! ha! ha!" the professor laughed and, in his vast amusement, he had to cling to the railing of the steps to keep from falling. "Ha! ha! ha! Excuse my hilarity. I was not at the baroness's party; nevertheless, I greet you as a poet. May I ask if you intend publishing any more verses?"

"Yes, honored sir; the Countess Hasenfels gives a party next week, when my Muse is to have *carte blanche.*"

"You are a lucky poet," cried the professor, as they climbed the stairs to the rooms of the censor, "you will never starve. If one profession gives out, you have the other. Lucky, lucky poet!" he cried, shaking his forefinger at his companion, who would as soon have expected bitterness in one of his own almond tarts, as irony in the professor.

The professor peeped curiously about, wondering in which of the labyrinths of corridors he should dive, when from one of the neighboring rooms there appeared a solemn being in black, who, seeing the manuscript under the professor's arm, asked his name, which he no sooner heard than he respectfully led the way into a small bare room, destitute of everything but a couple of pine chairs.

"As soon as His Excellency, the court poet, has finished with the censor, you may take your turn. In that room we let the herd wait," pointing to a closed door with his thumb. "But who is this?" and he turned on his heel and confronted the unhappy confectioner, who felt in his inmost heart that he belonged to the "herd" and had no business there.

"A friend of mine, pray let him stay," the professor answered, hastily.

The respectable man stared at the confectioner from head to foot with much contempt, who crept into a remote corner, and sat down, holding his hat between his knees. The professor stood looking out

10

of the solitary window, quite near the door of the room where the court poet and the terrible censor were closeted together, by which door some old locksmith, long since dead, had not done his duty; for the latch would not catch, leaving it open enough for the professor to hear distinctly every word that was uttered; a fact of which he would have remained unconscious, if suddenly a well known voice had not reached his ears—a bitter, biting voice that had called him, the author of *The Progress of Lucifer*, over-ripe, decaying, the day before.

"What can the doctor have to do here?" he thought, starting forward.

The next instant his doubts were set at rest when he heard that same voice say, "I am still a novice in my position, Your Excellency, but so much the more will I do my duty."

"Merciful Heavens!" the professor thought—"he the censor? he, the unsuccessful man of letters, a critic?   But they were wise who made this bitter foe to success the judge, for what sterner critic could they find?"

' "Sir," said this same voice with much dignity, "the insults you lavish on me but recoil upon yourself. 1 have read your poems, and I find in them no line worthy of you. Your Excellency, you wrong your genius, and some day you will thank me, for, in spite of your great name, I will not allow your poems to be published."

"Prevent me, if you dare," cried a passionate voice, and the next instant His Excellency dashed out of the room. But it is not often that a court poet hears the truth.

"Aha! you here, my good friend?" cried the doctor, and, rubbing his hands in high glee he walked up to the professor. "Let by-gones be by-gones. Come, shall we be on friendly terms again? For I must tell you that I feel contented; I like this position amazingly. It just suits my taste."

"Dr. Hagen," the professor began, "I did not come to see you; I came to see the censor of literature, in whom I regret to find you, though I believe you to be an honest man. You do not need or want my friendship, so I only ask you to judge of my work as impartially as you would that of a stranger."

"You are at least just," the doctor answered, with a malicious smile, "and so am I. You will acknowledge that I have the right to judge of your work, for I have been a silent witness of its progress. Oblige me by entering my office. Let me take your manuscript. Some men have the ridiculous idea that an original subject is to be desired. Your subject is not entirely new."

"Not new in the past, perhaps," and the professor grew excited, "but now in our practical nineteenth century, who would care to write on so mystical a subject."

"My dear professor, it is always the dreamers who deny their natures; and it is just the same with the nineteenth century. If we could judge of other ages with the same knowledge we do of this, I believe their romance would pale before ours. Let me give you a practical example.—Johann!" The man of service appeared, to whom the doctor gave instructions in a whisper, and as he turned his back to the professor, a grin of exquisite malice made his green eyes greener, and distended his wide mouth from ear to ear.—"My dear friend, I must give you a lesson," he thought.

At that moment there was heard a humble, faltering tap at the door.

It opened, and there entered a procession of seven. One of the seven was fat and wore a pompous look and a gold watch chain; he was an exception. Middle-aged men they were all, with anxious, harrowed faces, and a bewildered look in their spectacled eyes. Each carried a voluminous manuscript under his arm, and they all glared at each other with deep suspicion.

"Gentlemen," the doctor said with much friendliness, as if deprecating his new authority—"Gentlemen, I had Johann call you, fearing that your time would be lost waiting in such a crowd. It will be best if each of you will in turn leave his manuscript and address at the desk.—Herr Simponius," said the doctor, seating himself at his desk quite near the professor, and addressing the individual who had tapped at the door,—"Herr Simponius, pray advance," which he did, and apologetically dictated to the doctor: "Adolph Simponius, author of *The World and the Devil*," and apologetically laid his manuscript down, while the doctor, with a look of sly enjoyment, watched the surprise on the professor's face.

The next man had more assurance: "Dietrich Reinhold, author of *Demonology and Witchcraft*."

"Many thanks, Herr Reinhold: I shall be delighted to examine your fine library, and proud to meet your wife."

Number three: "Heinrich Hermann, author of *The Life of Satan*."

A glance of venomous amusement at the bewildered surprise of the professor.

So through the list till the seven had disappeared, and seven manuscripts alone remained as a token of their presence.

With his chin resting on his hand, the doctor, as if absent-minded, read the remainder of the titles out loud: "*The Devil's Book, Lucifer's Kingdom, The Club-footed Devil, Modern Demons.* Hum! hum! a pretty collection!" he muttered to himself, all the while sharply watching his victim.

"Good God! What do you mean by this farce?"

and a heavy hand was laid on his shoulder. "Why can't you be honest, outspoken?"

"Take your hand from my shoulder, sir," the doctor cried, turning haughtily on the old man. "As for understanding the drift of such expressions, I am afraid I am as much at a loss for a meaning as your readers generally are."

"What am I now? what am I now?" murmured the old man, as he turned away and buried his face in his hands.

"You are one of eight," the doctor cried with a mocking smile. "Eight there are in the good town of Döllingen alone who write about the Devil. You know they say—ha! ha!—that misery loves company. Yesterday I dared only hint; to-day I may—nay, it is my duty to speak openly. Would you put your name to that book?" he cried, placing his hand on the professor's manuscript. "Then you would be giving your name to a lie—a lie, I say. You did not write it: ages of long-forgotten men, have written it. It is their wisdom, their knowledge and—pray be comforted—their folly. You have read much in your life "—

"Stop, Hagen!"

"No, I will not. You have read much, but while you remember the contents of books, you forget their authors, and their ideas, and yours become strangely intermingled until you claim the paternity of all. Why, you have neither originality nor ideas—you, the learned man! Mark me!" he cried with a triumphant smile, pointing toward the half-opened door, "that little confectioner out there has more originality than you, and does more good to the world, for he at least amuses with his imbecile rhymes, while you, you great man, can neither teach nor amuse."

"Spare me! spare me!" cried the old man, sinking back into his chair, with a smothered groan.

"Why should I spare you?   The world did not spare me, but I had to learn the bitter lesson from every penny paper."

"You are a stern teacher," the old man cried, rising, and, as the doctor watched him with curious eyes, he seemed ten years older than the hale, hearty man who had entered the room only half an hour before—"you are a stern teacher,—you have unmanned me and seen the agony of my heart.   That I regret.   We often have to stand as we are before our consciences, and you are my conscience, which has been sleeping till now.   Could you have been gentler in your treatment of me, I—I forgive you.   Perhaps your way was the kindest.   My manuscript?   Yes, yes, I will take it.   O God! the ruined hopes! the lost years!" he cried, burying his face in his hands.

Recovering himself, and without another look at his enemy, he opened the 'door.   The confectioner sat dozing in his corner.

The professor shook him.   "Come! come home with me!" he cried in a dazed way.

"Holy Virgin! what's the matter, sir?" the little man exclaimed, so haggard and worn did the professor look.

"A blow, my friend—a blow."

"What?" cried the confectioner, understanding it literally, and evidently making for the doctor.

"Not so, not so," and the professor detained him gently.   "Nothing you can heal, my friend—nothing you can heal.   Only come now; let us go home."

So they went.   Johann shut them out with little ceremony, for they were of no account in the literary world or any other world.   They passed a new crowd going in with hopes full blown, but nobody noticed them, the bowed old man leaning on the little round poet.

So they reached the narrow street.   Again the well-known room closed about him, and at last even the green curtains of the bed ; and now, for the first time, he was alone—alone with his misery. In his despair and sorrow he buried his gray head in the pillow and burst into a wild, dreadful flood of tears.

"He has come back to consciousness," said the doctor, as he bent anxiously over the professor.

From the pillow two hollow eyes glared at him, and a feeble hand tried to push him away.

"You here?" the professor whispered.

"Why, of course—been here for a couple of weeks. In fact, had a bed put up here. You've been pretty sick, and I had a hard time pulling you through."

"You! After what you told me at the town-hall —I can never forget it—and what you said about *The Progress of Lucifer !*"

"Hush!" the doctor commanded, gently. "You are dreaming. For two weeks you have been dreaming : we call it brain fever."

"But — but what you said at the inn?" the professor murmured, bewildered.

"I have said many things that I have regretted sorely : that was one. I came here the next morning to bid you not mind an old misanthrope like myself, and I found you already delirious. Trinka said that you talked all sorts of nonsense to her when she brought you your breakfast. So I found you."

"Oh, forgive me ! forgive me !" and the professor grasped with two thin hands the doctor's right hand.

"Forgive you? I? Why, you should forgive me."

"No, no! I have been so unjust to you ! I thought of you with hatred. I dreamed you said *The Progress of Lucifer* was not original—that it did not contain one good idea," and the poor professor looked wistfully at the doctor's embarrassed face. "Yes,

yes, my dream has come true; I have wasted my life," he groaned, turning his head away.

"My dear professor," and the doctor, took the old man's unresisting hand in his own, "*The Progress of Lucifer* must be a forbidden subject to you. It has been your death, nearly; that is as much as you can give to one work. If you still wish to live, I forbid you thinking of it for one year at least. I have had all the damned histories of the Devil taken away; if after a year you wish them back, you shall have them."

"I obey," the professor said solemnly, "for I have had a warning."

There was an incredulous smile about the doctor's mouth, and a question in the end of his turned-up nose.

"Do not smile," the professor said sadly. "I have had a warning which I shall obey. You will laugh if you know that I have had a lesson in a dream, and that instead of waiting for the judgment of the world, I accept yours and abide by it. You came here grieved for your hasty words, but with unchanged opinions, I know."

"You have done wisely and bravely," thought the doctor, and pressed the professor's hand, and for the first time he loved him. Was he not on his own level now, defeated and unhappy? From this moment the contradictory doctor was ready to sacrifice everything to restore these shattered hopes.

"Take all these things away," the professor cried— "books, papers. Heaven knows, I wish you could take my memory also!"

"Nonsense! nonsense!" the doctor interrupted cheerily. "In a few days you will be well again, and you and I will quarrel as we used. The old times will come back with the old professor."

"Never, Hagen! The old times have carried away the old professor."

" There's Trinka come to see how you are. Trinka, bring me a chair and a pipe," the doctor commanded: " I want to sit down by your master and show him that as long as a friend remains and there is a curl of smoke in a pipe, the old times must surely come back."

A TRIFLE OF INFORMATION.

I.

FROM Miss Dorothy Outerbridge to her brother, Captain Richard Outerbridge.

Villa Bellevue, St. Severin on the Rhine,
June 2nd, 1890.

DEAREST DICK: Why didn't you take me with you! To say that no nice young man wants his sister tagging after him! Did I not offer to pretend not to be your sister, and you said that would not do at all? Aunt Mumler botanizes and comes home all mosquito bites. Such mosquitoes as they have here! I told Aunt we'd have to take to smoking, and she was awfully shocked.

It is so tiresome here, Dick, and I am just dying for a romance. I thought romances were commoner here than in New York, but Priscilla says that men who know anything, don't fall in love with things like me, and she may be right.

I have no chance when Priscilla's about! Sunday we went to church and everybody stared at her, and she captured a girl. It wasn't much, but it was better than nothing. The girl comes every afternoon to adore her and I just run, I can't stand it.

I have thought it over and I mean to form myself on Priscilla's plan,—my mind and my style, I mean, for I can't get my nose down straight, and that is a trial!

I've found just the loveliest place where I can be alone,—only don't tell! It is a garden. I practise

(154)

here raising my head and showing off my eyelashes just as Prissy does, while I hold my nose. A girl I knew did a great deal that way towards making hers Grecian, and she said it was a great deal worse than mine.

Perhaps when I am quite perfect the romance will come.

I heard the other day that there is an awfully handsome man here among the summer boarders, who forges bonds and things,—millions worth! I'd like to meet him! Perhaps after a while he would fall in love with me, and repent. Wouldn't that be a romance! But he'd be sure to fall in love with Priscilla instead,—I have no chance.

Do send me a box of candy from Baden-Baden; I think it would make life more endurable till you come back.

There's that dreadful Cordula (Priscilla's girl) and now I must run, for they're beginning!

Your loving sister,
DOLLY.

The hills about St. Severin on the Rhine were capped by gloomy mediæval castles, from which the noble proprietors gazed with scorn upon unassorted summer boarders, giddily enjoying themselves by means of donkeys, dancing and band concerts in the casino.

Beyond the village there were certain villas to be rented for the season, and one, the loneliest and most expensive, seemed to rent along with its other advantages, a vague claim to at least moderate civility from the (truly) upper circles, for the upper circles, after penetrating into a boarder's pedigree, were not insensible to the state of his cash account.

As this story opens, this desirable villa had been rented by an American family, upon whom St. Severin turned a perplexed scrutiny.

There was a lively young man who never ceased asking questions, and there was an old lady in spectacles who would have asked questions had she not been mercifully ignorant of the German language.

The other two members refreshed the sight of St. Severin the next Sunday at the Protestant chapel, where the select of St. Severin worshiped, the unselect being Roman Catholics, while the summer boarders, for unexplained reasons, were heathens.

A couple of old generals and a gouty baron or two, stared heavily as a very beautiful woman passed up the aisle, followed by a young person in pink.

It was at once known that this was the lady of the villa, Mrs. Oldecott from New York, and the young person in pink was her sister, Miss Outerbridge. The gentleman was their brother, Captain Outerbridge, U. S. A. on leave, and the old lady of the inquiring mind was their aunt, Mrs. Mumler.

It further transpired that Capt. Outerbridge, having exhausted St. Severin, had embraced his family and retired to the joys of Baden-Baden.

II.

FROM Mrs. Oldecott to her brother, Captain Outerbridge.

Villa Bellevue.
June 2nd.

My Dear Dick : You would have liked St. Severin better had you stayed. Aunt Mumler is *so* contented, she botanizes and keeps a diary for the people in Portland. I wish Dolly liked it better ; I think she misses you, and she dusts your room every day in melancholy remembrance. I found her crying over your cigarettes the other day. She has a way of disappearing after breakfast and if this were not so quiet and safe a place, I should certainly interfere,—she is too independent.

I have met some very pleasant people, quite the nicest here, a Baron and Baroness Von Stendal and their daughter, who is devoted to me. There is a brother attached to the German embassy in London. Cordula talks about him a good deal and that is rather tiresome.

Don't stay away too long, Dick dear, for we do miss you badly.

With much love,
PRISCILLA.

The Stendals firmly believed that they were as old as the hills and, indeed, the first Baron Stendal was of the 7th century, when he became at once a good Christian and the most scoundrelly robber on the Rhine. The present Baroness wore a breakfast shawl and had her hair cut short, and she nagged the Baron, her husband, in the intervals of knitting endless stockings.

They were, however, united in wholesome awe of their son, Baron Kurt von Stendal, and his occasional visits were the joy and terror of their lives. The young man did not realize what an event his coming was, nor how he upset that respectable establishment. His own infallibility bored him fearfully, and he had been known to disappear for a couple of days to breathe air unincensed, and even his good mother did not dare to remark on these abrupt departures.

The continental train was just leaving the London station, when Baron Stendal opened his sister's last letter and smiled absently at its enthusiasm. "I have a new friend who is so lovely, and how I wish you would fall in love with her, though—there!—she is a widow, and I used to think widows should not marry again. But her husband was old and she only married him because he was so distinguished, her Aunt told me. Her Aunt is a nice person who asks a great many questions.

"Truly, Kurt dear, this is the first woman I ever wanted you to marry. She is nearly worthy of you, and I adore her. There is a sister, but I do not think much of her."

III.

THE pride of St. Severin was its "Jaeger-hof," an old rococo hunting-lodge, all stucco-work and statues. Its owner, a prince of Prussia, had died, and the Jaeger-hof, with its concert-hall and ball-room decorated with fat, improper cupids and faded rose garlands, was deserted.

The gardens were overgrown with weeds, and time, aided by a tangle of vines, had arrayed the broken-nosed statues in a manner more befitting 19th century propriety.

In the midst of what was once a lawn, but which was now a wilderness of grass dotted by vagrant poppies, stood a huge gnarled apple tree, about which some considerate soul had built a wooden bench. Not a sound was to be heard but the drone of the locusts and the hum of the bumble-bees. Even the girl who sat in the shade of the apple tree reading, did not stir. It was so peaceful and yet the enemy was preparing for assault.

"Buzz--uzz--zz--z-pick!"

"O dear me, those horrid mosquitoes!" and Dolly lashed herself with a bunch of poppies, then leaned forward, her round chin in her hand, and dreamed a little. "A hundred years is a long time to wait for a prince,—I do think the poor princess must have felt a little old in her heart when—O dear me, do go away!" here she sat bolt upright and flicked the poppies about her head, for the mosquitoes were swarming merrily.

Constant and solitary possession had given Dolly quite a sense of owning this garden of the late prince of Prussia, and she never dreamed that any other person would intrude ; it was therefore with a sense of security that Miss Outerbridge practiced modifying herself on the plan of the stately Priscilla, raising her head and lowering her eyelashes, in the meantime holding her nose with commendable gravity.

Just then a stranger sauntered through the opposite entrance ; he carried a book and look bored. The heavy grass deadened his tread, and sitting down on the other side of the apple tree, he proceeded to entertain himself with a joyous report (statistical) of the German consular service.

He did pause to say, "The child is a perfect nuisance with her widow! What is her name? Never mind. Go to see her? I'll be hanged if I do," and he dived into his report.

There being a serpent in this garden of Eden, with historic accuracy he addressed himself to Eve.

"Buzz--uzz--zz-z-pick !"

"It's just too dreadful!" and Eve lashed herself with the poppies.

No sooner said, than she heard a masculine exclamation, and before she could struggle into an engaging attitude, there he stood,—her romance. He had appeared from the other side of the tree.

"Pardon me, but can I be of service?" he asked in excellent English, and it sounded so natural to Dolly, that she quite forgot to wonder, except as to what Priscilla would do in this delightful situation. In the meantime she sat up very straight and made a frantic effort to hide her feet ; then she wondered how long he had observed her, and at the thought, she blushed crimson.

Of course Priscilla would be gracious, but with a film of frost, and so Dolly checked a too friendly smile.

"Thank you, it is only the mosquitoes, they are so troublesome," she murmured.

"Please don't let them drive you away," this sympathetic stranger urged.

Here Dolly was false to her model. "I do have such times with them since Dick went away,—he used to smoke. Were you sitting at the other side of the tree?"

"Yes, I was reading. I am afraid I startled you."

"Never mind. Do you know I don't really want to go home quite yet! Perhaps you wouldn't mind smoking a cigar? I should be so awfully obliged. I know that will keep them away."

"With pleasure, if I have one with me. I am not much of a smoker."

However he found one, lighted it and looked beseechingly at the curve of the bench by her side..

But Dolly was alarmed,—what would Priscilla say if she knew!

"Please don't let me detain you any longer."

The accommodating stranger hastened to say that he had nothing else to do all day.

"I do like the smoke best at a little distance," Dolly urged.

The effect of this speech was instantaneous, the stranger retired to his side of the tree.

"I don't think that sounded quite polite," Dolly meditated, and she considered whether Priscilla in her place would explain that she didn't mean to be rude.

The sufferer on the other side of the tree pondered, smoking vigorously.

This young person was very impolite, but why should she let him take a liberty? Here he was seized with a longing for another sight of her face, and succumbing to temptation he looked cautiously around the corner and met the gaze of two inquiring eyes.

"I—only wanted to ask if the mosquitoes are still troubling you?" he faltered.

"They have all gone, thank you so much. And if—if you please, I wanted to say that I didn't mean to be rude—about the smoke, you know. Dick corrects me a great deal, but he's away now. It was awfully good of you to oblige me, but you needn't smoke any longer for that, as I'm going. Good-by," and she disappeared, and he stood there gazing after her, trying long after she was out of sight, to think of something brilliant and appropriate to say.

Mrs. Oldecott lay back in a low willow chair. She was a picture and she knew it. Beside her on a table were Cordula's roses. They had been sent the evening before with a message that she had been detained, as her brother had arrived.

"Now for a deluge of Stendals."

But Priscilla was mistaken, no Stendals came and even Cordula stayed away. Priscilla resented this defection of her slave and so she was cross to Aunt Mumler. When things went wrong, Dolly's shortcomings came triumphantly to the fore.

"What has become of Dolly? You don't look out for her a bit, Aunt!"

"Dolly is all right, Priscilla, this place is safe, safer than—Portland." Aunt Mumler was just writing in her diary. "I have seen a young man in Portland, but I haven't here."

"I don't mean that, Dolly is such a child; but one ought to think of appearances."

Here the culprit sauntered in. "Where have you been, Dolly?"

Dolly turned to the window and became engrossed in the landscape.

"Been reading."

"Dolly, you are frightfully rude."

"I'm afraid I am, Prissy."

"It is something that you realize it. I wish you had one of your dolls here, you need amusement, child."

"Why Priscilla, I play with dolls! Why, you were married at my age?"

"That is the only thing you don't need to imitate."

"I shall do just as I please—"

"I dare say you will, only don't surprise us too much."

Dolly gazed at her sister with a forgiving smile. To mention dolls to her,—Dorothy Outerbridge,— who had been spending the morning in the society of an interesting stranger with a cigar. A stranger upon whom even Mrs. Oldecott herself would gaze with charity, for Priscilla had in the strictest sense, charity towards all men.

Miss Outerbridge retired to a nook where, in her hitherto unromantic career, she had dreamed about nothing in particular.

She curled herself in the broad window-seat and turned her thoughts to the accommodating stranger.

"I mustn't go over there again, though it was so nice and quiet; or I might go in the afternoon, for I've just as much right there as he. I would be ashamed to meet him there again—he might think I—no, I won't go! How well he speaks English. I wonder what he thinks of me? I wish I had worn my pink dress! But that is too late now.—What would Prissy do? I simply can't go over there again. Oh, dear! and it was the only place where they would leave me alone!"

The next morning at breakfast Dolly's entrance excited some comment.

"Why, Dolly, you have on your pink dress."

"The blue one is all shrunk in the washing, Priscilla, and it doesn't near reach my ankles. You don't pay any attention to my clothes, you are so taken up with your own."

"Why, Dolly, what has happened? Didn't I beg you yesterday morning not to go tearing about in that dreadful buff gingham, and you said I was always bothering. The other day you said you wished you could live in a suit of armor and be scoured off once a week."

Dolly, confronted with her own inconsistencies, remarked with dignity, "It's a long time since yesterday morning, Priscilla, and I've changed my mind. It doesn't take twenty-four hours to do that."

After breakfast Dolly lingered irresolutely. She flattened her nose against the window panes and flung herself in turn on all the chairs.

At last, with a look of heroic purpose, she fetched her hat and a book.

"Why shouldn't I? It isn't his garden! Besides, he probably won't come."

.   .   .   .

Baron Kurt had finished a late and lonely breakfast in the ancestral dining-room. He strolled to the Gothic window and stared at the distant village.

"Yes, I think I will go down to the Jaeger-hof,— delightful place for reading.—Intrusion? Why, it's not her garden. Besides, she may not be there. I must not forget the cigars."

Just then Cordula came into the room.

"Will you come this morning and make that call, Kurt dear?"

"Do leave me alone, you absurd child," and he pulled her ear good-naturedly, "I am busy. Besides, don't try your hand at match-making. If you knew more of human nature, you would understand that a brother and sister never fall in love with the same woman."

When Baron **Kurt** reached the apple tree he found there a young person in pink reading with such intentness that, though she blushed furiously, she did not see him until he stood before her.

"O, good-morning,—there you are again," Dolly said with an engaging smile, "I've been wondering if you'd—I mean, I was wondering if there would be any mosquitoes here to-day."

"They shall not disturb you, I have brought plenty of cigars."

"How nice of you.   It is just as if Dick were here. Dick is my brother.   It doesn't seem right to let you smoke all your cigars to keep off the mosquitoes, does it?   But I mustn't interfere with your reading,—how wise your book looks."

Baron Stendal blushed.   In fleeing from Cordula he had grasped the first book at hand, and it happened to be a dictionary.

"May I smoke?"

"Isn't that what you are here for?"   The stranger retired to his side of the tree, injured, and Dolly meditated on the curious way she had of saying rude things with the best intentions.

On his side of the tree, the injured one smoked and nursed his resentment.

"So she thinks I am here only to smoke for her benefit!   She probably imagines I came here for a sight of her blue eyes and—well, to-morrow I rather think she will be surprised,—I won't come!"

"If you please," a contrite voice interrupted, "I'm afraid you must think I am very uncivil,—you'll excuse me, won't you?   I never thought how it would sound.   I do mean to say the nicest things and then they sound horrid, and Priscilla says horrid things and they sound nice, until you stop to think."

The injured one was at once reconciled.   He approached her curve of the bench and took up her book.

"Please don't look at it, please don't! You'll think I am so very young, and after all I am seventeen, nearly seventeen and a half."

It was a book of fairy-stories and it opened to the tale of the sleeping princess, and Dolly blushed as she thought how he must guess at once what she and the princess were waiting for. "I dare say you have decided that she lives in this old palace."

"Why, yes. How did you guess? She is sleeping on the loveliest white silk couch and she has long golden hair and a trailing veil, as fine as a cobweb,— and because she is a princess she wears a tiny crown all of diamonds. Some day the prince will come— and—and how I should like to be there.—What nonsense! You musn't think that I never read anything else, I've fallen asleep over nearly all of Aunt's books, and they are very improving.

V.

"I HAVE never seen Kurt so contented before," his mother declared, highly gratified. "He has not even suggested going away."

"I don't see what a man wants more than to be left alone," the old Baron growled.

"But he shouldn't hurry off to study, right after breakfast," the Baroness continued, shaking her head ; "strong as he is, he will wear himself out."

"My private impression is he has his French novels bound in law-calf."

Here Cordula appeared, a bunch of fragrant roses in her hand. She put on her eyeglasses and looked hurt.

"I only want to leave the roses at the villa, but I shall not call on Mrs. Oldecott until Kurt goes with me. It is very uncivil of him after all I have said to her."

But Kurt found a champion in his mother.

"Don't be so foolish, child, about this young person. Kurt has more important matters to attend to than to call on all the strangers who stray into St. Severin! Besides, she is an American and with Kurt's title and prospects—my dear, he must be protected."

.   .   .   .

Time was passing and the little apples on the old apple tree were swelling visibly.

"Ought I to tell Priscilla?" Dolly wondered.

After all, when one is seventeen one is at liberty to read under any apple tree, and she could not forbid the Nameless one,—so Dolly called him to herself,—occupying the other side ; besides, his conversation was improving and respectful, and his cigars were good. She only feared that he was smoking all his best ones in that enthusiastic battle with the mosquitoes.

The result of this meditation was that Dolly retired to Dick's room and examined his belongings.

The next morning the Nameless one was already there and his face brightened amazingly at sight of her.

She smiled and yet she looked rather embarrassed.

"Please take this," she said, and thrust a little package in his hand. "You see, I ought to do my share towards keeping the mosquitoes away, and—and as I can't smoke I—I—really thought it wasn't more than fair that—that—" here she broke down and blushed.

"I—I—hope you ar'n't offended at my asking you to take them?"

The Nameless one glanced with a smile at a red and gold bunch of cigarettes in his hand.

"You mustn't smoke them if you don't want to,—but I fancy they're good."

He took a meditative whiff. A peculiar taste. Never mind, they were from her—so he smoked on, resolutely.

"Will you allow me?" he asked, and sat down beside her.

Dolly observed him with some trepidation,—she couldn't help thinking that the Nameless one was taking a liberty; he had never shown such assurance before, for, though they generally happened together at the end, he always started respectfully with his own side of the bench.

Dolly pretended to read, but she watched him out of the corner of her eye while he smoked and looked at her with, yes, with frightful emphasis.

What would Priscilla say if she knew, and—Dick! She,—Dorothy Outerbridge,—had bestowed a bunch of Dick's cigarettes on a nameless stranger, whose only passport to her esteem was his improving conversation and his well-fitting clothes.

As it was, he smoked one cigarette after another and stared at her with equal perseverance.

For all practical purposes, considering what hearts are for, Dolly had hitherto been quite unconscious of hers, but now it began to beat in an unpardonable manner, and she looked desperately at her book.

Half of the red and gold package had vanished into thin air, and the Nameless one was beginning to regard life as a pleasant dream, the more so as he was decidedly drowsy.

"I'll tell Prissy all, and I'll never come here again! The idea of sitting there and not saying a word!"

She stole a glance at him. He had stopped smoking and passed his hand across his eyes, drowsily.

Dolly returned to her book. "I wonder who he

is,—the idea of not knowing his name. I beg your pardon—what did you say?"

With a faint exclamation the Nameless one rose to his feet, with one hand against the tree for support.

"It is nothing—a sudden dizziness," he murmured, and sank down on the bench again.

"Do come over to our house," Dolly cried, "we live only just across the way—and I am afraid you are ill."

He rose, made a few steps, then paused, covering his eyes again. "I don't think I can—I—I—this dizziness—"

"You must take my arm. No, that won't do, I'm not tall enough. Just put your hand on my shoulder—don't be afraid, I'm strong. Now you do feel steadier, don't you?"

He obeyed, and it took forever to cross the road to the villa. Dolly felt him swerve, and she grasped his arm with all her young strength. "Only two or three steps more. Courage!"

"Forgive me—I—I"—here he made a hopeless effort to grasp Dolly's hand, and the next instant he was lying unconscious at her feet.

Aunt Mumler heard Dolly's cry, and ran out to find her kneeling beside an unknown young man, trying to raise his head.

"O Aunt, help quick—he is dying! Call Priscilla—the gardener—any one!"

Aunt Mumler was paralyzed. "Get up this instant, Dolly,—are you hurt? Did he hurt you?"

"O Aunt, don't you see he'll die if you don't do something! He must be put into Dick's room at once."

Aunt surrendered, and the gardener and a strapping maid managed it between them, and by that time a doctor arrived.

Dolly waited for him outside the patient's room.

"What ails him," and she tried to rub some warmth into her trembling hands.

"He has all the symptoms of opium poisoning,—I think I found the explanation in his pocket, a bunch of cigarettes."

There was a cry, and Dolly, white and trembling, leaned against the wall for support. "Will—will—will he die."

"He is young and strong, and so—"

A touch of color crept back to Dolly's face.

"If I were to advise the gentleman—pardon me, I did not hear his name?"

Dolly stared at the little summer doctor with frightened eyes.

His name, indeed!

"B—Brown!" Dolly murmured, and clutched the nearest chair for support.

"Mr. Brown should beware of cigarettes unless he wishes to kill himself. Those he has been smoking contained, I should say, a murderous proportion of opium. Quite an instructive case, my dear young lady."

Aunt Mumler stepped softly out of Dick's room and found Dolly stranded on the hall-settle, crying torrents.

"Perhaps, Dolly, you'll now kindly explain—why, child, what is the matter?" For Dolly hung about her neck.

"Save me, Aunt, save me!"

"Save you?"

"Don't tell, Aunt, but if he dies, I'll have killed him!"

"What!"

"I don't know him, and I haven't any idea what his name is, but, all the same, I've killed him."

"You're crazy, child."

"I wish I were! but I am only disgraced, that's all."

"Dolly!"

"Dick's cigarettes killed him, and I gave him Dick's cigarettes—there!"

"Dolly!"

"That horrid doctor would know his name, and I had to say something," here she wept afresh, "and so I said it was B—Brown."

"And you mean to say, Dolly, that his name isn't Brown?"

"I told you just now that I don't know what his name is!"

"What would Dick say if he knew!"

"I couldn't be any more miserable if he did," here she shook out a morsel of a handkerchief dripping with tears, and hid her face on Aunt Mumler's shoulder.

"Auntie, if you ever really liked me, say that his name is B—Brown, and that he is a friend of yours from America—he—he speaks just the nicest English."

"But suppose, my dear, he says his name isn't Brown?" Aunt Mumler urged feebly.

"It's got to be."

"Dolly!" a voice called from above.

"There's Priscilla, and she'll want to know! It's just too dreadful!"

The wretched little criminal appeared before her judge. Her nose was red with friction and her handkerchief could absorb no more moisture.

"Please explain, Dorothy!"

"You see, Prissy dear, we were having such a pleasant time together until to-day. There was no harm, really. He went to the palace-garden to read, and so did I—and—and you know there is only one bench. His conversation was always very respectful."

"Oh, indeed."

"Yes, truly. But there were a great many mosquitoes about, and as he smoked just to oblige me, I thought I really ought to do my share. So this morning, I never dreamed of harm, I brought him a b—bunch of Dick's cigarettes—and—there he is now —downstairs — dy—dying — perhaps!" and Dolly gazed about for something fresh into which to weep.

"Take a towel and damp it right through, if you have any sense of propriety left."

"There's another thing, Prissy," a muffled voice urged from behind the towel, "you've got to call him B—Brown. The Doctor would know and so I had to say something, and so I said B—Brown, and he is supposed to be a friend of Aunt's, from America. She's ever so good about it. If I could see him just a minute, I'd explain. I know he'd be glad to say his name is Brown, to oblige me."

"That is accommodating. Well, you can't; besides, he is too ill to care what his name is."

"You must be dreadfully ashamed of me, Prissy!"

"Rather, Dolly, child."

"I don't mind that so much, but I couldn't bear to have Dick ashamed. Don't tell him, dear, and you shall see how grateful I can be."

Whereupon Dolly went in search of her aunt.

"Just as soon as he knows anything, tell him his name is Brown, that I told you so."

"I can't, Dolly, besides you said he doesn't know your name."

"That's true. But you tell him 'the girl in pink,' he'll know. He likes my pink dress very much—he said so."

"Certainly I sha'n't!"

"Then just let me put my head in the room and say—"

"Child, what are you thinking of!"

"Well, what am I to do! Don't be so unreasonable, Aunt! Shall I write him a note?"

"Don't you dare!"

"Then how is he to know his name? And what am I to do? Besides, he may be dying! Oh, Aunt, Aunt, I am too wretched. Do you think it is a broken heart? It feels more like that than anything else."

VI.

THE next day the Nameless one rallied and looked about perplexed. An old lady, beaming mild sympathy out of gold spectacles, came towards him.

"Where am I?" he asked in German.

"You must speak English, we are Americans."

"Why am I here," and he looked in deep disapproval at the bed.

"Because, my poor boy, you have been very ill."

"Humph!—Where am I?"

"In Mrs. Oldecott's house, dear. Well, I don't suppose you would know. You were taken ill here."

The Nameless one suddenly remembered.

"You don't mean to say that she is married," and he stared at Aunt Mumler with gaunt eyes.

"Who?"

"That is just what I don't know—who! But it seems that Dick is her brother, and that Priscilla is her sister."

"You probably mean my niece, Dorothy Outerbridge," Aunt Mumler said with dignity, and added under her breath, "who is a little fool, or you wouldn't be here, young man."

However she treated him well, in fact spoiled him, and gave him a hand-glass so that he could measure the ravages of disease.

"When he is stronger he shall explain," she decided severely. The Nameless one had no intention of explaining, so he took refuge in weakness.

Confess his name, indeed, and have his family come pouring down upon him, or, worse still, to be packed off home—never!

"To-morrow you will be on your feet again, Mr. Brown," the Doctor said to him that afternoon, "but, ha! ha! not independent of me."

The Nameless one stared. Here the German maid appeared. "Is Mr. Brown to have soup or a bit of chicken for dinner?"

"Mr. Brown?" he repeated, in growing amazement.

"He is ready for a good dinner," the Doctor said, genially.

"As an American how well you speak German, Mr. Brown. I suppose you spell your name with an 'ow.' We Germans spell it with an 'au.' You are quite like a German, really, and Miss Outerbridge surprised me when she said you were an American."

"Miss Outerbridge said so? Yes, I spell my name with an 'ow,'" and he smiled. Shades of his ancestors! What melody in the plebeian name of Brown with which she had favored him.

When dinner time came he was famished, and he suffered tortures for fear that he should recover too soon. ·

Mrs. Oldecott was very severe with Dolly. "Nursing a man we don't know from Adam! A man who doesn't tell his name, too, Dolly; that looks like a very bad conscience."

"I am sure that he is a gentleman," Dolly remonstrated, much subdued.

"He is probably something dreadful."

"Don't, please, Prissy!"

"What would Dick say if he knew?"

"But don't make it any worse, Prissy! Dick is in Baden-Baden."

Priscilla strolled into the garden,—she was greatly annoyed. A familiar voice roused her from her unpleasant meditations, and two arms were thrown about her neck.

"Dearest Mrs. Oldecott, I have not seen you for an age!"

"Why, Cordula, where have you been?" Cordula looked at her divinity through eyeglasses that twinkled as in a mist.

"Dearest, you knew that my brother came? A few days ago he went away without saying a word, and we have not heard from him since, and we are so anxious! He has done this before, but he never stayed away so long. We don't know what to do."

"He'll be sure to come back, dear; don't worry. When he does come, give him a good scolding. You spoil him terribly."

As Cordula went away, an aged man hobbled towards·Priscilla with a telegram. He was a familiar visitor, for Dick did most of his correspondence by wire, but Priscilla stared at this message in consternation.

"Homesick for you and Dolly. Am on the train to St. Severin. Dick."

"What shall I do?" was all she could say, but, indeed, there was little to do, for at that moment a dilapidated depot-carriage turned in at the gate.

"Here I am, Prissy; glad to see me? Where is Dolly?" and the next instant she was in Dick's arms.

"Just what I expected,—telegram and I came together! A regular one-horse country! I say, are you glad to see me?"

"Don't be foolish, Dick," and she struggled out of his grasp.

"Is this the welcome for which I have been pining? Same room, eh?"

In a moment he would have dashed in, only Dolly barred the way.

"Why, Dolly, old girl, what's up?"

"There—there—is some one ill here, Dick."

"Don't say Aunt is laid up."

"N—no—it's a—a friend."

"Didn't know we had friends here on such intimate terms. Anything catching? If she is a real, nice, jolly American, why—I say, Prissy, what is up?"

"I—I—meant to say, Dick dear, that it's a gentleman, a—a friend of Aunt's," Dolly interposed faintly.

"I see, some crony of Aunt's,—old Baptist parson from down East on a Cook's excursion. Got banged up and lets himself down on a parishioner. What's his name, Dolly?"

"B—Brown."

"Thank Heaven, that won't wear my memory out as most of these infernal foreign names do. Don't bother about me, girls, stow me anywhere."

Aunt Mumler found Dick in the midst of chaos, in his new quarters. He lit a cigar and resigned his wardrobe to her care.

"I say, Aunt, how is the old man?"

"What old man, Dick?"

"Why, your sick old man downstairs."

"O but he isn't old, he is young."

Dick whistled softly. "From Portland, eh?"

"No—no—not exactly. He's a German young man," and Aunt Mumler tried to hide her confusion in a bureau-drawer.

"By the name of Brown?"

"Y—yes, O yes."

"Humph,—been very ill?"

"Dreadfully. But he's up now and dressed."

“What kind of a chap is he?”

“Perfectly charming and so handsome.”

“I’d like to see your paragon.   Guess he’ll be glad to talk to a man for a change.”

“I’ll inquire, Dick,” and Aunt Mumler fled in search of Dolly.   “I simply can’t keep Dick out of that room, child.”

“Very well, then, but I must speak to him before Dick does,” Dolly cried in despair.

The Nameless one was in very low spirits when there came a hesitating knock at the door, and Aunt Mumler appeared, followed by a young person in pink, whose lips quivered at sight of him.

“At last,” (or words to that effect) he stammered, and rose rather unsteadily to his feet.

“Forgive me—do forgive me! it was all my fault,” Dolly cried, though that was not at all what she meant to say, and she let him hold her hand as if he could never let it go again, and that was not at all what she meant to do.

Aunt Mumler coughed back the proprieties.

“I—I—came to tell you that my brother has arrived, and that he wishes to see you.”   Here Dolly paused and looked at him with tragic eyes.

“I shall be delighted to meet—”

“Yes, but you don’t see how dreadful it is for me, for I—I—have been telling such awful — — lies! And Dick will find them all out and I shall be disgraced,” and she burst into tears.

“You— —disgraced!   Surely you are dreaming!”

“N—no,” she sobbed; “I felt obliged to give you a name; the doctor would ask, and there was Dick, and so—so we’ve called you—B—Brown, and that— that’s what I’ve come to tell you, so you’ll know what to do.”

“Do forgive me, though I hardly can forgive myself!   I never thought to what my silence might expose you. My excuse is that I was too ill at first to quite realize. My name is— —"

"Don't tell me, I don't want to know," Dolly cried in a reaction of emotion. "Everybody will know then, and that I tell lies. All I beg of you is that you call yourself B—Brown as long as you are here, for if Dick should know he'd never forgive me. I—I— was considered a very truthful person," and her lips trembled.

"I understand; you think it is easier to forget me without a name."

"I couldn't forget you!"

"Dolly!" Aunt Mumler interposed.

"I—I—couldn't, Aunt, I have had such a horrid time ever since."

"You may be sure I shall release you at once from my troublesome presence," he retorted, injured.

"I don't mean that, either," and she held out her hand to him with a gesture of entreaty. "You know I mean well, but I do somehow say the wrong things. Priscilla never does; you'll like her a great deal better than you do me— —"

"Dolly!"

"Well, I'm going, Aunt. I dare say Dick is dying to come in and ask questions. O dear me!"

VII.

CAPTAIN OUTERBRIDGE examined Mr. Brown with thoughtful curiosity, as that gentleman expressed his sense of obligation.

"As a friend of Aunt Mumler's they would do anything for you—Mr.—a—Brown."

Dick spoke the name so deliberately, that its temporary possessor turned crimson.

12

Captain Outerbridge gazed at him as one who is searching the recesses of memory.

"What excellent English you speak, Mr. Brown."

"I—I—live in London."

"London? Nice place except on Sundays.—In business?"

"I am attached to the German embassy," the Nameless one explained, off his guard.

"Indeed,"and Dick leaned forward on one elbow. "I was at a ball there last spring. Delightful quarters. Fine supper, too. Our own minister feeds the free and independent, and somehow it flavors the cookery."

As Dick finished his cigar that night he turned to Dolly, who gave a nervous start.

"Come upstairs, Dolly, I've something to say to you."

"Please say it here."

"Do you think I want my remarks tacked down in Aunt's diary and sent to Portland?"

Captain Outerbridge lighted his lamp with elaborate slowness.

"Now then, Dolly, about—Mr. Brown."

There never was so eloquent a pause as preceded Mr. Brown; Dolly surrendered at once.

"What is his real name?"

"I—I—don't know."

"Yet you turn this house into a hospital for a man whose very name you don't know!"

"Please—please, don't be angry, Dick."

"Now, how did this all happen?"

"I—I really can't tell you."

"You'd better, if you wish me to get you out of a scrape."

Then Dolly hung her head and confessed how the Nameless one had been poisoned by Dick's cigarettes, bestowed on him by Dick's own sister.

" By George, but you gave him a dose ! " and Dick whistled gently. " Why, they're not fit to smoke. They're Sam Mallory's experiment—he sent them to me and said the effect was blissful. Two nearly floored me. I meant to throw them away, but I forgot. I say, Dolly, if this man didn't tell his name as soon as he came to his senses, it is because he is either afraid or ashamed."

"Oh, no, no, Dick !"

" Then prepare yourself, my child. Your Mr. Brown is no stranger to me." Dolly stared, spellbound.

" Do you remember what you wrote me about a suspected forger who is moving in the best society here ? Not a common forger, you said, but decidedly aristocratic ? You rather hoped he would fall in love with you—"

" Dick, don't say another word ! I cannot bear it, —I have been punished enough ! O I'm so wretchedly unhappy."

Captain Outerbridge the next morning strolled into the Nameless one's room and found him drumming a dreary tune on the window pane.

" You will be sorry to hear that my sister Dolly is ill," he said politely, " and she so regrets not tb see you again before you go."

The Nameless one looked helplessly at the Captain, but he was bound in honor not to explain.

Was the Captain really so obtuse as not to see that though he was an impostor, he was a very respectable one ?

That night, like the prodigal son, Baron Kurt returned to the home of his ancestors with a look on his face which forbade interrogations.

The fatted calf took the shape of an extra fine bottle of Johannisberger, and Cordula hung about her brother's neck, dissolved in tears.

"She said you'd come back."

"Who?   Your widow?"

"She said we were spoiling you."

"Perhaps she would like to try a hand at it her-self."

"You are greatly mistaken, Mrs. Oldecott would never—"

"Cordula!   Who?"

"My dear friend, Mrs. Oldecott."

"Why didn't you tell me her name before?"

"You never listened."

Serenity returned to Baron Stendal's heart.   With Cordula's help he would again penetrate into that enchanted abode, with colors flying and drums playing. He was prepared to sacrifice the whole Stendal tribe, a diplomatic career, and his own untrammeled affections, on the altar of a young person in pink, who read fairy tales and who had bestowed on him, Baron Stendal, the plebeian name of Brown.

Now that the prodigal had returned, the family underwent a reaction, and glared at him.   Kurt declined to inhale this reproachful atmosphere any longer. He strolled towards his sister and kissed her with unusual warmth.   "I'll call on Mrs. Oldecott with you to-morrow, child."

"I have no intention of taking you, Kurt."

Here again, like the prodigal son, Baron Kurt proceeded to pick up the crumbs of what had once been a goodly feast waiting his pleasure.   Such is life!

VIII.

A HAMMOCK swung under the linden trees before the drawing-room windows.   In it lay Dick, smoking and meditating.

To him appeared Aunt Mumler with an air-cushion,

which she proceeded to blow up, like an ancient cherub.

"For your head, Dick, child. Hadn't we better send for the doctor,—Dolly looks so ill."

"Serve her right!"

"Serve her right? Why—what do you mean?"

"She is worrying, of course. What business have you fools of women to take in a strange man, and to coddle him! You'll be town-talk next."

"We only did our duty,—he was sick and we took him in. I'd have done it in Portland just the same—such a lovely, considerate young man, and such a gentleman!"

"Have you heard that this place is the headquarters of a band of forgers, Aunt Mumler?" Dick interposed, gravely.

"Bless me, yes, so I have," and she stared at him.

Dick turned away.

"At the same time what has that to do with this young man? I don't understand! Dick, I insist, I really must insist! You don't dare to tell me that this gentleman, this perfect gentleman, is connected with— —Richard, why don't you speak!"

"I have nothing further to say," he replied, in a faint voice, and before Aunt Mumler could ask another question, he swung himself out of the hammock and strolled away.

She turned—still aghast—at sound of a light footfall. It was Dolly, a picture of woe and humility.

"Goodness, child, how you look! There, lie down. Don't worry, it will all come right."

Dolly obeyed and turned her poor little face from the sight of mankind in general and of Cordula von Stendal in particular, who came up the garden path in search of her divinity.

She found Priscilla in the summer-house, bored

with St. Severin, indignant with Dolly, and frosty
with Cordula herself.

"You were right, dear Mrs. Oldecott, my brother
has returned. He looks very ill and he is cross.
But even mamma doesn't dare to ask him where he
has been. Do you know, I have punished him."
Cordula was triumphant. "He was coming to call
on you; he just begged me to take him, and do you
know what I did? I left him waiting for me at one
door, while I ran away by another."

Priscilla declined to be amused—she was pining
for society, and she thought that even a heavy diplo-
matist might be better than nobody.

"My brother has come back from Baden-Baden,
Cordula. There he is, don't move."

Cordula made an awkward bow in answer to the
Captain's graceful salutation, and becoming a prey
to shyness, she bade her adored friend good-by and
fled, with a desperate nod to the Captain.

"'Pon my word, Prissy, she is just like a green
apple," and Dick's face puckered up, as if he had
taken a bite out of something very sour.

Cordula ran until she reached the foot-path to
Castle Stendal, where she met a tall man, who greeted her as one injured and indignant.

"I waited half an hour at least, and then I found
you had gone."

"I hate to go calling with a martyr," she replied,
pertly.

"I told you distinctly that nothing would give me
greater pleasure."

"Don't you think I understand, Kurt? You have
fallen in love with Mrs. Oldecott,—I dare say you have
seen her somewhere. Don't think I am blind! but I
sha'n't help you!" and Cordula retreated in just resentment, partly on account of Kurt, but principally

in remembrance of that elaborate bow with which she
had been favored by Captain Outerbridge.

.   .   .   .

Dolly felt so humiliated that the very sight of her
reproachful family was unendurable.   So she avoided
everybody and sought a spot where she could be alone
with her disgrace.

Instinctively she strayed into a certain deserted
garden, where, under an apple tree, there stood a man-
trap in the shape of a wooden bench.

She sank wearily down in the old place and closed
her eyes, oblivious to all things.

Just then another person sauntered in, his tread
dulled by the heavy grass..

He had come for the simple reason that he wanted
to see again the divine spot where for the first time he
had found a little person in pink ; perhaps to discover
in this inspired place a solution for his happiness.

He looked up from meditation and stood spellbound, for there, in the old place, sat the girl of his
heart, her dear eyes closed.

He sighed for very happiness, and Dolly looked up.
The quick blood flushed her face, and she gazed at
him with mute reproach, while her heart beat so fast
that she could not speak.

"Why are you here?" she stammered at last.

The Baron was so astounded that he hesitated, with
the semblance of a very bad conscience.

"Had I known you were here," he said, recovering himself, "I should, yes, I should have been sure
to come."

"How dare you speak so to me!" and Dolly hid
her face in her hands.

"Dare?   If my presence is so hateful to you
I— —"

"I—I—hoped that you had left St. Severin," she
sobbed, "but it is best to tell you—I know—all."

"Who told you?"

"My brother."

"I thought he recognized me. But, surely, you must confess that I am not quite to blame?"

"I—I—am very sorry for you,—I dare say you were terribly tempted."

"Indeed I was," he cried eagerly, "and you may well be sorry for me, if such a trifle has caused me to lose your regard."

"A trifle?" and she looked at him aghast.

"If you knew what those days were to me, you would understand."

"Don't—don't, I want to forget them forever!"

"If you but knew how I love you, you would— —"

"Don't—don't speak of love to me—the man you are!"

"The man I am!—Miss Outerbridge?— — —"

Here Dolly dried her eyes, and made a little speech.

"I'll tell you something, though it is just too dreadful!—I—really do like you—there! Perhaps it will help you in the future, and you will—repent."

"Repent?"

"And I'll just as lief promise never to marry anyone, if you wish. I don't mind, for I feel too dreadfully old."

"Miss Outerbridge—Dolly—"

"Please don't touch me! Oh, if I had only known who you were!"

"Was I quite to blame for not telling you at once? When I found myself ill and in your house, I could not give up the joy of being under the same roof with you—foolish and wrong though it was. I could not bear to be taken to Castle Stendal— —"

"Taken where?" and Dolly held her breath.

"Love makes us so selfish," he continued, heedless of interruption. "To be under your roof, for the sound of your voice—for a possible glimpse of your dear face, I sacrificed my whole family, and all I get for this is to be told to repent, as if I had committed a terrible crime," and he turned away without another look.

"Forgive me,—forgive me!" and an appealing hand was laid on his arm. "I—I did not know that you were—I mean, I—I—mean I thought you were some one else."

"Did you not say that Captain Outerbridge told you—"

"I—I—can't explain! But please say you forgive me—and—and—I suppose you don't care a bit now whether I ever do get married or not."

"I should care, my darling, unless you married me," and he held her in his arms.

"Do you really mean it? And you won't repent? And what do you see in me to love? But please don't repent, dear!" and she put her arms about his neck and hid her face, and so Dick found them as he strolled over in search of Dolly.

"Now, Captain Outerbridge, will you kindly explain?"

"Pardon, Baron Stendal, will you kindly explain," and Dick glanced at Dolly, blushing and crumpled.

"Dick, you knew who he is, and yet you told me— —"

Dick was as calm and sunny as a May morning.

"Dick, you spoke of—of forgers the other day."

"I believe I did."

"And you said that—that this gentleman was one of the— —"

"I didn't! But if you will jump at ridiculous conclusions— —"

"Dick!"

"I have been looking for you, Richard."

It was Aunt Mumler. "Priscilla wants you."

Here she started back in dismay, at sight of Baron

Stendal, while Dolly grasped her arm with painful emphasis.

"What did Dick say about this gentleman?"

"That—that—there! I can't and I won't believe it!"

"He said he belonged to the forgers!" Dolly declared, with tragic denunciation.

"I didn't," the culprit replied, unmoved, "for that would have been absurd, since I recognized him at once as Baron Stendal, for I saw him in London at a ball at the German embassy. But I was rather surprised to meet him again in our house as Mr.—Brown."

"Will you please explain about the forgers, Dick?"

"All I said was that there is supposed to be a band of forgers here. Don't you remember, Dolly, writing about them?"

"What has that to do with Baron Stendal?"

"I am sure I don't know," and Dick opened his cheerful eyes very wide. "It was simply a trifle of information, and anything is interesting in this dull place."

Dolly began with withering scorn, and ended by laughing on Dick's shoulder.

"You see it was only a little misunderstanding, Baron Stendal. Dolly, I really must go. Suppose you stay and explain. After all, you are to blame."

The morning passed, luncheon time came, but neither Dolly nor the Baron. So Dick sauntered across to the apple tree, to announce the prose of existence.

At sight of her brother, Dolly tried to draw her hand out of Kurt's.

"The explanation seems rather long?"

"For life," Baron Stendal answered gayly, and drew Dolly still closer.

She looked up at him with laughing eyes.   "We'll be grateful, and put up a monument here."

"A monument?"

"To the mosquitoes, of course! Don't you see, if it hadn't been for those dear mosquitoes, we would never — — —"

And that was true!

MR. CARMICHAEL'S CONVERSION.

A NINETEENTH-CENTURY MIRACLE.

I.

THE gout and whaling-voyages not being compatible, Captain Jonathan Dunlow gave up the latter to attend to the former.

He anchored in the old Portsmouth harbor for the last time, and would have felt much sadder as he passed the harbor-light, if at that moment a twinge of his enemy in the great toe of his left foot, had not warned him that it was high time to settle down. So Captain Dunlow anchored the *Lovely Sal* at the weather-beaten wharf, and watched her a moment after he landed with a choking sensation in his throat. The only things he took with him to remind him of his past career, were his telescope and speaking-trumpet; indeed, unimportant as this fact may seem, had he left them behind there would have been no story to tell. With these under his arm he lounged down the silent streets of Portsmouth town, with the afternoon sun blinking lazily on the hot cobblestones, and at last knocked at the widow Curdy's front door.

"My goodness, mum! it's the capt'in, come home for good," the maid-of-all-work cried, hanging out of a convenient window.

"Open the door, you! D'ye think I like to broil!" the captain shouted irritably; and in a moment more he was ushered from the glaring light of day into the coolness of a long, broad corridor—cool by reason

(188)

of generous doors, cooler for the presence of the widow
Curdy gliding downstairs, thin and long and exasper-
atingly chilly, the captain justly thought as he threw
himself into an easy chair and mopped his head mean-
while with a bandanna handkerchief of a fiery scarlet.

Captain Dunlow was a short, thick-set man, weather-
beaten and heavy-featured, but with shrewd gray
eyes, which he winked knowingly. Being the widow
Curdy's only lodger, he was the subject of fond speculations to that estimable woman ; still, in spite of the
undoubted advantages she possessed, the captain's
heart remained untouched, and three days after his
reappearance, he collected his luggage, paid his bill,
and, with his telescope and speaking-trumpet once
more under his arm, disappeared forever out of the
widow Curdy's horizon.

II.

COULD Fate, in connecting the lives of people, at
the same time draw between them a thread of
light, in what a curious mesh we should be entangled !
Could such a thing be, then would there have been a
delicate connecting link between Mr. Carmichael of
Milboro' and Captain Dunlow, at that moment hazard-
ing his life on the top of a New Hampshire stage-
coach, and still clinging to the telescope and the
speaking-trumpet. His disappearance from under
Mrs. Curdy's roof was not nearly so mysterious as it
might at first seem, for he had long since contemplated
occupying a certain little farm on Milboro' hillside,
as soon as he could get his sister Dinah to keep house
for him.

Mr. Carmichael was at that identical moment in
his own home in South Milboro', lying on his bed, with
a vacant look in his eyes, and an unkempt aspect to

his hair, which, with the perfume of bad whiskey about, if it did not explain, at least hinted at Mr. Carmichael's condition.

There was a boot and shoe factory in Milboro' which in prosperous times had given Mr. Carmichael sufficient work to do, till one day, elated by too much prosperity, he came near taking to himself a wife ; of which, for reasons best known to himself, he had thought better. But from that day, curiously enough, his good luck deserted him, till he had no work and could get none, and there seemed no hope in living. It being injudicious to kill himself outright, Mr. Carmichael concluded to stupefy himself, which he proceeded to do as fast as he conveniently could. Mr. Carmichael, then, lay on the bed in a stifling little room that late summer afternoon, just as the captain, having at last reached his destination, was sitting on the veranda of his farm on the hill, while he smoked a comforting pipe, and watched the eastern hills turn purple, and the western capped an instant with the last superb radiance of the sinking sun.

"Dinah "—and the captain turned to his sister, who was knitting near him—"it may do well enough for landlubbers," nodding his head at the offending mountains, "but it just chokes me. If I'd been the Lord, I'd made the world all water."

Miss Dunlow looked up to heaven in pious horror, and felt certain, of what she had before only suspected, that Jonathan's soul needed saving very badly.

Mr. Carmichael, too, could see the mountains from his solitary window, but they did not trouble him much, and he would have remained passive at least, if an inquisitive hen had not wandered in at the open door, which so unexpectedly incensed him that he sent his solitary pillow flying after her, with little damage to either. So the summer sun sank behind the hills and hid them from Captain Dunlow's protesting eyes, and at the same time kindly extinguished the man named Carmichael, who at that moment had in his low soul neither courage to live nor courage to die.

III.

MISS DUNLOW called it a freak, but the captain declared, he'd be darned if he cared what she called it.

The matter was, that the captain, with a fond recollection of the deck of the *Lovely Sal*, had taken possession of the rotunda on the roof, which was, however, in common language, nothing but a small square room with a window on each side. Here he placed his telescope on a stand of his own construction, and on the wall behind it he hung his speaking-trumpet, occasionally amusing himself by bellowing down at unwary passers-by ; and, what with scanning the whole neighborhood with his telescope, Milboro' might be said to be an open book to the captain. Sometimes, by gazing fixedly at the sky through his telescope or staring steadily at the small stream in the valley as it rippled by, he could delude himself into the innocent belief that he was still sailing the *Lovely Sal*, especially if he accompanied the act by a vigorous motion of his rocking-chair.

The house lay quite high up on the side of a hill, with a fine stretch of cultivated ground about. But, beyond the sloping fields, there were acres of dense woods, with a bit of clearing in one place showing a tremendous rent in the granite rocks, with a few lonely pine trees overshadowing the black chasm, where nothing grew but dogwood and poison-ivy ; the whole, from its gloom and foreboding sternness, called " Purgatory " by the country folks. The captain in his tower, half a mile away, could see this dimly, but every inch of ground was distinct to his sight as soon as he put his faithful telescope to his eye.

Strange as it may seem, Mr. Carmichael's good angel kept guard over this telescope, seeing he was certainly not in the society of that gentleman, who was by this time plunged in such depths, that it was a delicate question whether he would leave this world sober or not.   Mr. Carmichael's faults and misfortunes, till he took to drinking, were mostly of a negative kind ; which was at this time his misfortune, for had he committed a serious crime he might have been hung respectably.   But now he had made up his drunken mind that on the whole it would be better to die than to live on forever in this way, with nothing to hope for, and only the jail or a poorhouse staring him in the face.   It was no fault of his, so ran his argument ; and on the third day after Captain Dunlow's arrival in Milboro', Mr. Carmichael borrowed—if he did not steal—a ragged halter in the tumble-down barn behind the house, and with shambling gait and hanging head, shuffled along under Heaven's bright sunlight, in the perfect loveliness of a summer's day, unmoved by the birds or sunshine, by flowers or passing breeze, and unconsciously took the path that led to the place called Purgatory.

Mr. Carmichael's fate ordained that Captain Dunlow should be in his rotunda reconnoitering the neighborhood with his spyglass, much after the manner of the Arabian sorcerers.   The scraps of information obtained were, however, of the prosiest description, and were each in turn shouted down, through the trapdoor in the floor, to the unfortunate Miss Dinah below, who, suffering from delicate nerves, was hardly soothed by having " Cows ahoy ! " " There them confounded turkeys in the potatoes ! " " Boys in the cherry trees ! " yelled at her every few minutes.   Suddenly a death-like silence prevailed, and Miss Dinah, taking advantage of the lull, folded her thin, respectable hands and dropped into a doze.

Mr. Carmichael's good angel had so arranged mat ters that when the captain had examined the fields of grain swaying in the afternoon breeze, and had looked at every conceivable object far and near, he should bring his glass to bear on that open space in the woods which Carmichael had reached in his reckless deter-mination, and where Dunlow overtook him like a nineteenth-century magician, and not too soon! God knows, not too soon, and the captain's hair stood on end in horror.

Down below, in the clearing, he could just see a man with a wild, despairing face — a rope — the high, strong branch of a tree.—God's mercy on the wretch ! he was going to hang himself!

For a moment the captain's heart stood still with the horrible sense of his helplessness to save the man, who would be dead before the quickest could reach the spot—even if a straight path led through the dense woods—when, suddenly, an idea flashed upon him. He grasped his speaking-trumpet, and with his eye glued to the fatal spot, he shouted with all the strength of his strong lungs, "Sinner, beware! The eye of the Lord is upon you !"

The man named Carmichael had already hung the rope on the tree, and fashioned a good strong noose ; perhaps, in a moment more, there would have been little left to tell, had not the words come to him through the still air. Rough, hardened man though he was, his strong hands shook, and his knees so trem-bled that he fell flat to the ground. A sickening fear took possession of him as he stared stealthily about the lonely spot and saw no one, heard nothing more ! Carmichael knew of Heaven. Why, he'd even been in the church in Milboro'—a church that had a familiar trust in Divine Providence, believing it would go out

13

of its way and upset all known laws to save one sinner, however unworthy. So this man, with shaken nerves, in the midst of terror and cowardice, had a vague belief in a miracle performed, and so slunk away through the woods, leaving the horribly suggestive noose still hanging on the tree, to darken and disgrace the sunny afternoon.

IV.

A CURIOUS age, the nineteenth century, with its bad reputation for skepticism, and at foundation a touching desire to believe everything, in default of believing nothing. There is no doubt that the Church needs a periodical stirring up, and it happened that at that time any religious incident with a flavor of excitement, was welcomed rapturously.

These things were known to Mr. Carmichael, in a vague and rude fashion. This man, who would have faced death with immovable stupidity, had at the eleventh hour been utterly shaken by a voice without an attendant body, where there could have been no one, it seemed on close examination; therefore, it must have been a voice direct from Heaven, from which Mr. Carmichael concluded, in his by no means clear mind, that he was reserved for something better.

There is no doubt that the world is glad to give unsuspected merit a lift; and Mr. Carmichael, having entered on his new lease of life, washed and shaved—processes which he needed extremely—and after having had a private interview with the pastor of the Milboro' church, felt certain that Heaven had interposed in his behalf, especially after his story leaked out so much to his advantage that he was called upon to repeat it at a revival-meeting in the market-town. This he did with such unbounded success that he went from one place to another in the character of a hardened sinner saved from the vilest and lowest fate by the grace of God, till he grew fat and oily with too much temporal prosperity, and in the course of time developed an unconscious but artistic talent for adding trifling touches to the original story, at which Mr. Carmichael of that summer's day at Purgatory, would have stared in drunken surprise.

V.

CAPTAIN DUNLOW was a scoffer. So Miss Dinah said, and it was the object of her life to enlighten his soul and to take him to church; both of which projects were eminently unsuccessful. The captain hated regular church-going, and he had, too, religious opinions of his own, which, if not quite after Miss Dinah's respectable pattern, probably answered quite as well in the eyes of an all-wise Creator.

Milboro' was the proud possessor of a town-hall of the barest and most angular description, warranted to contain no object which could divert the most thoughtless mind from religious contemplation. The early autumn had come, and that mansion of grace was hired by the piously disposed for a religious revival. The cold winds were beginning to blow rather rudely, so it seemed best to hold the meetings here, instead of on the camp-ground.

Miss Dunlow was in a ferment of excitement all the time, and the captain was in a corresponding state of fury. " I'd like to know where your duty begins," he shouted in a passion. "At home, it seems to me. D'ye know, I haven't had a hot mouthful to eat since that confounded show started. Charity and duty begin at home; d'ye hear me, ma'am ? " and the captain rushed off, with passion at white heat.

Miss Dinah shut her eyes and let the bottled wrath pour over her head without a murmur.

Matters had by this time come to such a pass that no revival was anything without Mr. Carmichael and his story.

"Carmichael? Carmichael?" the captain asked gruffly one day. "Carmichael? Who's he?"

"Oh," Miss Dinah said with a sigh and a pitying look at her brother—"oh, he's one of the saved. He was a dreadful drunkard and a sinner, but now he's full of grace."

"A precious shining light!" the captain interrupted in great disgust: "it must do folks a darned sight of good to hear him!"

"Jonathan," his sister said, as pleadingly as possible for her undemonstrative nature—"Jonathan, come with me this afternoon. It'll do you good—indeed it will. Mr. Carmichael speaks for the first time. They say"—lowering her voice mysteriously—"they say he's had awful experiences."

Captain Dunlow, moved by an unexpected curiosity, not only consented to go, but hitched the horse to the "shay," and he and Miss Dinah were off to the town-hall in good time.

There was a peculiar delicate flavor of excitement about Mr. Carmichael's appearance, as he was a native of the town, and people had some curiosity to see the saint who had been developed from such a vagabond. So Milboro' and all the surrounding towns turned out in full force to do him honor, and the open square before the town-hall was filled with any and every kind of vehicle which would hold together enough for the occupants to reach their destination. An enthusiastic multitude had preceded the captain and Miss Dunlow, so they could barely squeeze into a back settee between a door and a window, through which blew a brisk breeze that began to tell on the captain's temper.   However, there was something in the air, an excited earnestness, which made the unhappy scoffer even forget himself.

The hymns were sung with tremendous fervor, and the women's voices rang out shrill and high with excitement.   The prayers, too, were fervently listened to, and wet eyes, and bony, hard-worked hands wrung in repentance, spoke more in honor of trusting hearts than of the preacher's eloquence.

Even the captain became excited, and ran his stubby hand through his gray hair till it stood on end, and then took out his scarlet handkerchief and blew his nose, till the people about turned round in disgust, not knowing the captain's way of showing his emotions.

Suddenly there was a commotion; the people stood up and stretched their necks, till the captain, who was a short man, and wedged into a corner as well, turned this way and that in balked curiosity, vainly dodging his head in between his neighbors.

"Confound it!" cried the captain, and leaped on the settee.   Looking over the heads of the people towards the platform, he gave a gasp and a start as he saw a man standing there with a half-conquered, hang-dog air, a defiant look in his eyes and a snarl and a whine in his voice—in other words, Mr. Carmichael in his well-known character of a rescued wretch.

"Bless my soul! who's he?" the captain thought, but had no time to recollect, for Miss Dinah, red with shame and horror, pulled at his coat-tails.

"Down! down there!" shouted an outraged worshiper; and so the captain descended, and Mr. Carmichael began.

He had no intention of giving himself a good character; he reveled in every vile epithet he could use against himself, and groveled in such dire abasement that his admiring hearers acknowledged that

Heaven had stooped a long way to pick him out of the mire ; while a certain choleric old gentleman in a corner, with a distracted mind and two clenched fists, wished he'd had Mr. Carmichael alone on board the *Lovely Sal* with a rope's end handy, when that re-formed sinner suddenly threw an unexpected light upon himself.

" Heaven," said Mr. Carmichael, and raised his eyes to the ceiling—" Heaven saved this poor wretch for its own purposes. A miracle was performed : there came a voice from the clouds saying, ' Sinner—' "

The choleric old gentleman in a corner gasped for breath, and turned fatally red.   The choleric old gentleman wanted to get up, but was held down by the hands of a middle-aged gentlewoman.

" ' Sinner,' " continued Mr. Carmichael—" ' sinner, beware !   The eye of the Lord is upon you ! ' "

" You lie ! "

It rang through the place, and Mr. Carmichael stopped open-mouthed and glared down on the red-faced old gentleman in the corner, who had leaped upon the settee and was waving a scarlet bandanna handkerchief like a flag of defiance.

" You lie, you—you landlubber !   'Twa'n't a voice from the clouds.   'Twas I with my speaking-trumpet ! Don't you go round telling such darned lies ! "

Mr. Carmichael came to himself ; he tore off his coat and leaped down from the platform, where he was, however, grasped by several stalwart worshipers, who held him struggling and frantic and using language unbecoming an object of grace.

" Put him out ! out with him ! " the crowd yelled at the captain ; and so the good man was hustled out, and Miss Dinah, without a moment's reflection, fainted right under the settee.

Three hundred years ago such boldness might have cost the captain his life : the angry religious feeling of the nineteenth century cost him his hat, at which sacrifice the captain was disgusted.

"Blamed if I do a good turn for another feller!" he thought as he climbed into his "shay." "Let 'em go hang and welcome.—Go 'long!" he said to the horse, and so disappeared up the hill.

The fine effect of Mr. Carmichael's spiritual experiences was, however, spoiled by the interruption, and it was amazing to see how popular interest in him languished at once. That he had without doubt been indirectly saved by Divine Providence was of no earthly concern to Milboro', in its keen disappointment that he had not been saved directly. Milboro' pined for a direct miracle.

So there was nothing left for Mr. Carmichael to do but to disappear, which he did very soon, leaving behind him nothing but a vague rumor sometimes referred to as "Carmichael's Conversion."

JACINTH.

I.

TWILIGHT began to dim the corners of the large, low-studded room, and to obliterate the family portraits on the wainscoted walls. It softened the worn face of Miss Penelope Macilvaine as she sat before the open fire, occasionally glancing over her shoulder towards the nearest window, and sighing. At the two farther windows sat her sisters, Miss Sarah and Miss Judith, as they had done for thirty years. They also looked out of their respective windows once in a while, but they did not sigh, that was Miss Penelope's privilege.

They were three old women, for even Miss Penelope, and she was the youngest, would never again see fifty, but they were all secretly stirred at sight of young Malcolm Dunston walking by Jacinth's side at the foot of the garden, where the hawthorn hedge divided the soft green lawn from the high road.

"So to-morrow you leave Rothmere and Scotland, Miss Jacinth," he was saying. "You will return to America and forget us!" He could not look into her face and command his heart, and so he watched the river over the way as it rippled and tumbled under the rustic bridge.

For a moment Jacinth's lips quivered, but then she lifted her eyes, and there was a quiet strength in their tender depths as they met his, that troubled him, and his heart rebelled against his practical Scotch mind and his self-made barriers.

(200)

"I have had a long holiday, and if I do not go now I shall forget how to work, for my aunts are so good to me," she said, and looked lovingly at the old brick house, unconscious of being watched by eager eyes.

"I hope," said Miss Sarah, "that it is settled; then the dear child can stay with us until they are married."

"I can't understand you, Sarah; he is poorer than Job; he's only a clerk in the bank, and he hasn't any prospects."

"He is Mr. Dunston's son, Judith."

"A nice, shiftless lot that, though I shouldn't say it of the minister."

"Oh, hush, please," Miss Penelope interrupted; "they are coming up the walk! Fetch the lamp, Sarah, do—oh, I'm all of a tremble."

The door was quietly opened just as Miss Sarah came in at another with the lamp. She placed it among the books on the table, and then, as if with one accord, all three stared expectantly at Jacinth.

"Where is Malcolm?" Miss Sarah broke 'the silence.

"He bade me good-by and went back to the parsonage across the pasture."

"Is that all, Jacinth?"

"All, Aunt Sarah," she answered, smiling, and drew a chair to the table, while they still watched her as if spellbound.

"I am glad of it," Aunt Judith cried and broke the spell.

Aunt Sarah shook her head, but she did not trust herself to speak, and after a moment of stupor, they both left the room.

No sooner were they gone than Jacinth's face slipped into the palms of her hands and lay hidden, until, at a soft touch on her shoulder, she looked up with hopeless eyes.

"You, Aunt Penelope?"

Between the two had stood the wall of Aunt Penelope's grief, a luckless romance upon which she had built the sad structure of her existence, by right of which she enjoyed unstinted melancholy, which her sisters bore with the patience of long habit, but which, in the uncharitableness of youth, Jacinth called selfishness.

"My dear," Aunt Penelope said, and a faint flush crept to the border of her lace cap, "my dear, out of my sorrows and mistakes I speak to you. Thirty years ago the man who once said he loved me, told me that the old feeling had changed. There was nothing to do but to bear it, but, God forgive me, how ill I bore it, how selfish I was. Child, be better and stronger than I, and you will yet be happy. You are young, dear, and prettier than ever I was, and you will forget."

"Aunt Penelope," Jacinth cried, "he never once told me that he "—she paused and hid her face on the old woman's breast.

"I know, child, I know, it is not only words that speak."

"It was a mistake, that is all," Jacinth murmured, trying to smile; then, with a cry that broke down the barriers of her good resolutions, she threw herself forward on the table and buried her face in her outstretched arms.

"Have patience with me, Aunt Penelope."

"My dear, it is not for me to tell you to do at once what I could not do in thirty years," Aunt Penelope said humbly, when the door opened, and Miss Judith appeared. For a moment she stared in consternation at Jacinth, and then she sank into the nearest chair with an eloquent bounce.

With a quick movement Jacinth was by her side, and threw her arms about the old lady.

"I love you so dearly, Aunt Judith, forgive me for my foolishness, for to-morrow I shall be far away, and who knows when we shall see each other again?"

"See each other again!" an indignant voice repeated, and there stood Aunt Sarah, with the tea-tray. "Don't talk nonsense. You are coming back next year, sure! Now come and have tea by the fire." So they sat about the blazing logs on the hearth, with Jacinth in their midst, resting her bright head on Aunt Penelope's lap, while Aunt Sarah held her hand and Aunt Judith patted her head softly; and there was peace in the still room and even in poor Jacinth's heart, while, a mile away, in the Rothmere parsonage, Malcolm Dunston was pacing up and down the floor of his shabby room. "I could curse my destiny if I did not mean to conquer it," he cried, stopping short in his walk.

"Yet if I had said to-night, 'Jacinth, be my wife, wait and be patient until I have earned enough to support you in comfort,' why then she would still have had to go away, and there would have been the misery of waiting, for her as well as for me. Now I alone have the sorrow of parting, the fear for the future, and the hope," something seemed to whisper. "Yet she shall be my wife, some day with God's help! When I can make her happy and when poverty shall not drag her down as it has my mother. I can work, and, by Heaven I will," and he stretched out his strong arms like a young giant trying his strength.

"Yet suppose," he thought of a sudden, "she sees in the meantime some one she can love, free from any promise to me?" He stood still and pondered. "Then I shall have kept the sorrow out of her life with the hope."

So Malcolm Dunston took Fate into his own hands.

II.

IN a dreary, shabby New York street, Jacinth Macilvaine looked out of an attic window and watched
the forest of chimneys that stood out against the steel
blue of the spring sky, and for once she was idle.

It was a shabby, whitewashed attic, with a dim
window, a bare floor, and the cheapest of furniture.
In a corner hung a couple of gowns, elaborately decorated and boldly proclaiming themselves sham.

"Ten years ago, on just such a day, I sailed for
Scotland," Jacinth thought, as the afternoon crept
away, "and now I am thirty instead of twenty, and
Eve is as old as I was then."

"After all, it is good that I have so little time
to think," she murmured, when an unceremonious
hand rattled the broken door-knob, and then the rat-
tler shot in with a celerity which astonished even
her airy self. A wonderfully pretty young person, in
a dress that proclaimed itself a near relative to those
on the wall.

"From Aunt Sally," she remarked, tossing a letter to Jacinth, pirouetted about once or twice in the
very wantonness of spirits, slammed the shaky door,
and was gone.

Yes, it was from Rothmere. They had not once
forgotten her during these ten long years. "Come
to us, Jacinth, child," Aunt Sarah wrote. The same
old story, repeated every year with loving persistency.
But every year a new baby or an illness, and an invalid, fretful mother, had tied her down to duty, and
so she refused, with pretended cheerfulness.

"But Eve is old enough now to take your place,"
Aunt Sarah wrote, "and we long for the sight of you.
Besides, we are old women and who knows when—"

for a moment Jacinth's eyes filled with unaccustomed tears. "One has a duty to perform even to one's self," she read, "and it is the only one you have neglected. We send you a check, so that you cannot have any excuse for not coming."

The letter fell in her lap, and her heart leaped with joy at the thought of seeing them all again, and perhaps—why not?—seeing him once more, and for a moment she grew faint and dizzy with longing. Then came the awakening.

Deliberately she placed before herself her faded image, with the touch of care on her forehead ; the prim lines of her gray gown, the dawn of old maidhood, to which she had surrendered without a struggle.

"If I should see him again and love him, for I am so weak, so weak! Oh, Jacinth, what is there in you that he would care for? Old, even for your age, and careworn, and faded. Better, you poor thing, the quiet of your daily life, looking forward to no hope, than such unbearable pain."

For a moment she sat quite still, when suddenly she saw one of her sister's gloves lying on the floor. Why not Eve instead of herself? Was she not as much Aunt Sarah's niece? To transplant her into the purity and peace of Rothmere would be worth any sacrifice.

"She is so pretty," Jacinth thought fondly, just as the door flew open and Eve skipped in.

"There it is !" she cried, and picked up the lost glove, and prepared to skip out once more.

"Eve, wait a moment ; I want to speak to you."

"I can't wait, for I'm to take a walk in the cemetery."

Eve's admirers being as a rule rich in hope, but poor in purse, tokens of their devotion were mostly confined to these lugubrious strolls.

"My dear," Jacinth said, putting her arm about

her sister, "would you like to go to Scotland on a visit?"

"Do they really want me, old girl?" Eve cried in a glow of delight. Then Jacinth explained that she hardly cared to go (God forgive her), and Eve should go in her stead, if father and mother were willing.

"Oh, they'll let me go," and Eve, in rapture, scampered towards the door. But as she reached it she ran back and flung her arms about Jacinth, and gave her an affectionate dab of a kiss nowhere in particular, and pronounced these words: "My dear, it's no use being too good in this world. It's nice for others, but it's bad for yourself. Folks take it for granted after awhile, and don't even thank you." Then, with a parting hug, she added: "You're a dear old thing, and of course I'll go." At the door she looked back. "Any men in Rothmere? Good gracious, I forgot! They must have been babies in your time. Still, I do hope there are one or two—I should die of nothing but old women."

So Eve disappeared, and Jacinth, looking out into the shabby street and seeing nothing, felt that she, also, had taken Fate into her own hands.

III.

TIME, that ruthless joker, had, in spite of his bad character, dealt tenderly during the past ten years with the old ladies of Rothmere. To be sure, he had turned Aunt Sarah's hair quite white, and given Miss Judith a twinge of rheumatism, but he had left Aunt Penelope her gentle grief, and a fondness for soft gray gowns and dainty lace caps.

The long, quaint house was still the same, the only change being that the luxurious ivy had so entangled the sprightly legs of the weather-cock, that this unreliable bird had settled himself permanently due south. About the house was a subdued air of welcome and festivity, and the opening of the distant kitchen door sent delicious whiffs through the old-fashioned hall.

The Misses Macilvaine sat in their usual places, trying to work, but they gave it up and looked expectantly out of the windows. Miss Penelope spoke.

"I wonder if she is much changed? She has had a hard life, and at thirty—"

"I can't understand," Miss Judith interrupted irritably, "why she did not write to say that she was coming by the next steamer, as Sarah suggested. It was thoughtless! She may not be coming at all."

"I am sure she will come," Miss Sarah spoke with decision. "I said so to Malcolm last night."

"Mark my words, Sarah, you're making a terrible mistake. If ten years ago Malcolm made a mistake, and made Jacinth unhappy, don't you help him to do it again. Do you believe that Malcolm Dunston, good looking and rich, with half the girls of the county running after him — do you believe he will fall in love again with the poor child, after all these years? Do you believe he will fall in love with her again, when, ten years ago, when she was young and pretty, he could let her go without a word or a promise? Is it natural, Sarah?"

"No, it isn't natural, Judith," she replied, sighing. "But he loved her once, and I believe in his faithful heart, for we know why he did not speak."

"Nonsense! Believe in his fiddlestick. What right have you? When he should have spoken, he was as dumb as an oyster. Lord! he's only for money-making—he's always calculating. He's been at it now for ten years without stopping. I tell you, Sarah—"

Down the road at that moment came the rattle of wheels, and Miss Sarah sprang to her feet. "God bless her, it's Jacinth," she said, and the next instant she was down the garden path, her spectacles bobbing up and down on her nose.

The ancient cab which served Rothmere drew up at the gate, and the first sound that greeted Miss Sarah's horrified ears was a choice selection of " swear words," as the cabby wrestled with a gigantic trunk atop. Then, to cap Miss Sarah's surprise, there stepped out of the vehicle a youth with an eyeglass, and a young person in an astonishing toilette, who threw her arms about the struggling Miss Sarah, and imprinted a kiss upon the end of that good woman's nose.

" Heaven preserve us ! who are you ? " she gasped, freeing herself.

" Good gracious me ! I quite forgot. I'm Eve, aunt. You see pa forgot to post Jacinth's letter, and so I brought it myself."

" And who is he ? " and Miss Sarah turned severely on the young man.

" O we met on the train, aunt. He's been real good to me. I told him I was a stranger."

For a moment Aunt Sarah was staggered, then she collected all her strength, and in a moment the young man with the eyeglass, the rickety cab and the swearing cabby had disappeared as chaff before the wind, and Eve, calmly seated on her trunk, listened with a faint smile to the angry old lady.

" A heart of gold, loving and generous—which will be all the better for your love and gentle ways." So Jacinth wrote, and the three discussed it with many a sigh, as they sat about the fire, while Eve was upstairs, emptying the amazing trunk.

The sitting-room was deserted when she opened the door with a propitiatory smile on her pretty face. The smile died away, and for the first time, perhaps, in her life, the quick tears rushed to her eyes.

With a stamp of her foot, she dragged Aunt Sarah's

sacred chair to the fire and threw herself with much spite into its wicker embrace.

"Why did I come?" she cried. "Of course they hate me, for they've hardly been civil. As for Aunt Sally, the idea of her flying like an old cat at that nice young man, who was so very polite." This sent her light thoughts off at a tangent, and she only looked up at the sound of a firm tread, and the opening of the door.

In an instant life in Rothmere exhibited one point of interest at least; for a grave, handsome man, holding in one hand his hat and riding-whip, stood in the door-way.

"I came to see Miss Macilvaine," he said, coming forward, but the eager look in his eyes vanished at sight of Eve's pretty face. "She was expected to arrive to-day from America."

He had a low, steady voice, and he seemed to take the girl's measure, body and soul, at one quiet glance.

That young person bowed graciously.

"I am Miss Macilvaine, and I'm sure I shall be delighted to know to whom I have the pleasure—"

"Surely there must be some mistake," he interrupted. "Pardon me, I must find Miss Sarah." And quite unmoved by the younger Miss Macilvaine's toilette, her big eyes, and her small feet, he left the room.

"Well, I never!" she exclaimed, then with a bound she was at the window.

There they were, sure enough, walking up and down the garden path. He, with grave, down-bent face, listening to Aunt Sarah's eloquence. For she was eloquent, anxious, exasperated, and her cap-strings shook with indignation, as she glanced towards the house. So Aunt Penelope, coming in, found Eve watching them.

"O, Aunt Penelope, who is he?"

14

Miss Penelope sank into her usual place and watched her niece with a hard line about her mouth, for there was something in the pretty face and volatile temperament, that turned Miss Penelope's comfortable sadness to gall.

"That is Malcolm Dunston,"—"The richest man in Rothmere," Miss Judith added. She had just come in.

"You don't say so! Why, then he'd do to marry!"

There was a moment of stupor, during which Aunt Penelope smiled with scorn.

"Marry whom? What are you talking about?" and in came Miss Sarah.

"Eve means to marry Malcolm Dunston," Miss Penelope exclaimed, with a sharp laugh.

Aunt Sarah pulled her spectacles down to get a better look at the girl, and, with a sinking heart, she silently acknowledged her loveliness. .

"Marry him!" she cried with indignation. "He isn't the man for every chit! Better girls than you have tried."

"Do you really think it's so hard to fall in love with me? There, you don't know. Why, I've had no end of offers! Mostly bad ones," she acknowledged, "but this is a chance," and she rose and faced her astonished relatives. "So, first he shall fall in love with me and then," here she looked back at them with undutiful defiance, "and then he shall marry me!"

Having, so to speak, flung down the gauntlet, Eve scampered upstairs and left the three old women staring at each other in speechless consternation.

"Poor Jacinth!" Miss Penelope broke the silence.

"For Jacinth's sake," Aunt Sarah said, "I think we'd better send her home as soon as possible. After all, he is only a man" (Miss Sarah had a very poor opinion of men), "and there is no knowing. If we can only keep Malcolm away," she sighed, "and as he is the only man who ever does come here, I think she will be ready to go."

IV.

THE monotonous days passed, and poor Eve was much like the Lady of Shalott, with the difference that any Lancelot would have been welcome. It was the necessity of her nature to make an impression on some one, and at last she was reduced to flirting with the ancient gardener. As he was wholly deaf and half blind, she found, one day, nothing left for her to do but to lean over the hedge and stare up and down the road. Then, in default of other amusement, she opened the gate and strolled down the road into unknown regions, sheltered from the sun by a huge Japanese parasol of flamboyant colors.

Rothmere was still barbarous and, while Eve was only conscious that she was making a very pretty picture, she was roused from a contemplation of the queer old houses of Rothmere, buried in honeysuckles and roses, by a most diabolical "whoop!" and the next minute she was surrounded by a lot of dirty ragamuffins who greeted her umbrella with derision.

Miss Macilvaine was no coward. "Go away, you little wretches!" she cried, with a stamp of her foot, but as that effected only another "whoop," Eve, holding her umbrella as a shield, made a regular onslaught, when, of a sudden, it was torn from her grasp, and the next instant it was borne triumphantly down the street.

She looked helplessly about.

"Why, Miss Macilvaine, what has happened?"

It was Malcolm, who had come upon her from a

side path, and she had not heard the sound of his horse's hoofs.

He swung himself down from the saddle while she explained; and throwing the mare's bridle over his arm, walked beside her and listened with rather absent-minded amusement to Miss Macilvaine's chatter.

Aunt Sarah, trimming the roses about the porch, saw them coming, and stood rooted to the spot.

"Now there's a man about, she'll never go," she groaned, gifted as if with the power of prophesy. But in a few weeks it was not of a poor solitary man that the old women complained, but of what they were pleased to call "hordes of men."

One afternoon Miss Sarah, opening the sitting-room door, turned into stone upon the spot. In the Misses Macilvaine's sacred chairs reposed three young men. Three men, where once only Malcolm had dared to enter.

"Mr. Parkins, is it parish business?" Aunt Sarah demanded, recovering herself.

The wretched young curate turned purple to the roots of his sandy hair, and the others, one from the circulating library and the other from the apothecary store on High street, kept him company.

"And I suppose you, sir," and she glared at the first, "have come about the book club." Then she closed like a steel trap on the apothecary's young man. "You'll excuse me, sir, if I can't imagine why you are here!"

Then up sprang Eve. "They are calling on me. I asked them."

"I beg your pardon, gentlemen; this is a new custom. I was not aware of it. You'll excuse me, I'm sure. Pray don't let me hurry you; good morning," Miss Sarah concluded with much irony, and out she stalked.

The truth is, it did hurry them, and they departed as if they had been shot out of a gun. Eve took a long breath as Parkins's clerical coat-tails disappeared.

"How I hate her!" she cried; "how I hate this place! Why did I ever come? O, if I were only at home again." She ran out of the house, slamming the doors, and leaning over the hedge she stared at the river through a haze of angry tears.

"Why, Miss Eve, am I always to find you in trouble?" At the sound of Malcolm's voice, she dashed her tears away and forced a smile.

"If everybody hated you and you hated everybody, you'd be in trouble, Mr. Dunston."

"What has happened now?" he asked, perplexed at the footing of warfare upon which the Misses Macilvaine stood with regard to their niece.

"Were you coming in?" she asked, heedless of his question.

"Well, to tell the truth, no. I was only strolling by."

"Are you busy? No? Then do me a favör; ask me to take a walk."

"I shall be only too glad. There is Miss Sarah; I will talk to her while you fetch your wraps."

"I sometimes feel," Eve explained to Malcolm as they left the house, "as if I should die of badness up there. They act on me like a—a plaster—well, perhaps it is for my good to have the badness drawn out."

The three old women, with unspeakable dismay, watched them until they disappeared down the road.

For a moment Eve was silent, but at last the signs of conflict smoothed themselves out of her face, and she looked up with her old smile.

"Do you think I am so very horrid, Mr. Dunston?"

She was rather afraid of him, but she enjoyed the emotion.

"You may lay it up against me if I tell you what I think of you."

"What an idea!"

"The truth is, perhaps you are a little selfish."

"Mr. Dunston, I should like to go home."

"I thought so."

"You are mistaken," she said, pouting; "on the whole, I prefer to go on."

"Why can you and your aunts not agree?"

"It is Jacinth."

"Jacinth!" As he repeated the name, his face flushed.

"They expected Jacinth, and Jacinth sent me instead. It wasn't my fault that she wouldn't come. I'm sure I wish she had!"

"And so—Jacinth is alone at home?"

"Alone? O, dear, no. No one is ever alone in our house, there are so many of us; it's the only thing we're rich in. What Jacinth has to do? Everything. *She* likes to work; I don't. Of course you know we're poor; it's no use pretending. As for goodness, why, if you come to that, Jacinth is goodness itself."

"Does she look like you? I don't quite remember." Listening with a smile and a far-away look in his eyes.

"Oh, dear, no! She's over thirty, and you know light-haired people fade soon. Besides," she added with much importance," she has no style. Now, I'm stylish; at least so they say. Still, how can she have any style! She never goes anywhere, not even to the theatre; she never sees anyone but father and mother and the children, except her pupils, and they are poor and haven't any style. She really hasn't any ambition—any go. Now pa told me that ten years ago she was very pretty."

"Prettier than you are!" her companion interposed quietly.

"Oh, no," Eve replied, shaking her head. "Of course I don't pretend to goodness, as she does, but—"

"But does she pretend?"

"Oh, no, no! Not pretend! She is goodness itself," Eve cried, "but I can't make believe not to know that I am decently good looking."

"What shall you do when your sister marries and leaves you her work to do?"

"Dear me, Jacinth will never marry. She says so herself. People's tastes are so funny! Now I know that I'm a horrid, selfish little thing, but I've more offers than you'd believe, while Jacinth, who is the dearest, cheerfulest, most unselfish of creatures, why," and she stood still, to give emphasis to her climax, "I never heard of any one being in love with her in my whole life."

Malcolm looked down at her with a frown, and bit his lips.

"We'll go home now, Miss Eve," he said abruptly, and led the way back at such a swinging pace, that she had to scamper over the ground to keep abreast.

The moral atmosphere was all wrong, and when she entered the sitting-room, the three old women looked at her with speechless disfavor.

She went up to the round table, looked at them, and then she spoke. "Aunt Judith, Aunt Sarah, and Aunt Penelope, I am going home by the next steamer." There was an awful silence.

"We just can't get on together. I suppose it's my fault, for it seems that I am horrid and selfish. I am not really as bad as I'm here. You've frozen me and haven't given me time to thaw."

"We couldn't think of letting you go—what would people say?"

"Not let me go?" Eve interrupted Miss Judith, "why, then I'll run away, for I am just dying, I'm so homesick," and, throwing herself down by the nearest chair, Eve burst into tears.

Miss Sarah, conscience-stricken, laid her hand on Eve's shoulder. At the touch she sprang up, with a faint quiver of her lips.

"If you'll only let me go, I'll think kindly of you all. I'm selfish, I found that out to-day; but I didn't mean badly. I'll go home and send Jacinth instead, then, perhaps, you'll forgive me for coming. I never thought," she confessed, "that anyone would like Jacinth, and not me. I'll be willing to scrub and take care of the babies, if I can only go home and sometimes go to the theatre with pa," and at that reflection she brightened.

So, somehow, it was tacitly decided that Eve was to return to America, and in a few days the impossible trunk was once more lifted to the top of the Rothmere cab.

At the railroad station Malcolm was waiting for them, and at sight of his erect figure, Eve's heart gave a thump.

As he helped her into the railway carriage she turned and said softly, "I am going home to try and learn from Jacinth how to be unselfish."

For a moment she wondered at the light in his face, and that he should stoop to kiss her slender hand. Then her light heart beat fast as he said, "We shall see each other again, for I am going to America in a few weeks. For the first time in ten years I shall be idle. Wish me happiness, little Eve, and—God bless you. There is no need, you see, of saying good-by."

V.

SO Eve came back again to the shabby street in New York. Jacinth stood at the door, waiting for her, with all the small Macilvaines clinging to her skirts.

"We've missed your bright face sadly, my darling," she said, as Eve hid her face on her sister's shoulder and began to cry, to the anguish of the little Macilvaines and the sympathetic interest of the hackman.

It seemed to Eve as if she looked at Jacinth for the first time. What business had she to wear that mean, faded, skimpy gown? Why did she brush the fair, soft curls from her forehead, till each wrinkle (and there were wrinkles) stood out for its full worth? Why need her blue eyes look so unreasonably kind and quiet?

Eve pitied her with impulsive remorse, and she continued to sob until, in a pause, she looked up with a faint laugh into Jacinth's distressed face.

"It's because I'm so happy," she explained. "But you just wait, Jacinth, after I've seen mother I'll tell you something."

Under the branches of the hat-rack in the entry, Eve at last made her confession to Jacinth. "I promised some one that I'd be good, Jacinth," and she looked down with a smile. "Just now I said I hated them all. That isn't true. I like one, and that one, well, that one is a man."

"Thank God, my darling. You will be happy, and you will make him a good wife," and, with a quick impulse, Jacinth drew the pretty face to her breast and kissed her sister.

"It hasn't gone so far as that," Eve confessed. "He is coming to America, and, to tell the truth, it

was only what he said at parting that first made me
think that he really liked me. He's a great deal
older than I ; but he's really a fine match and—well,
I like him. Just imagine, Jacinth, why, he knows you,
and admires you very much. Indeed, he gave me to
understand that I was a horrid, selfish little pig. The
first day he called he expected to find you. Perhaps
you remember him—Malcolm Dunston ?"

Did she remember him ? She had tried to cheat
her heart and now she stood shrinking together as if
she had received a blow. Then, to punish her own
weakness, she said, " I thank God for it, my darling,
for he is a good man, and you will be happy."

.   .   .   .

There was an air of smouldering excitement in the
Macilvaine dwelling. Mr. Macilvaine had received
a letter, the object of which—for the Macilvaines disdained all mystery—was known even to the youngest.

The letter was from Malcolm Dunston. He had
come to New York on purpose to see Mr. Macilvaine,
and he took this opportunity to ask for the honor of
Miss Macilvaine's hand in marriage. In deference
to his own old-world notions, and as a simple man of
business, he first addressed Mr. Macilvaine. At the
same time he begged permission to call that evening
to learn his fate.

" So I suppose I may consider you as good as
married, Eve," Mr. Macilvaine remarked, patheti-
cally. " I'm sorry that I have to go out to-night
when Mr. Dunston comes, but I guess you and Jacinth can take care of him."

In honor of the occasion, one small Macilvaine
was delegated to open the door ; to which end Jacinth scrubbed him, and cheered him with promises
of candy. Then she hurried up to the room where
Eve was dressing.

" Why, darling, you're worthy of the king," she

said, fondly, examining the pretty figure, when, suddenly, unmindful of her dress, Eve flung her arms
about her sister.

"O Jacinth, Jacinth, how I love you!" she cried.
"How good you are ; if I could only once show you
that I am truly grateful."

From below there came the tinkle of the door bell,
and Jacinth freed herself gently, and listened. There
was the sound of scuffling feet, for five young Macilvaines had supported their brother in the trial of
opening the door ; the next instant a shrill, small
voice, ignoring gentility, called up from below, "Here
he is, sis, come down."

Rather pale, but all the prettier for that, Eve kissed
her sister and went slowly downstairs.

Jacinth roused herself with an effort, and tried to
put order in the confusion about, but to no purpose.
Shivering, she took up a little red knit shawl, and
drawing it about her shoulders, she sat down on the
bed and softly rubbed her hands.

She dared not think. "I am so wicked, so selfish," she cried in her despair, when the door was
quickly opened again, and Eve stood before her.

"Eve, my child, my dear, what has happened ?"

Eve's face was as white as her own, but she smiled
as she laid her hand on Jacinth's shoulder.

"Jacinth, Jacinth, you know that I love you."

"For heaven's sake, Eve, what has happened ? "

"You know what a hare-brained, fickle-minded kind
of a creature I am. I — I don't care a snap for —
Malcolm, Jacinth ; I never would have thought of
him, if he hadn't told me the day I left that he was
coming to America. I—I thought that he meant me
all along—I'm such a little fool," and Eve smiled
even more brightly.

"Eve! Eve, what does this mean!"

"It means, my dear, dear, that it was all a mistake."

"How dared he!"

"O, Jacinth, it's all my fault. For my sake forgive him. I should die if he ever knew how foolish I had been. See, he has been so faithful, waiting and working for you for ten long years. If you had only seen the light in his eyes when he asked me, 'Why doesn't Jacinth come?' He has no idea how silly I was. There, let me curl your hair about your face—let me put in this bit of ribbon at your throat. No? Oh, Jacinth, Jacinth, you grudge happiness only to yourself."

With a bewildered start Jacinth came to herself, and, drawing the shabby knit shawl tightly about her shoulders, she crept downstairs to her fate.

She paused at the threshold of the shabby parlor and, for a moment, she listened to his impatient stride.

"He shall see me just as I am" she thought. She would not spare herself. At the sound of the slowly opening door he turned, and so he saw her once again: a slender, faded woman in a little, faded shawl, with the sign of trouble in her blue eyes and on her open forehead. But she was the woman he loved.

"Jacinth! my love, my darling, at last!" he cried, and held her in his strong arms, and bending his handsome head, he kissed her with something of compassion born of the most innocent self-conceit.

"The sorrow in her face was all for me," he thought, exulting.

. . . .

And so they were married, and happiness, the great magician, made Jacinth young and fair again.

A FREAK OF FATE.

I.

BERTHOLET declared gloomily that he meant to see something of "life."

You would not believe how he clung to youth, or, rather, the wild fantasies of Parisian youth, in the shape of wide trousers, cuffs that scratched his knuckles, and a shirt collar too tall behind and too low in front. He nursed his sparse dyed hair with pathetic anxiety, and so pomaded and perfumed himself, that he carried about his own sacred atmosphere, to Madame's disgust.

Madame Bertholet's objections to her husband dated from their wedding-day. He was not her ideal when his hair was brown, not green,—accidents will happen,—and when his teeth were his own, and after thirty years of married life, custom had failed to reconcile Madame to the inevitable.

Thirty years ago Madame was round and rosy, with a slightly hard line about the corners of her mouth. Time, that jester, amused himself by exaggerating these characteristics: Madame's roundness had developed into fourteen stone, and her complexion to what it would be false politeness to term rosy. The hard line had crept up to her black eyes, and found congenial outlet in a prayer-book with a steel clasp.

Madame was Calvinistic, and life was to her neither a pleasure nor a joke. Neither was it to Monsieur. He was not Calvinistic, but he reflected Madame's moods, and so distorted them that when she spoke of death, with the profound indifference born of the toughest life, Monsieur, pulling his stiff cuffs over his lean knuckles, imagined he was already dead.

The trouble was that Monsieur Bertholet was rich. He had amassed a fortune in supplying Paris with horse-flesh in the guise of joints and cutlets, till at last Madame, who was ambitious, suggested selling out, and retiring into the gloomy grandeur of a mansion whose noble occupant had left his fortune on various roulette tables, and who gladly disposed of his family mansion on condition that a single room was reserved for his own use.

Madame's soul rejoiced in the gloom of her new acquisition. It did her good to see her family struggle over the slippery floors, or lean their harassed backs against the perpendicular stiffness of the chairs.

Two vulnerable spots there were, however, in her rigorous heart: Monsieur le Pasteur and "the little one." Madame's pastor was a comfortable sight, sitting by the fire in the only easy-chair, sipping curaçoa or crunching chocolate *confits* sacred to his coming, while he and Madame pronounced damning judgments on heathen, Jews, and Christians.

"I do not often see Monsieur Auguste at church, my daughter," M. le Pasteur would say.

"My poor little one, he works so hard, and Sundays he is so tired. You know he is delicate."

Whereupon M. le Pasteur brushed a few crumbs from his priestly coat and coughed. However, he only crunched some more chocolate and said nothing.

There was a fiction in the family called "the little one," otherwise Auguste. He was Madame's hot-house growth, and at the age of twenty-eight—in the intervals of studying law—was fed by her on the most harmless pap of knowledge. It was his mother's mission in life to show him the nice, straight path of existence, which would lead him to the fortune of a Calvinistic maiden.

Monsieur Bertholet was early sacrificed to the fiction of "the little one's" innocence, and, not to contaminate the infantile purity of his own son, the unhappy man was restricted to a life of such monotonous misery that, driven to extremity, he had even tried to make friends with Madame, and M. le Pasteur. In both efforts he signally failed. Then he lingered about the kitchen, and being, so to speak, ejected, prowled about the stairs. The noble occupant of the third floor back, coming down one evening, recognized, with a grim smile, in the solitary figure leaning against the banisters, a humble imitation of his own scant hair and generous linen.

"M. le Comte," Bertholet murmured, gratefully, as that nobleman threw him a smile.

The next day the same meeting ; M. le Comte said a word or two. Three days after, Bertholet confessed to Madame that M. le Comte had invited him to his club.

"Is it a righteous place?" Madame asked M. le Pasteur, lifting her black eyebrows.

M. le Pasteur was in his usual place by the hearth.

"Heavens, yes! To be sure they play a game or two at cards, of an evening ; but it is very noble and select ;" and so Bertholet was allowed to go.

Bertholet went, and sensibly kept the secret of the five thousand francs he had lost to his accommodating tenant.

M. le Comte being a gentlemanly blackguard, and, having present supply, dropped his landlord, who, however, preserved the fiction of this friendship, and, under its shelter, even reached a certain theatre whose very name suggests the world, the flesh, and the devil.

There was something of good in Bertholet's sinful heart, that the thought of " the little one " should haunt

him as he sank into the velvet arm-chair, and looked
stealthily at the audience.

"Think of .the 'little one,'" the fiddles scratched
and the flutes piped, while the double-bass and the
trombones added, ominously, "and Madame."

Monsieur Bertholet's gaze wandered enviously toward the stalls where the *jeunesse dorée* lolled in aristocratic laziness, and beheld, to his gasping amazement, "the little one,"—M. Auguste,—in claw-hammer,
an inherited fondness for a too expansive display of
linen, and a fashion of studying the stage through his
opera glass that but too surely betokened much practice.

"*Mon Dieu!*" M. Bertholet gasped, then a faint
grin dawned over his face. "So! These are the
prayer meetings he attends—ha, ha!"

As father, M. Bertholet was, for a moment, overcome, but he was, however, mortal, and a feeling
of joy stole over his heart to think how Madame was
being deceived, and, being human before being a
father, M. Bertholet smiled again, sat a little more
at ease in the shadow of the lace curtains, and devoted his undivided attention to the stage.

From that day M. Bertholet, having lost all interest in making a shining example of himself, quite
forsook the path of virtue, and hardly again darkened
the slippery threshold of Madame's *salon*. "Life"
was to M. Bertholet an awful phrase, unbefitting the
Calvinistic sanctity of the parlor. Indeed, it was
only to be dreamed of far away from Madame's presence ; so M. Bertholet, having weighed the pros and
cons in his distracted mind, determined to flee to
some congenial land, where plunging into mysterious
depths was compatible with personal security. In
other words, he decided to take his fortune and, in
disguise, to fly to parts unknown.

II.

THREE days after, M. Bertholet disappeared from the bosom of his family.

Gradually it dawned on Madame and "the little one," that something unusual had happened, but they bore the uncertainty with calmness till the third day, when they both hurried in secret to M. Bertholet's lawyer, for information about the will. There, to their momentary confusion, they met.

"Little one!"

"Mother!"

M. Auguste was round, like his mother, and his hair lay over his forehead in a shining sweep. He pressed his hat to his heart, and remarked gently—for he was always polite—that if his sainted father had left no will, the greater part of the property would revert to him, M. Auguste.

Madame looked up with a gasp, and, for a moment, her face turned to a dull yellow. Was this her Auguste, her "little one"?

"In fact, I may as well tell you that I mean to marry, now that I am my own master."

"You—marry, 'little one'?" Madame gasped.

"Confound 'little one'!" M. Auguste replied, with some exasperation.

"Little one!" and Madame stamped her foot, "I—I forbid it!"

M. Auguste turned on her with a most unfilial look in his small black eyes.

"Suppose, mother, your 'little one' were already married?"

With astonishing quickness Madame leaped to her feet and boxed M. Auguste's ears.

"I—I hope he isn't dead! I hope he'll come back and send you begging, *misérable!*"

15

"But then, mother, you will not be able to marry M. le Pasteur."

An angry red swept over Madame's face, and, with the last of her by no means feeble strength, she gave her child another blow, and sank exhausted into a chair.

One side of his face was white, and the other red with the marks of five fingers.

He stood before his mother, hat in hand, and said, quite politely:

"Come and see us—bring M. le Pasteur. My wife is an angel.—She dances at the 'Variétés.'"

"Wretch."

M. Auguste turned with a shrug, and nearly fell against a little man with a quill behind his ear.

"Madame!" He held a brown snuffbox, which he snapped with nervous violence.

"Well, M. le Notar?"

"M. Bertholet cannot be dead."

Madame's eyes flashed triumphantly, while "the little one," turning the door handle, muttered an oath.

"I fear," the little notary said, turning from mother to son,—"I fear, from all I have discovered, that Monsieur Bertholet has run away with his own fortune, five hundred thousand francs, and that he has left nothing behind."

Madame did not faint, but she leaned back in her chair and stared into vacancy.

"Not dead, but gone! Gone with all the money —our money—my money!"

"You are no better off than I, mother."

She looked up. M. Auguste stood before her, twirling his cane. "I am going in search of him, poor old man; and when I find him I shall make his life pleasant. Good-by, mother—come and see us," and so with a polite bow he left the room.

"Little one!"

A man who can run away with five hundred thousand francs is not to be despised, and Madame felt that she had, perhaps, been a little unsympathetic in her treatment of Bertholet.

She rose in unfeigned trouble. "He must be found," she said to the lawyer. "He must have been mad to have deserted me. Employ detectives—anything—but bring him back. Five hundred thousand francs," she said, laying her hand on the little man's arm,—"five hundred thousand francs left without guidance in a sinful world, will come to no good."

III.

MONSIEUR BERTHOLET, trying to lose himself in the great Northern Railway station, felt the by no means strange sensation that the eyes of the world were upon him. A flaxen beard and wig, marvelous checked trousers, and a tall gray hat, had transformed him into the Frenchman's ideal of an Englishman, and filled his French soul with disgust.

In a frenzied effort to discover whether the train destined to bear him to Calais—and to London and liberty—ever meant to start, he tangled himself in the meshes of wheelbarrows, porters, and travelers. He was jostled about and hurried along, till at last he stood, aching and battered, behind three broad-shouldered fellows, in whose shadow he hid himself, while he hugged to his breast a small newspaper parcel, his only luggage.

He breathed more freely, and looked with silent envy at the broad backs before him. They were only common soldiers, these three—poor devils, with the prospect of a third-class ride, and a meal of dry bread out of the forage-bag each carried slung across his shoulders.

A whistle and a shriek from the engine. "Calais! Calais!" and then a skurry and rush of people down the platform.

"*Tiens!* Duval, the old Englishman has gone," and one of the soldiers looked over his shoulder.

Gone? Poor M. Bertholet had made a dash for a *coupé*, when a couple of arms were thrown about his neck, and an affectionate kiss resounded on each of his cheeks.

"Little one!"

"I knew you," Auguste cried, gleefully. "I knew your walk."

"Let me go!" and M. Bertholet struggled to free himself.

It was an unpropitious time for explanations; bells were ringing, and barrow-loads of luggage threatened destruction to their legs.

"Come home with me, and you shall have a rousing good time!" Auguste shouted, just as his father leaped towards the train, with the cry:

"*Dieu!—Dieu!*—your mother!"

Sure enough, there was Madame, struggling through the crowd, and searching with keen black eyes.

M. Bertholet was appalled; but he had also the strength of utter despair. How he freed himself from Auguste's encircling arms he never knew; but he struck wildly out, leaped into an empty *coupé*, and slammed the door, just as, with a puff and a shriek from the engine, the train glided out of the station.

Madame stared blankly into "the little one's" face. "*Imbecile!*" she cried, and turned her broad back on him, and wrung her hands under her lady-like shawl.

M. Auguste had traced his father easily enough, and Madame had watched M. Auguste, and this was the end of their successful scheming. Tears filled her angry eyes, and so blinded them that, as she turned she stumbled against a broad-shouldered soldier, who muttered something under his curly dark mustache, before he saw that it was a lady. Then he made a hasty military salute, and rejoined his two friends.

"Ah, Chelot, the day is out of joint with you!" the man called Duval cried, as the other came up, and he kicked at an unsightly newspaper parcel, that had been rolled and pushed along, till it touched his hobnailed boots. The package was rather small, round, and dusty, and did not invite inspection.

Chelot said nothing, but a look of pain came into his honest brown eyes, as he watched the other two play at foot-ball with the accidental plaything.

As for M. Auguste, he stood for a moment perfectly helpless, grasping his inoffensive, retreating chin with one hand, while he wondered angrily how everybody could be so calm ; wondered what those three men would do if they had lost five hundred thousand francs—those three men who, he hoped, would get shot some day for the way they grinned as he pushed past them.

In a *coupé* of the train tearing Calais-ward at the rate of fifty miles an hour, a mysterious old gentleman was rolling over the seats and beating his bald head against the cushions.

"Lost! lost! lost!" he screamed, over and over again. "Five hundred thousand francs in a newspaper parcel! Guard, for heaven's sake, stop the train!"

"Five hundred thousand francs in a newspaper! Monsieur is wild," the guard said, looking in. "But if it will quiet Monsieur, he shall be listened to at Calais."

But nothing would persuade M. Bertholet to be quiet. He tried to leap out of the window, and, being held back by force, flung himself at full length on the floor.

Quick as lightning the guard tied his hands behind his back with a handy cord, and left him, after he had made a neat pile of a yellow beard and wig, a tall white hat and a pair of blue spectacles.

As for M. Bertholet, he lay prone, and, having struggled all the strength out of himself, he could only gasp:

"Lost—lost—lost—five hundred thousand francs wrapped in a newspaper!"

IV.

THOSE were the days of the third Napoleon and Mexican ambition. That glittering bubble, the Empire, had soared its highest, was glittering its gaudiest, and, like all bubbles under the same circumstances, it was about to burst.

Chelot, waiting for the train to Merle, strode up and down the platform, with thoughts far away in the village, three miles beyond Merle, where Claude used to wait for him, under the big chestnut tree before the mill with its red gable.

Of the other two, Duval, still kicking the improvised foot-ball, remarked that such a wet blanket of a friend as Chelot he had never seen.

"In six days he'll be sick—deadly sick," the other, Jean Pierre, added, tilting himself up and down, ship fashion.

"In three weeks, Chelot, you'll be making love to a Mexican ma'm'selle."

"In three weeks Ma'm'selle Claude will be forgotten."

Chelot turned his back on them, and strode to the edge of the platform, just as the train came alongside.

"*Ah ciel*, the old boy is angry! I say, Chelot, forget bad jokes!" Duval cried.

But Chelot was sick and sore, and, somehow, he couldn't turn his honest face about with a pleasant smile, so he sprang on the *coupé* step and paid no attention. Duval gave a parting kick to the dusty newspaper and hurried after him.

"Old boy," he said, with a friendly blow on his shoulder, "why be angry at foolish words? We were always good friends; so come, now, and shake hands. You're going far away, and who knows the fortune of war. Bah!" he cried, hastily, "I mean to dance at your wedding till I drop!" And he wrung Chelot's outstretched hand.

"Now, there's Jean Pierre; take his hand; he's a good fellow."

Jean Pierre, who had strolled up, was a bit of a joker, and while he shook Chelot's hand, he secretly thrust a battered newspaper bundle into his forage bag, rejoicing, with the hollow joy of all practical jokers, to think of the disappointment in store when he should pull out the dirty paper, instead of the piece of bread underneath.

Chelot leaned out of the car window and watched them sadly, till the train swung around a curve and tore its way into the golden summer afternoon.

Chelot was young, and five days ago, before the news came that his regiment was ordered to Mexico, he had loved all the world in his honest fashion, because Claude was his world and Claude loved him. But now, in six days, his regiment was ordered to sail; but six days of youth and love are better than ten years of old age, he thought, and he stroked his brown mustache and imagined Claude's surprise at sight of him. Five days of happiness, and then he would gently tell her that he must leave her for a long time, perhaps forever. He leaned his head against the window, and watched the wheat fields bend beneath the sweep of the summer wind, that touched the frail petals of the scarlet poppies, till they hid beneath the ripening grain.   The apple trees were heavy with fruit, and between the orchards and far-spreading fields, the red-roofed farmhouses twinkled into sight.   Flocks of sheep, nibbling peacefully in the pastures, followed the bell-wether, and scampered into safe distance.   At last came Merle, where Chelot leaped out, gave himself a shake by way of toilet, and looked down with pride at his scarlet trousers and smoothed his blue jacket.   He swung his forage-bag a trifle farther back, gave a cock to his cap, and trudged down the highway with an easy, swinging gait that sent the blood to his brown face and made his eyes sparkle.   "In five days? Ah, bah ! *Vogue la galère !*"   He whistled a merry tune, trudging up and down hill to Plaileroi and Claude.   At the foot of the hill, just beyond the bridge, lay the mill with the ancient chestnut street standing before the door, where the time-worn millstones were piled, step-fashion, to the broad threshold, where Claude sat, summer evenings, spinning and waiting for him. Chelot knew every stone and tree on the road.   The children came up and touched him with friendly, black paws, and the landlord of the " Pot-au-Feu " shook his tasseled nightcap at him.

"If thou art not too tired for a dance in the kitchen, bring thy sweetheart after dusk and show us what thy legs can do."

No wonder that the landlord of the " Pot-au-Feu " was *maire* of Plaileroi : he knew how to make himself necessary.

The young man shouted back a joyous acceptance, and sprang down hill, while his heart beat like a sledge-hammer, as he crossed the bridge over the mill-stream and saw the huge wheel turn noisily.   He was sc

near that he could distinguish a dusty, white figure
in the door-way—the miller—scraping and bowing to
a retreating figure, who passed Chelot just as he
reached the chestnut tree,—a long, lank personage,
with a yellow face, in the ominous elegance of broadcloth, baggy at the knees and too short at the wrists,
and with a huge bouquet on his breast. Chelot glanced
after him, with an instinctive desire to punch his shiny
tall hat a foot or two deeper over his face and dusty
hair; then he turned towards the house. The miller
had disappeared, and he stood alone under the chestnut tree, with the exception of a donkey hitched to a
cart, who was examining his legs with profound attention. So this was the coming back to Plaileroi
and Claude!

He sat down disconsolately on the bench, and the
next instant a shower of chestnut burrs and leaves
rained down upon him.

He sprang to his feet, and looking up between the
dark branches, caught sight of a laughing, rosy face
peeping at him through the clustering chestnut leaves,
and tantalizingly out of his reach.

"Claude!"

There was a sparkle of white teeth and a funny
nod of a brown head toward the figure plodding down
the road. Then, with a warning "Chut!" Claude
glided and scrambled out of her hiding-place, and
fell into her lover's outstretched arms.

"I have you again, beloved," she whispered, hiding
her rough head against his breast; then she tore herself away with a little laugh, and stood before him,
shading her face with a bunch of poppies. "Are you
sure that you love me?"

With one quick motion he clasped her to his heart,
poppies and all.

"Why do you ask, my torment?"

"Because *he*" (nodding down the road) "says he

loves me.   He wants to buy the mill and the miller's daughter, and he is rich—oh, so very rich.   Every day I have to hide from him and father."

"Your father? and we betrothed?"

"Yes, father favors him," she said, with a troubled look toward the mill.

"And you, Claude?" and he grasped her hands.

"Doubt me, Bertrand?   If I could only show you how true I am!"   Then with a sigh, "If you were rich you might buy your discharge, and then we could marry, and you would be the miller."

"And if not?"

"Why do you ask?   What is the matter?" she cried, in sudden alarm, clinging to his arm.

"Nothing; nothing shall come between us but death."

"Death?   Why do you speak of death?   You are well and strong, and God is good.   Bertrand, Bertrand, what has happened?"

"I am a fool!" he cried.   "Because I am so happy, I fear something may happen."

She shook her head, and it seemed as if the twilight that was creeping over the valley, the mill, and the stream, had touched her sunny face, as without a word but with a wistful look at Bertrand she led the way to the mill.

V.

IT had grown so dark that the oil-lamps twinkled throughout the village.   In the huge kitchen of the "Pot-au-feu" two fiddles and a trumpet twanged and tooted a rollicking galop, and whatever of Plaileroi had a pair of sound legs, went scampering up and down the bare floor, till the whole village was in a whirl, from the fat cook with a huge ladle in her hand, to Claude.

It seemed to Claude as if the world were spinning about, so did Bertrand whirl her up and down to the music.

Plaileroi balls were primitive enough—the world went as it stood, and hardly smoothed its hair, and so Chelot: he hadn't even taken off his forage-bag.

"If we could only dance forever!" and faster, faster he went, clasping her more tightly, knowing that it was, perhaps, his last dance.

"I am tired, Bertrand."

He stood still, holding her hand as if in a dream.

Some one in black broadcloth, and with a withered bouquet on his breast looked in at the door, over the heated crowd, and watched the two jealously. Chelot brushed past him and Claude turned her face away.

So they went through the porch of the "Pot-au-Feu" into the garden. The crickets chirped and the soft breeze touched the leaves of the poplars lining the roadside.

"See!—a falling star. I have wished," Claude whispered.

"A fine dance, Ma'm'selle. To last a year—eh, Monsieur?"

Like an unpleasant ghost in broadcloth, he stood beside them, with his tall hat on the back of his head and his hands in his pockets.

"Monsieur Garbelle."

"Another kind of dance in Mexico—eh, Monsieur Chelot?"

Claude looked up at M. Garbelle with a white face.

"What do you mean? Tell me! Mexico—for God's sake, what is it?"

Chelot turned on his rival in a quivering rage, and one strong hand nearly came in fatal contact with the withered nosegay on M. Garbelle's breast.

"Claude, wait till I tell you," he cried, and grasped her hands in his.

"No, now!"

"Monsieur Chelot's regiment is ordered to Mexico for a year. Perhaps Mademoiselle don't know that there is a war in Mexico? It is a wild country, far away, and M. Chelot will have to cross the sea before he is there. The big sea—so big," and M. Garbelle spread out his lank arms to give an adequate idea of the ocean.

"Is this true?"

"It is true. I thought we might be happy five days more in this world. Forgive me, Claude," he implored, looking into the dull misery of her eyes.

As for Monsieur Garbelle, having succeeded in his little plan, he slunk away. From the rambling old tavern the shrill fiddles and the trumpet struck up a new tune, that floated gayly down the hill after them. But the old charm had fled; it was all discord. With her head on Bertrand's breast, Claude was weeping bitterly.

It was high noon the next day. The miller in the kitchen was cutting huge junks of bread from a long loaf on the table, washing the bites down with coffee.

Across the other end of the table Chelot had flung his forage-bag the night before, and there it still lay. The miller, with a scornful laugh, leaned across the table, and took it up, and out dropped a crust of bread and a dirty roll of newspaper.

"Not much to bring from Paris," he said, with great contempt. He knew some one—with a sly look at poor Claude, who was standing listlessly at the window—who at least would bring home a silk gown from such a journey.

The girl paid no attention. Her father was talking nonsense. The miller was a weasel-faced old man in a smock-frock and a nightcap. He had ambition, and fortune was favoring him. He rose to leave the kitchen, giving a parting push to the bag, when Claude turned upon him suddenly.

"Father, what will make him free?"

He knew what she meant, without explanation.

"Money—much money."

"We are poor, are we not?"

"Yes, poor as rats," he answered, with great cheerfulness, knowing the drift of her thoughts.

"Where he—Bertrand—is going is a wild and dangerous country?"

"Oh, yes; very dangerous."

"He may never come back," she murmured.

"Very likely. If they are not shot, they are starved."

She grew so deadly pale that the miller was alarmed.

"Can no one save him?" she cried, wringing her hands. "Oh, for a little money!"

"Monsieur Garbelle," he suggested.

"Do you think he would lend us some?"

"Not for nothing," and he scratched his head. "But I'll send him to make his own terms. He's always about the mill nowadays," and the miller tried to suggest a shattered existence, and shuffled out of the kitchen.

M. Garbelle was there, and came sneaking in, doubtful of his reception. He was not an inviting-looking object, covered with a thin layer of flour, from too much prowling about the mill.

Claude sat with her back to him, her head on the table against Bertrand's bag. She looked up as he stood beside her. It was a new look to Garbelle, and he liked it. She was wonderfully handsome.

"Ma'm'selle, you want money? I have it, and I will give you what you want, if—"

She looked at him breathlessly.

"Well, M. Garbelle?"

"If you will marry me."

VI.

POOR Chelot went away in the early dawn, and came back with a heavy heart. He had been to all the Chelots to borrow money. It was a wild endeavor. They shrugged their shoulders, and declared that men were cheap and money dear. So he returned to Plaileroi at twilight, with empty hands and quite hopeless.

He looked up drearily, for some one called to him from the "Pot-au-Feu." It was M. le Maire, waving a letter. The "Pot-au-Feu" and the post office were one in primitive Plaileroi.

A letter for him—Chelot! The miracle did not happen once a year, and so he turned it in all directions in his perplexity.

"It was left for you an hour ago. For heaven's sake, open it, man!" the mayor suggested, with some irritation. He was dying of curiosity.

It was a soft letter with a downhill direction in one corner; a pleasant letter, M. le Maire concluded, for, after a second of bewildered delight Chelot leaped in the air, seized M. le Maire and hugged him passionately."

"Free, free, free!" and he shook three one-hundred-franc bills in his face. There was a bit of paper inclosed, on which was written, in crabbed writing, "From a faithful friend."

"God is so good!" and a film dimmed his eyes, and his lips quivered under his brown mustache.

Then, with a laugh, he swung his cap in the air and sprang downhill. He had escaped a great danger, and, in his sudden joy, he never once thought of the cause.

Free! and Claude his forever!

Monsieur Garbelle was crossing the bridge; he looked up at the other's radiant face with a frown. But Chelot did not care; in his great happiness he was willing to love even his rival.

"I am free, M. Garbelle. See, all this money is mine!" and he thrust it into the other's face.

"Have you received it already?" and M. Garbelle retreated to the moss-grown stone railing.

"What do you mean? Who sent it?"

M. Garbelle had had an unpleasant courting, and an expensive, so he needed something to soothe his soul.

"Ha! ha! It is a little bargain: Ma'm'selle Claude accepts three hundred francs from me, and I take Ma'm'selle Claude."

"Sold herself for me!" Bertrand thought over and over again, as if he could not grasp the idea. However, there stood M. Garbelle, grinning, until with one hand the young man grasped his broadcloth collar, and with the other stuffed the bank-bills into M. Garbelle's pocket, and then, with a vigorous kick, sent him staggering uphill.

"The debt is repaid, M. Garbelle," he said, and, turning his back on him, went towards the mill.

That whole afternoon the miller had been happy in his chosen son-in-law—M. Garbelle. As for Claude, she said nothing but she worked with feverish activity.

After M. Garbelle had given her the money he tried to reward himself by clasping her arm with one bony hand, but she shook him off like a spider.

At dusk she sat down by the open hearth, shivering in the fire-light, and the miller put on a fresh log and the flames went blazing and crackling up the chimney.

She was still sitting there when Bertrand came in. For a moment they looked silently and sorrowfully at each other.

"Claude," he said, at last, drawing her towards him, "I shall come back to you again—I swear I shall. The price you paid for my life was too dear—I—I have given the money back. Have patience, my darling, for a year—only a year."

She hid her face on his shoulder and wept, but something of peace touched her heart. God only knew how patient she would be! It grew darker, and the fire-light cast red shadows across the floor; a yellow glimmer pierced through a crack in the door.

It was the miller who came in holding a lamp, followed by M. le Maire, longing to know what the letter and the money were about.

The miller caught sight of Bertrand.

"You here again?" he asked, with much disfavor. He would have said more, but he was afraid of Claude. M. le Maire pricked up his sharp ears, but he was also a Frenchman, and polite, and he had no interest in family skirmishes.

There was an ominous silence, and M. le Maire, sitting down by the table, stretched out his fat hands to a ragged newspaper parcel, lying beside a forage-bag and a crust of bread. Anything to break the dead silence.

"*Tiens!* A paper from Paris!" and, without a moment's hesitation, M. le Maire began to unroll it with nimble fingers.

"It is the only thing Chelot brought from Paris," the miller said, with much scorn, while he filled a couple of pipes, and dived into the recesses of a huge carven chest for a bottle of wine, for M. le Maire was an honored guest.

"In the name of heaven, what's this?"

Only to hear M. le Maire, it was no wonder that the miller leaped to his feet, and dropped the bottle with a crash. He wasn't dreaming, but——money? The table was covered with it, and the ragged paper that Bertrand had brought from Paris, was bursting with more. It strewed the table and fell on the ground, and the numbers on the bills were fabulous. Between all stood M. le Maire, open-mouthed, petrified, and pointing a fat forefinger at Bertrand.

For a second Chelot was bewildered; then a sudden light dawned upon him.

"To be sure—yes, I remember! Jean Pierre thrust it in my bag yesterday, as I left Paris. He and Duval were kicking it about till Jean Pierre dropped it in there," pointing to the bag, "I suppose some one lost it," Bertrand added, indifferently.

It seemed like a nineteenth century fairy-tale, as they stood about M. le Maire, while he counted the bills with a moist forefinger. The miller watched each motion with open-mouthed wonder. After the first few thousands, his ears were dulled, he could comprehend no more; while Claude thought of the happiness such a bit of paper could give her and hers.

She turned to the window, and looked into the darkness till the last bill was counted and the whole was safely tucked into an inside pocket of M. le Maire's waistcoat.

Bertrand looked on with calm indifference.

"If we had all that money," she whispered, laying her hand on his arm.

Something of his old bright smile came back as he stroked his mustache and looked down at her.

"But we haven't," he answered, lightly, and that was all.

"Five hundred thousand francs. Some one has lost half a million," M. le Maire said, impressively. "Whoever it is, will cry loud enough to be heard. If it hadn't been for me, that money would have lain there till doomsday. What would you do without me—just tell me? I shall ride to Merle to-night, and telegraph to the chief of police in Paris. As for you, Chelot, the money is yours till the owner appears; so you must sleep at the inn to-night. I shouldn't like all the world to know what's hidden in the 'Pot-au-Feu.' Come, Chelot! You, miller, bring a lantern. Good-night, Ma'm'selle Claude."

The miller accompanied the two to the inn. To say that M. le Maire was excited was to say nothing. He was magnificent!

"Legends," he declared, as he harnessed his fat horse to a square box on four wheels,—"legends will be handed down about that money, Chelot, my boy; and you, miller, won't be forgotten. But I ——" and M. le Maire paused a second and laid his forefinger against his nose, " I—oh—I——"

Language failed to provide him with words suffi· ciently eulogistic, and, like other artists under equally impressive circumstances, M. le Maire remained silent.

VII.

M. LE MAIRE was still snoring placidly in the early morning, when a coach tore down the highway and pulled up, with a sweep, at the " Pot-au-Feu."

He sat up in bed and rubbed his heavy eyes, when a thundering knock sent him to the window like a shot.

Two men stood below; one looked up with a stern, official eye.

"I am a police commissary; this gentleman "— pointing to his companion — "has lost a package containing a large sum of money that answers the description of the one you found. Let us in!"

For a second M. le Maire stared at the happy possessor of so much money, though he wasn't much to look at. Of course it was Monsieur Bertholet; but

after a day of unspeakable misery and an early journey, a pea-green haze covered his features ; but with
the last remnants of energy he pulled down his cuffs.
He trembled with joy and eagerness, and M. le
Maire, enveloped in a mysterious, long garment,
had hardly unbarred the door before M. Bertholet
fell about his neck.

"My preserver!"

"No, not exactly."

"Well, then, who is he? Where is he? Let me
see him!"

"He is in bed ; I'll send him down directly."

That did not satisfy M. Bertholet's grateful impatience. He followed M. le Maire's fluttering garments down the winding corridors, and burst into a
small room where Bertrand, dreaming of Mexico with
the magnificent fantasy of a Frenchman, suddenly
awoke to find a queer old man sitting at his bedside,
clasping his hand,—a strange old man, with wisps of
thin, green hair, and a limp but generous display of
linen.

"You shall have the reward, twenty thousand
francs!" cried Bertholet, over and over.

"He is mad!" Chelot thought, and shuddered.

"Day before yesterday I lost the money in the
railway station in Paris. In Calais they said I was
mad, and sent me to Paris by the next train, with two
keepers."

Chelot watched him, horror struck.

"I remember, I saw you at the station, my fine fellow ; I'll make your fortune."

A light dawned on Chelot.

"I'm the owner of the five hundred thousand
francs," M. Bertholet explained.

"And you are not mad?" Chelot asked, still doubting M. Bertholet's feverish joy.

M. Bertholet mad? He was mad the night he

had been left to recover his reason at leisure in a
police cell, after a forced journey back to Paris, with
two keepers and a pair of handcuffs. He was mad
the next morning, when Madame and "the little
one" came, each in turn, and overwhelmed him
with reproaches. But mad now? No, he was coming to himself; he had learned a lesson. Madame
was nothing without him, and "the little one" less
than nothing.

Experience has been an extravagant luxury ever
since Mother Eve ate an apple and lost Paradise. It
cost M. Bertholet twenty thousand francs.

It was a great day for Plaileroi and the "Pot-au-
Feu." Bertholet sat beside M. le Maire in the great
kitchen, and watched him brew wonderful drinks. All
Plaileroi came and stared at the rich man, who had
lost a fortune in Paris and found it in Plaileroi.
They drank to his health and to M. le Maire's, and
stared again when they heard that he had given the
miller's Claude a dowry of twenty thousand francs,
and remembered M. le Maire handsomely.

Chelot would accept nothing, even when he was
told that twenty thousand francs was the advertised
reward. However, after a moment's consultation with
the host of the "Pot-au-Feu," Claude was transformed
into an heiress by the mere scratch of M. Bertholet's
pen.

"It's all one," M. le Maire said in explanation,
as Claude came shyly into the room, followed by
Bertrand.

"Am I mad?" M. Bertholet asked the young man,
and patted Claude's blushing face. It was an expensive pat. It was all he had seen of "life," and it
cost a pile of money. Still he did not care, though
he watched them rather enviously when the fiddlers
arrived, and in a trivet set Plaileroi scampering and
spinning down the long kitchen.

"They have the best of it," he thought, catching sudden glimpses of a laughing face, the glitter of white teeth, and Bertrand's brown mustache in dangerous proximity.

Grandeur begets solitude, and M. Bertholet pulled down his cuffs, rasped his throat, and wished M. le Maire to the devil.

"Will Monsieur dance with me?" asked a shy voice, and Claude stood before him, blushing.

Would he? Good heavens, yes!

He leaped to his feet, pulled down his cuffs, the fiddles struck up a new tune, and, after thirty years of inaction, M. Bertholet's feet cracked their old muscles to the tune of a dance, and M. Bertholet's elbows forced a way through the population of Plaileroi with superb effect. In the midst of it—

"*Mon mari!*" said a familiar voice.

M. Bertholet thought he was dreaming, and danced on.

"*Mon mari!*" said the voice again, plaintively.

He stopped as if he had been shot. There stood Madame at the open door, travel-stained and humble.

"My friend, I heard that you were here, and so I followed you."

"And now you can go home again," M. Bertholet interposed, politely, and, taking her by one fat elbow, he led her through the garden to the vehicle in which she had come.

"Will you not come home with me, my friend?"

"Not till I choose, my dear," he answered, shutting her into the coach.

"Perhaps you haven't heard the news," she said, spitefully, looking out of the window. "Our little one is married."

"Then I pity him," M. Bertholet replied, with much feeling.

"She's a dancer—a ballet dancer!" Madame

screamed, as the coachman, with a crack of his whip, started his lank beasts toward Merle.

It was sinful and not fatherly, but he laughed till he ached ; he was still laughing when he reached the " Pot-au-Feu," and the merry tune of a dance tickled his ears.

" Now," said M. Bertholet, and he pulled his cuffs down for the last time in this story,—" now I shall begin to live. Madame is crushed, and 'the little one' is—ha! ha! married."

The fiddles twanged and the trumpet tooted, and M. Bertholet and all Plaileroi whirled about in the kitchen of the " Pot-au-Feu."

MONSIEUR PAMPALON'S REPENT-ANCE.

I.

MONSIEUR PAMPALON had no care: that was the trouble—a solitary case in the world, I'm afraid.

He would go out of his way to make himself miserable, and finding everything as it should be, he grumbled because he had nothing to grumble about.

Monsieur had been in the confectionery business on the most magnificent scale—so unlimited that it embraced all the varieties of dainty boxes and bags and flowers and fancy papers with which Parisian candy is decorated, to tempt a morally weak world. Being candies, you would naturally imagine a dainty little shop, at whose contents you could gaze with varied emotions and then buy a franc's worth. Don't flatter yourself; you could never buy a franc's worth,—the business was wholesale, fearfully wholesale.

Monsieur's warehouses stood in the midst of Old Paris. They were reached through a labyrinth of narrow streets, above which the tall houses towered in a fashion that kept out very much sunlight and all fresh air. You crossed a small courtyard, and then you were irrevocably lost unless some one came to your aid; for the three small doors that opened into the courtyard, and the tall, narrow windows, with their iron shutters, were all deserted. So you wandered in at the first door like a stray sheep, and meandered among a wilderness of pasteboard boxes until, fate propitious, you were rescued by a gentleman in a paper cap and white garments, who would politely give you the clew to the labyrinth, and lead you to M. Pampalon's presence in a dim counting-room, very dusty and very full of samples of candy and fly-speckled flowers of some bygone fashion.

M. Pampalon was very short and very fat, with a large, smoothly-shaven face surmounted by a thick crop of stiff gray hair. First you would notice his ears, and then his gray eyes, with their heavy, melancholy lids. The nose was blunt and large, and the mouth, with drooping corners, was moved by the same machinery as the melancholy eyelids.

M. Pampalon was born with a natural pity for himself, in which he was quite unjustified. As a boy he was affected to tears by his virtuous school-record; at the age of fifty his eyes would grow dim as he gave a sou to a cripple, not owing to his sorrow at misfortune, but because he was moved at his own philanthropy. He had, besides, a strong tendency to look at the dark side of life, in which, again, he was not justified, for if ever a man was controlled by the most blind and stupid of good luck, Pampalon was that man. So true was this, that a saying went about among his neighbors, "La chance à Pampalon," in which everybody agreed but himself.

Madame Pampalon was short and broad, like her husband. While his, however, was a flabby stoutness, hers was good and solid, and there was not a fraction of melancholy in her bright black eyes. Madame had been a pretty shop-girl before she became monsieur's wife, and her loyal soul never forgot that he had raised her from that condition to be the ruler of a most desirable country mansion within two miles of Paris.

On Saturday afternoons, about three o'clock, madame appeared at the warerooms, gorgeous in her finest attire, followed by Dodé, who cast down her brown eyes and blushed crimson, whenever a stray clerk made his appearance. There was a curious sympathy between father and daughter. M. Pampalon rarely surprised this young philosopher, and though he was affectionate by spasms, Dodé was always ready to meet him halfway. Though she loyally defended her mother, when family skirmishes obliged her to give up neutrality, still in her heart she felt for her father and praised him and spoilt him, setting him up for a stubby, wayward, outwardly unattractive idol, which she worshiped blindly. These were the two kind fairies who rescued M. Pampalon from his sugar-coated chains, and bore him off, melancholy but re-signed, to the desirable country mansion.

Monsieur Pampalon was no silent martyr. A faith-ful audience of two admired and pitied him, and would have henpecked in the usual innocent, feminine fashion, had not this husband and father, in the midst of their cooing, always said to himself, "Why do they pity me? I know I suffer, I know that I am miserable, but there's something back of this : they're too ten-der by half. I'll watch."

By which will be seen that the good man was a hyp-ochondriac of the deepest dye. There was, too, a fiction in his mind of the fearful sacrifices he was mak-ing for his family. No man, he declared, slaved as he did ; he used to cast it at his wife and daughter, as if to bid these unfeeling tyrants reflect before they goaded him too far. So, of an evening he would come up from Paris on the top of the omnibus, smoking a cigar and talking politics with a chance neighbor, quite forgetful of his griefs till, coming in sight of the desirable country mansion, he suddenly returned to his normal condition, and appeared crushed and care-worn.

Among other peculiarities, M. Pampalon reveled in the prospect of old age, and he had a way of hinting at his years which made Methuselah a rollicking young blade in comparison. That he was a devoted patriot was a matter of course. He read all the newspapers, beginning with the advertisements. During the siege of Paris he had threatened to enlist, and had gone so far as to describe to his harrowed listeners, with tears in his eyes, how he would like to be buried should he fall for his country. But he never enlisted. However, these sentiments gave him a right to grow eloquent on the duties of a patriot. It was terrible to hear him hold forth after dinner over a cigar and a cup of coffee, and madame was heartily glad that a man of such reckless courage should not be in the midst of carnage.

Said M. Pampalon to madame one evening, as they sat on the veranda, and monsieur was gloomily heaping up a pile of that day's miseries: "I am growing old. There comes a time after a man has worked like a cart-horse"—with a faltering voice and a look of silent reproof at this wife—"when he, too, would like to enjoy something of life."

"Well, papa"—she always called him papa—"why don't you sell the business?"

"'Sell the business!'" monsieur echoed with much contempt. "Much you women know! Sell it? Who'd buy it in such times? No, there's no hope for me. I shall have to grind and wear my life out in the usual way. Had you been economical—"

"Papa! papa!" madame interrupted, with good-natured decision, "we are economical enough."

"Dear little papa!" and a soft small hand caught him right under his fat chin, "do sell that tiresome business."

"Dodé, be quiet! You're too young to give advice."

Dodé—whose real name was Rose—retired into a corner and pouted, but after a moment, a feeling of her extreme age came to her rescue—a trait inherited from her father—"After all, I'm eighteen," she thought, triumphantly. "When a person's eighteen it doesn't take very long to grow old." Which is a lamentable fact.

Pampalon's blind luck following him, he came from Paris one day and told his wife, in the deepest dejection, that he had an offer for the business. He declared that he was breaking down, and he considered it his duty to preserve himself to them. However, he did not mention that the offer was so brilliant that it was a subject of nine days' wonder among his business friends. Madame and Dodé having been called upon to admire such self-sacrifice, Monsieur Pampalon further announced that he meant to devote the rest of his existence to peaceful agricultural pursuits.

II.

M. PAMPALON'S desirable country-seat was situated in Ligny, that charming suburb of Paris where Arcadian bliss is tuned to the keynote of Parisian bourgeois luxury — where the honest French republican turns his back on the city and lives in the contemplation of ripening apricots.

Perhaps there was a sameness in the houses, which were mostly of a chocolate color, with a mansard roof, a veranda in front, and under the veranda a hammock. Each house stood in the center of a little garden, whose flowers thrust their inquisitive heads out of the fence palings and became pale with the dust of the highway, where the omnibus rattled by every hour, kindly leaving each resident at his own door.

The Pampalons were at breakfast. The dining-room was not large, but two low windows opened on the veranda, and let in the concentrated freshness and fragrance of a summer's morning. It was already quite late, for M. Pampalon, in spite of his agricultural pursuits, had overslept himself. He was reading the morning paper, and had just emerged out of its depths to ask for a second cup of coffee from madame, who sat, smooth and dark and neat, behind the coffee urn.

Monsieur was cross, and he eyed his wife with a great deal of slumbering conjugal wrath. "There, now! you're putting too much water in the coffee," he exclaimed, peevishly. "You know I hate dish-water, and I won't drink it."

"Papa, you are growing near-sighted," madame answered, unmoved, "don't you see this is milk?"

"It's all the same," monsieur muttered, foiled.

"If it is all the same, we had better buy a pump instead of a cow—it's much cheaper," madame replied calmly, as her husband growled himself back into his paper, while Dodé, who sat between them, smothered an untimely laugh.

There is no knowing what monsieur might have done at such a lack of feeling in his daughter, if he had not started up, in sudden excitement, "Madame, command yourself!"

"In Heaven's name, what is the matter?" she cried in consternation.

"The matter is," monsieur began with exasperating slowness—"the matter is that we are beggars: the Russian National Railway bonds, in which I have invested the greater part of my money, have fallen to absolutely nothing. I told you so! I knew how it would end!" monsieur cried with a great groan, and again groped his distracted way to the alarming piece of news. All at once there succeeded an embarrassed pause, and monsieur raised his paper and coughed apologetically.

"I suppose you have made a mistake?" madame said with some iciness, for she knew her husband's familiar ways.

"The fact is, my dear," monsieur said, quite subdued, "I read 'Russian National Railway bonds,' and, looking to see their value, I accidentally followed the wrong line."

Madame rose and went toward the window: she had lost her appetite for breakfast. Mademoiselle Dodé played with her coffee cup, but had her young ears unconsciously very wide open, for, hearing a faint sound in the distance, she cried, "The coach is coming!" and ran to the window.

The family Pampalon, reunited by a common excitement, buried the hatchet and stood on the veranda to see the omnibus pass. Instead of galloping on as it had done ever since M. Pampalon retired from business, it stopped before the gate. There was a letting down of steps, a banging of doors, and the creak of a gravel walk; then a jovial voice cried to M. Pampalon, in execrable French, "How are you, old fellow?" the question being followed by a vigorous slap on the shoulder which made the wretched victim jump.

"Karl!" Monsieur Pampalon faltered, "why—"

"Surprised, are you?" Karl said, unconcernedly. "Didn't you get my letter? Sent it to your office— said I was coming, and meant to bring the captain instead of my wife.—My son, the captain—family Pampalon. Now, that's settled. Where's Rose? Why do you call her Dodé?—vile name, Dodé! Ah, ha! gone, has she? I know why; she had her hair in curl papers. So you didn't get my letter? Queer! queer! Sent it to your office."

The captain made a military salute, while M. Pampalon stared at them both in speechless consternation. Madame, being the first to recover, held out a very pretty hand to her unexpected guests. "You know that you are always welcome, and how much more after so many years! And this is your son? Albert, is it not?—I am glad to see you, not only for your father's sake, but for your own," she said kindly to the young man, who stood aside, evidently greatly embarrassed at finding their visit so unexpected.

There was no need to say that they had come from Berlin; it was enough to see them, enough to hear the old president murder the French language.

Officially, the president was the chief magistrate of a Prussian criminal court; privately he was under subjection to a very decided little wife, in spite of whom he enjoyed hugely all such chance pleasures as came in his way.

The captain was a newer, handsomer edition of his father—a great broad shouldered fellow with a fine head, kind blue eyes, and in his buttonhole the ribbon of the Iron Cross.

Extremes will meet. M. Pampalon had met the president in Germany while there on business. Strange to say, they had taken a fancy to each other, and in the course of long intervals M. Pampalon would drop in at Berlin, and the president would surprise the Pampalon family at Ligny.

"Glad to see me, old boy? And you mean to say that you never got my letter?" the president cried cheerfully, slapping his host on the knee.

"It seems you don't know, Karl, that I am out of business," M. Pampalon answered, making a desperate effort to raise his spirits. "Sometimes they forget to send my letters as promptly as I could wish."

"Rolling in riches, are you? Well, I'm glad of it."

"No, not at all; times are bad."

"Why, what's the matter with you?" the president exclaimed, quite overcome by his host's misery.

Madame came gracefully to the rescue, and burdened monsieur with a fictitious attack of rheumatism from which he vainly tried to free himself.   The captain sat by and twisted the ends of his fair mustache and thought of the pretty girl in the curl-papers.   This is, however, not the captain's story, it is M. Pampalon's, and poor Pampalon might indeed have melted the heart of a rock as he sat there listening in misanthropic agony.   You see, he had noticed the sparkle in Madame's eyes, and he hated to have her pleased even by this long-legged old judge of a Prussian criminal court.

III.

M. PAMPALON was impressed with the belief that all marriageable men had Dodé's hand as their aim in life, with a wary eye opened to pecuniary results.   This feverish problem, being studied by an impartial mind, resolved itself into—Monsieur Alphonse Gaspard.   Alphonse Gaspard lived next door to the Pampalon's, and was the sad spectacle of a weak young man with a strong-minded and widowed mother, a nice income, and no visible occupation but to stare over the garden-paling at Mademoiselle Dodé.

Monsieur Pampalon patronized Alphonse.   Alphonse played piquet, écarté, vingt-et-un—in fact, all those pleasant games without which retirement becomes an unbearable bore.   Besides, Alphonse enjoyed being patronized by Dodé's father, and Dodé's father had, without much ado, made up his mind that it would be a great convenience if she should marry Alphonse and live next door, with an income independent of himself.   He was not a cruel father— Heaven forbid !—but he had made up his mind to that effect without consulting anyone, and he considered the matter as good as settled.

No one could expect Monsieur Pampalon to waste much romance on his chosen son-in-law: he viewed him practically—not from the heart, but from the pocket—and found him extremely desirable, so M. Pampalon being a tyrant and Alphonse a willing slave, there was a bond of accommodating friendship between them. M. Pampalon hated to be forgotten; and now this poor misanthrope felt his eyes grow dim as the president and madame talked and laughed together, unmindful of him, and the captain looked cautiously about for some one in curl-papers.

Just then fate sent Alphonse up the front walk in a magnificent morning toilet, as she sent him twelve hours in the twenty-four. M. Pampalon, forcing back some tears, rose and welcomed Alphonse vehemently—flung himself, so to speak, on the poor fellow in a manner which all but said, "You see how I am forsaken!" Alphonse was highly flattered, but when he saw strangers he would have fled, only that M. Pampalon clung to him.

The blunt old president stared at Alphonse in undisguised wonder, and the captain bowed stiffly, and twirled his mustache.

There was a moment's awkward pause, then a light step came down the veranda. The captain and his father turned with quick military precision.

"Coquette! coquette! where have you left your curl-papers?" the president laughed, threatening her with his forefinger. "What! you won't kiss Uncle Karl because you are eighteen? There! I knew you would!" and he gallantly kissed Mademoiselle Dodé. —"Albert," he said to that young man, "I am sorry for your sake that you are not your father. Rose, my child, this is my son the captain. By the way, the captain saw the curl-papers. He is very sharp."

Dodé smiled and blushed, and looked shyly up to the captain till she reached his blue eyes that were so much more eloquent than his poor lame tongue.

So you see how all these *dramatis personæ* came together—how the president laughed loud and long with madame; how the captain smiled and Dodé blushed; how M. Alphonse hid himself behind M. Pampalon's broad back, and felt an unknown emotion of jealousy beneath his magnificent waistcoat; how poor M. Pampalon, our unhappy hero, felt life to be a burden to him, and, hating everybody as he did, hated most of all long-legged guests who burst upon you unawares and make life miserable.

IV.

"MADAME, I hate people who come visiting without being invited."

M. Pampalon had retired to rest one night, and only the outline of a lowering face surmounted by a tasseled nightcap could be seen among the bedclothes. Monsieur addressed madame, who was tying her nightcap under her double chin, and wisely made believe not to hear. "Are you deaf? I say it's a confounded impertinence for people to come visiting without an invitation!"

"Well?"

"Well?" monsieur echoed, "is that all you have to say? At your age you should do something else than encourage these—these idlers."

"At my age!" madame was angry. "At my age I might be doing something else than listening to your nonsense."

"What do you say, madame?" monsieur cried, and raised a wrathful head from the conjugal pillow. "You're a coquette—a coquette, madame!"

"Monsieur Pampalon, you're a fool!" but madame was mollified.

"This to me?" and with a sudden change of voice from the wrathful to the lachrymose, M. Pampalon sank back on his pillow and groaned at the misery of his life.

"If you dislike them, why don't you tell them to go?"

"I tell them? It's your duty. You say to them—"

"Indeed I shall not. I like them both, but if you want them to go, why don't you tell them so?"

"It's abominable!" monsieur groaned.

"You're a coward," madame remarked, kindly.

"You shall repent this!" and monsieur half rose in bed.

However, madame had a fine temper well under control. With a firm hand she extinguished the candle, then saying quite unmoved, "Papa, go to sleep now—your threats always end in words," lay down and shut her bright black eyes, preparatory to sleeping the sleep of the unromantic just.

V.

M. PAMPALON was in despair. One day he cut across his front garden into Alphonse's, and threw himself on young Gaspard's neck, crying out piteously, "I am deserted! They—I mean she, my wife, has deserted me for an enemy of her country!"

"Have you followed them?" Alphonse asked with great sympathy.

"No, I scorn to," and monsieur relapsed into melancholy wrath.

"Where's mademoiselle?"

"Gone with them."

"What!" and Alphonse started back and absolutely

forced some expression into his small black eyes—
"what! you allow your daughter to stay with a mother
who is disgraced?"

"Yes, that is it—disgraced!"

"And you—you call yourself a father?"

"What else should I call myself?"

"And the captain?" Alphonse groaned.

"Gone too."

Alphonse took off his smoking-cap and wrung it.

"They've taken everything to eat in the house,"
monsieur continued gloomily. "The captain sat by
the driver holding two bottles of champagne and one
of sauterne. Madame had a whole goose in a basket
at her feet, and that German beggar, the president,
laughed in my face as they drove off."

"You saw them go and never stopped them?" Alphonse cried, in such undisguised horror that M. Pampalon paused in his anguish to ask, "Why should I?"

"What! when madame elopes—"

"M. Alphonse, you misunderstand: madame has
gone to a picnic. She has left me alone, and, as if
that were not enough, there is nothing to eat in the
house. Can you give me something?"

For a moment monsieur's stomach conquered his
emotions, but when the mistaken Alphonse had disappeared to order a lunch, the wretched man, seeing,
in his mind's eye, the champagne, sauterne, goose and
sandwiches vanishing down the throats of his enemies,
felt his wrongs rising in double-distilled strength, and
vowed vengeance.

Monsieur had indeed been deserted. There was,
to be sure, some excuse for madame. Being of a joyous nature, she had little chance in the companionship
of her husband to cultivate that side of her character.
What wonder that she liked the president's society
and shared all the amusements of that benighted for-
eigner? The president had soon remarked the sink-

ing of his host's hospitable thermometer, but madame growing more cordial in the ratio of her husband's iciness, the jovial old fellow lived in a constant state of mental see-saw, and could only encourage his own visit by remembering how often his capricious host had lodged in the Königsstrasse in Berlin.

As for the captain, by this time he was in love, quickly, frankly, incurably. They were so constantly together, he and Mademoiselle Dodé : they had been as clearly forgotten as the babes in the wood, in the midst of the president's pleasure excursions, madame's gayety and Monsieur Pampalon's unspeakable jealousy and misanthropy. This is not the captain's story, and so I will not tell how Captain Albert and Mademoiselle Dodé found themselves in the garden one summer's twilight under the dense shade of a noble evergreen, and—well! well! the gallant captain stooped and whispered something, and some one looked up at him very shyly with eyes full of tears and smiles. But, as I said before, this is not the captain's story, it is M. Pampalon's.

So what wonder that Mademoiselle Dodé looked at the world through rose-colored glasses, until even her unhappy father partook of the general hue : truly, only love can be so blind.

To be sure, madame was not in love. Her daily flights with the president were of the most prosaic character, even M. Pampalon being cordially invited to join. He, however, received the invitation with such utter gloom, muttering something about extravagance and carriage hire, that it was never repeated. Madame, though not in love, closed her eyes willingly ; so monsieur was alone with his grievances, roaming about with hanging under-lip and melancholy eyelids.

Misery not only loves company, but generally finds it. Not that Madame Gaspard was miserable, by no means; she was only miserable when she had to pay a bill. Madame Gaspard was Alphonse's mother and lived next door, and it was a great convenience—for M. Pampalon was lazy, even in his unhappiness—to pour into her ear the tale of his misery and his expenses. Madame had a fellow-feeling when her afflicted neighbor spoke of bills. She had also made up her maternal mind that Alphonse should marry Dodé and Dodé's fortune. So she watched the captain with suspicious eyes, and saw through his feelings with a clearness that should have put the Pampalon family to the blush at their marvelous stupidity.

It would be impossible to do justice to Madame Gaspard's emotions as she saw the captain gallantly escorting Mademoiselle Dodé through the garden, carrying the watering-pot and the garden shears, while her own Alphonse lay under a pear tree reading Alfred de Musset. He had neglected Dodé of late for he was desperately shy in spite of Alfred de Musset, and it was with a sinking heart that he obeyed his mother's stern commands to go to the Pampalon's and be fascinating.

Fascinating? Why, he never had a chance, for he always encountered M. Pampalon on the veranda, who forgot the emotions of a father in his hunger for sympathy. So Alphonse listened, sliding about on the hard veranda chair, a prey to terror, fearing that somebody would come.

There was no need, for in the sunlit flower garden the captain and Dodé were gathering roses.

VI.

" A PARTY, madame ? "

" Yes ; why not, papa ? "

" What ! a party—a party at my house ? May I ask what you intend to do with a party ? "

" Amuse myself."

" Never ! " " never in *my* house ! To have it torn up for German beggars, and my money wasted ! Never ! never ! never ! "

" M. Pampalon, you forget that I, too, have a word to say," madame interposed. "As it is, perhaps you had better know that we have already set the day for the party, and the invitations are out. Dodé is to have a new dress—so am I. The captain has gone to town to hire the band, and the president—"

Madame did not end, for monsieur, in a frenzy, grasped his head with both hands and tore out of the house. He fled down the well-worn path, and stood gasping and furious before Madame Gaspard, whom he awoke from her afternoon nap.

" What is it now ? " madame asked in a hard, rasping voice, looking at her visitor with much disfavor, for she had an unacknowledged feeling that had monsieur been her husband he would have been managed differently.

" A party ! my wife is going to give a party ! " monsieur gasped, and in his despair thrust his hands through his hair and made it stand on end.

" Are we invited ? "

" Madame, do you not see that I am in despair ? I—a party—to have my money flung to the dogs— rioting and feasting ! But I'll spoil their pleasure yet ! "

Madame had brought her son up on *eau sucré*, and

had found it efficient in keeping down the manly temper. To M. Pampalon she brought a glass of this innocent elixir. "Drink it, my friend. You should be careful not to excite yourself ; you are stout, with apoplectic tendencies."

"Thanks! thanks! you are a true friend," monsieur murmured. "But I — I must go — I'm unstrung."

"See that Alphonse gets an invitation ; he hasn't had a chance with Dodé since that monkey of a captain has been dancing attendance."

"Don't speak of him," monsieur said, with a slight shudder. "But I'll spoil their pleasure. I'll—"

What monsieur meant to do remained unsaid, for just then Alphonse appeared with an immense envelope in his hand, out of whose contents he read with much satisfaction that Madame and Monsieur Pampalon requested the pleasure of his company, etc., etc. "We are very much obliged," said the grateful Alphonse, shaking Pampalon's limp and dejected hand.

"Don't be! It's a lie!" was that gentleman's far from satisfactory reply.

"What?"

"It's a lie!" M. Pampalon repeated with passion at white heat, "but I'll be hanged if they don't have a good time, a high old time!" and he fled out of the house leaving Madame and Alphonse to wonder if the last promise was not to be taken in a figurative sense.

VII.

THE night of the party came—a lovely evening with the blue-black zenith radiant with stars, and the air full of the perfume of flowers heavily laden with dew. Everybody knew that there was a party at the Pampalons', for a double row of Chinese lanterns led from the gate to the entrance, to the great satisfaction of the captain, who had arranged this decoration, and the great satisfaction of Mademoiselle Dodé, who admired everything the captain did.

Mademoiselle Dodé had herself made a hurried and shy appearance before that gallant officer in the drawing-room an hour before the party, and quite overwhelmed him with a vision of airy lace and delicate rosebuds, and a pair of brown eyes that dared him to say that the lace, the rosebuds and the aforesaid brown eyes were not the loveliest of their kind, and, it being quite dark in the room, the captain—I am afraid one of the band heard, for he was discovered in a corner blowing his nose with unnatural violence.

Madame Pampalon was gorgeous in yellow satin and scarlet poppies.

"Upon my word, ma'am, you are magnificent," the president said ; which madame would have continued to be had she not gone into the kitchen and had a violent altercation with the caterer. The emotions so excited caused her face to turn of a fine crimson, which would not and could not harmonize with the poppies.

Monsieur had a plan—alas for him !—and for once he was a silent martyr. As silent martyr he arrayed himself in a claw-hammer coat and a white necktie, and made a dismal effort to put one half of a light lavender kid glove on a perspiring hand. But there is a point when even the worm will turn : it was not monsieur's time to turn quite yet, but he already bade defiance to the world, as it were, when he made his appearance in society with only half a glove on. Society, consisting of madame at that time, looked at him critically from head to foot, and concluded, very wisely, that this votary to pleasure was in such a state of exasperation that it would be best to leave him alone.

Society began to arrive at half-past eight, and its individual members trod on each other's heels, so exactly had Ligny calculated the time of coming. Madame had even been successful enough to include one count and half a dozen "De " Something-or-others among her guests. In fact, everybody who was anybody in Ligny was invited, and madame's heart beat high with gratification under her yellow satin bodice.

A bow, a curtsy, a scrape, and madame welcomed a new arrival, then turned him over to monsieur, who received him with speechless resentment. Still, how was the victim to know monsieur's secret thoughts as he pressed that unhappy hand and congratulated himself on being in the distinguished society of monsieur and madame and their amiable family?

The amiable family was at that moment dancing with the captain, and casting lace and rosebud thunderbolts at Alphonse. M. Gaspard was very unhappy, but madame his mother was grand and proud in black velvet, and made mental disparaging remarks about Madame Pampalon's yellow satin.

There were other beauties there besides Dodé, and they looked encouragement at Alphonse, for dancers were scarce ; but Alphonse was loyal, so he remained alone and silent, leaning against a door-post till his turn should come to claim Mademoiselle Dodé's hand for the cotillon.

M. Pampalon was strangely passive : he allowed madame to dictate his line of conduct with such speechless meekness that she patted him on the back with her fan and said, " After all, it is a good child," but overlooked a curious flaring up of the light in her husband's eyes, which boded ill.

So he went off on duty, as directed, to a certain hard-featured, gray-complexioned, thin woman who persisted in sitting solitary and alone as near the band as possible. Her M. Pampalon rescued, or rather he gave her a companion in misery, for he brought a stiff chair and sat down beside her. Though they said not a word, for the crash of the instruments hindered all conversation, still they felt that they were a couple of congenial souls.

Madame Gaspard, if she had been tasting of unalloyed bliss that evening, did not look so. To soothe her ruffled feelings, Madame Pampalon delegated to her husband the pleasant duty of leading his sympathizing neighbor to supper. She had organized an intricate pilgrimage through the hall and the parlor, *ad infinitum*, preparatory to getting up an appetite for supper, which pilgrimage she proposed to lead off with the president. The band had begun a hopeful march in anticipation of supper, when, as she was on the point of starting, madame discovered Madame Gaspard still seated alone and neglected in the shadow of a window-curtain, with feelings she took no pains to conceal. "Dear me, Madame Gaspard! where's my husband?"

Madame Gaspard, like a forlorn Ariadne, denied all knowledge of her truant swain. Here the lady of the musical shower-bath volunteered the information that when monsieur left her an hour ago, he declared that he felt far from well.

"I must see where he is," madame said like a good wife, feeling some internal and nameless compunctions.—"Excuse me for a moment, will you not, president?" she said, and left that gallant man, who was enjoying himself hugely making love to every woman with whom he danced.

Madame disappeared, and the orchestra, like clock-work wound up, still continued its runs and flourishes, when, through the brightness, the talking and laughter, —more horrible for the contrasted gayety—there rang a sudden, piercing cry. It was madame's voice, and it had hardly died away before the president, the captain and poor Dodé were already in M. Pampalon's room. On the floor madame lay senseless in crushed yellow satin, and on the bed Monsieur Pampalon lay—dead.

VIII.

THE five doctors whŏ were at madame's party hurried up at the first alarm. Each applied different remedies, yet the body of M. Pampalon refused to be reanimated.

Poor M. Pampalon, who only meant to sham illness and have all the house in an uproar for his sake, had taken laudanum to give his wife a good fright when she should find him. Supper-time being propitious, knowing he should be missed, he had set to work and had surprised himself completely by taking a trifle too much.

The spirit of M. Pampalon was not in his body, for that lay limp and lifeless on the bed, animated by nothing nobler than earthiness. The spirit of M. Pampalon had fled from its body as far as the foot of the bed, and there it stood and wrung its hands, as for the first time, in seeing the bitter grief of wife and child, it realized the happiness it had placed at stake. M. Pampalon, unfettered by a body, saw with clearer eyes and wrung his hands in mute repentance, and for the first time, when he would have gladly wept, M. Pampalon, being a spirit, lacked tears.

The house was still lighted ; the Chinese lanterns still burned brightly, but the guests had gone. The remnants of the night's gayety lingered about like wretched ghosts.

Poor Madame Pampalon, having recovered from the first terrible shock, returned to her normal condition of a helpful little woman, though her eyes were

red and swollen with weeping ; and the spirit of M.
Pampalon, looking on, became strangely humble and
repentant, for the soul of M. Pampalon had received
a lesson.

The doctors called it apoplexy, and the doctors
called it heart disease, while the spirit at the foot of
the bed shook its head wofully, for the soul of M.
Pampalon wanted to return to its body, and life seemed very sweet now that it was so nearly lost.   The
chances for the life of M. Pampalon were becoming
fainter, when one of the physicians, in lifting monsieur's head, displaced the pillow.   It was lucky that
the unhappy sinner had not hidden that bottle more
successfully.

"I have it, gentlemen!" the doctor cried, briskly; "it's laudanum.   He has tried to kill himself.
There is some hope now, though, really, he has made
it a very delicate case," and he nodded approvingly
at the body.

The spirit of M. Pampalon hung its head in shame
and wrung its hands again as his poor child, clasping
the hand of what had been M. Pampalon, whispered
in eager defence, "Not my father—oh, not my father!
he loved us so much!" and fell back in the arms of
madame's Brittany maid, who bore her young mistress
away.

I could tell you very much about the distracted
captain, who stood guard at Dodé's door, but, as I said
before, this is not the captain's story.

.   .   .   .

A flickering of the eyelids, a gasp, a sigh, and the
doctor had conquered, for Monsieur Pampalon's spirit
returned to its normal condition, and, being M. Pampalon, groaned.

At that moment the door opened and the captain
came in.

"Monsieur is out of danger," the doctor cried.

"Then come at once to Mademoiselle for she is very ill," the captain interrupted, harshly, for the captain was human and not at all in love with M. Pampalon.

In an instant that self-made invalid was deserted except by the captain, who stared at him with half-fascinated eyes.

Another gasp, another sigh, and M. Pampalon opened his eyes and looked at Albert in a dazed way.

"What do they mean by deserting me?" he whimpered.

"Mademoiselle is—is ill."

"What is that to you?" for M. Pampalon resented the captain's undisguised emotion.

"I love her," the young man replied simply.

M. Pampalon was the soul of honor, but he muttered "Alphonse Gaspard."

"What is he to her?"

"Her future husband." And M. Pampalon closed his eyes and the conversation at the same time.

Albert looked with helpless rage at the exasperating form of M. Pampalon, shielded by weakness, and with a heavy heart he left the room. Not for an instant did he doubt her. "I'll wager it's some confounded family arrangement of which she is ignorant," he thought with a groan. "I'll join my regiment," and as he stalked out of the room he nearly fell over Alphonse, lingering on the threshold.

M. Pampalon was in a state of weak rage because of the captain's desertion. As if it were an every-day occurrence to see him, M. Pampalon, die! Just then Alphonse knocked. "Come in!" M. Pampalon said in an expiring tone, and groaned aloud. It was really unnecessary, but M. Pampalon felt that this was the least you could expect of a man who had been at the point of death.

Alphonse stared at his prospective father-in-law with damp, sympathetic eyes.

"Sit down, Alphonse; I want to speak to you about Dodé," monsieur said, with a vivid recollection of the captain.

The unhappy Alphonse obeyed.

"Now, if she were here we might settle a certain little matter."

"Oh, monsieur, don't you know—" Alphonse stammered.

"What?" cried monsieur.

"The shock of last night—she is threatened with brain fever," Alphonse exclaimed, regardless of monsieur's feelings.

"My God! I—Let me go! I tell you I must go to my child!" and the poor old culprit tried to get out of bed. But even Alphonse could manage him now, he was so weak. The unhappy father buried his head in the pillows and shed bitter tears, and knew that if his child died he had killed her. Alphonse looked helplessly at the wretched man, and begged him to look up, for it might all end well. To all of which M. Pampalon paid no heed, for he was repenting at leisure.

IX.

A FEW days afterward President Karl sat in his room, nursing his leg, with a perplexed look in the only eye capable of expression. The captain was packing; he had decided to go, with a look as stern as a pair of naturally sunny eyes could assume.

"It's a pity—" President Karl began, when the captain interrupted him unceremoniously: "Father, we must go. How can I stay here, when I love that girl more than my life? When I know she's to marry that confounded jackass?"

"Mildly, my son—mildly."

"It's easy enough for you to say 'mildly,' but you'd be the last man to give up a girl if you really wanted her."

"There is truth in that;" and the president was highly flattered, "but it won't do to say so.—Consider, Albert," he said aloud, "she may never marry anyone. You know she is very ill, and we might as well look facts in the face."

"Don't speak so, father; I cannot bear it!"

"Albert, be a man. Do you think you are the only man who has lost the woman he loves?"

"Will you go, father?" and the Captain ignored the philosophy.

"Well, if I must."

So the fiery steeds of the Ligny omnibus once more reined in at M. Pampalon's front gate; again there was the creak of the gravel walk and the letting down of steps. Captain Albert looked wistfully back at a certain little room with closed windows, but the unfeeling coachman gave him no time for reflection.

They had gone without leave-taking, for the whole house was in confusion. Only Alphonse saw them start, and his emotions were of unequivocal joy, for, after all, Alphonse was a man, and he hated his rival.

"They've gone!" Alphonse cried triumphantly to M. Pampalon as that poor man came out of Dodé's door late that evening, looking haggard and careworn.

"Who?"

"The president and the captain."

"Gone? The captain gone? The very man I want to see!" The poor father groaned and hid his face in his hands.

In the closed room a small restless head was tossing about on the pillow and moaning, "Albert! Albert!" till the doctor said, "Who is Albert?" and

M. Pampalon, after a moment's reflection, with a sinking heart confessed it must be the captain.

"Bring the captain; he may save your daughter's life," the doctor said.

Bring the captain? Why, he would have brought the moon to save her. So he went humbly to bring the captain, and the captain was now on his way to Berlin at the rate of fifty miles an hour.

"I'll go after him," M. Pampalon cried as he hurried past the bewildered Alphonse. "I must bring him back. Bear it like a man, Alphonse," and M. Pampalon disappeared.

For an instant M. Alphonse stared about him, then a blur dimmed his eyes, so that he could hardly find the way to his own gate.

Madame Gaspard was knitting by the lamp in the family sitting-room when Alphonse came in. "Mother, I'm going to London to-morrow."

"Are you mad?"

"The captain is coming back; Monsieur Pampalon has gone to Berlin for him."

"My poor child, take some of this," and madame offered him a glass of *eau sucré*, "it will do you good."

"Mother, pray don't!" Alphonse cried with aversion; "you seem to think that sugar and water will cure everything."

"My son, it cured all the emotions of your late lamented father."

For the first time in his life Alphonse rebelled; the next morning he rebelled for the second time when he took the train for London without as much as saying to madame, "By your leave."

Whether Alphonse ever recovered from his passion is not known. Yet I do know that a retributive Providence sent a very tall and bony woman into the Gaspard house in the course of time, who tyrannized over the tyrant Madame Gaspard, and called her mother-in-law, and who, hasn't called on the Pampalons to this day.

X.

M. PAMPALON had followed in the footsteps of President Karl, but not of the captain, for the captain had deserted his father just as they reached Paris in the omnibus. He was unspeakably wretched, and could not tear himself away from Ligny; he could not return to Berlin with the haunting thought that the girl he loved might be dying. But he wanted to be alone in his misery, so he escaped from his father, seeing that unhappy man for the last time as he was defending himself from enthusiastic cabmen.

The captain returned to Ligny that same evening, and met madame's Brittany maid in the narrow lane behind the house. Mademoiselle was worse, much worse, the faithful follower sobbed, and hiding her face in her sturdy arms, bawled very sincerely.

The wretched captain said nothing, but he looked unsteadily at her for a few seconds, then turned away with a face pale and worn.

"He'll do himself something!" cried madame's Brittany maid, with a dim remembrance of certain well-thumbed romances.

But the captain did not lay violent hands on himself; in fact, the thought did not enter his mind. He lingered about the house, hoping to hear more; he would have gone in, but he dared not. In his restless misery he trudged down the country roads about Ligny till the church bells sounded midnight. Then he retraced his steps, and paced up and down before M. Pampalon's front gate until the light in the hall changed to a flash as the door opened. There was the sound of a man's tread on the gravel walk, and

18

in a moment more the doctor was lifting the latch of
the front gate. He paused at sight of a man pacing
up and down. Something familiar about the figure,
or some sudden suspicion, made him pause. "Who
are you? What are you doing here?"

The other stopped, and the two men faced each
other.

"Why, it is the captain!"

"Is there hope?"

"Where is M. Pampalon?"

"How should I know?" the captain cried, with an
impatient stamp of his foot.

"True! true! he only went to-day. Yes, now there
is hope; you're just the man I want; you bring hope
along with you. Come!" and the doctor led the captain, bewildered and with a beating heart, into the
familiar house, where the Brittany maid received them
with satisfaction, where madame was too unhappy to
be astonished, where poor Dodé grew quiet when the
captain laid his hand on hers.

You cannot, of course, expect the Ligny omnibus
to have human sympathy: therefore you can hardly
lay it up against the horses that they galloped just as
gayly down the highway and left M. Pampalon with
as much of bustle and clatter as in the happy days
when he was devoted to the candy business. However, the man who alighted two days afterward with
an aching head and a heavy heart, was a different
M. Pampalon from that one. A man who begins to
repent after he is fifty generally means it.

"He is not in Berlin," he said hoarsely to his wife,
who ran to the gate to meet him.

"My dear, Heaven is very good to us," and there
were happy tears in her eyes. "Come and see."
Taking him gently by the hand she led him to

Dodé's room.   "Softly!" said madame, and opened the door.

Mademoiselle Dodé was sleeping quietly, with a smile on her lips, and beside the bed, in the easiest chair of the house, sat the captain, with the light of perfect contentment in his blue eyes.

"What!" and M. Pampalon stared at the captain.

"He never left Ligny," madame cried, with an approving nod at Albert, for she dearly loved a bit of romance.

Of course Dodé recovered and married the captain,—but then this is not really the captain's story.

As for M. Pampalon, no one ever said that he became an angel instantly, and that he never grumbled again.   To tell the truth, he and madame had their little differences just as they used to, both being human.   I *do* say, however, that from that time M. Pampalon gave up the habit of brooding and took to thinking, and there is a delicate distinction.   Madame Pampalon, being a sensible woman, appreciated the difference.   When, once in a while, she saw that poor inborn misanthrope battle with some particularly disagreeable emotion, and after a hard tussle conquer, madame would write it up high in her memory of her husband's good deeds, and say gently, "It is Monsieur Pampalon's repentance."

A LEGEND OF OLD NEW YORK.

I.

OVER two hundred years ago where the great city of New York now stands there stood the town of New Amsterdam, and Peter Stuyvesant of blessed and hard-headed memory was governor : peace to him !

In those days there were no elevated roads, no crowded tenement-houses, no deadly spider-webs of electric wires overhead. Instead, there was a market-place with a town-pump, flanked by queer Dutch houses with dazzling brass knockers against the green front doors. Cows grazed on Wall street, and the good citizens strolled along the Battery of an evening and watched the setting sun.

The Battery of those old days was overgrown with grass and clover, and shaded by spreading elms and sycamores, beneath which the children played and made posies of dandelion blossoms.

On the outskirts of the Battery, facing the sea, stood a lane of curious gabled houses, one of which " De Blauwe Druif " (The Blue Grape) was a tavern famous for its *poffertjes* and *wafelen*, Dutch delicacies as cele-brated as the victories of Admiral de Ruyter. On the benches beside the porch the good fathers of the town smoked their long clay pipes, meditating about nothing in particular, while the young folks danced to the tooting of Kristoffel Sauer's trumpet. Exhilarat-ing were Kristoffel's strains, and delicious were the crisp poffertjes and the sweet cider with which the gallant swains revived the exhausted energies of the fair juffrouws, while the summer breeze swept up from the bay and lightly swayed the trees, tempering the heat of the fiery sun.

There was no turmoil of ships in the harbor as in these days, and it was a six months' wonder when a Dutch brig as broad as she was long rolled into the bay and cast anchor. It gave the good mynheers inexhaustible food for reflection as they smoked their pipes before "De Blauwe Druif" and stared sleepily into the sunset.

Even old Governor Stuyvesant lightened the cares of government occasionally by stumping down from the Town Hall on the market-place to the Battery for a sniff of sea air, and it was his privilege to pat the cheeks of the prettiest juffrouws with a condescending forefinger. There was nothing in this attention to excite gossip, though it was faintly whispered if Mevrouw Stuyvesant were no more,—and she was very lively,—and old Peter were fifty years younger, then would young Mistress Van Witt have the best chance to be in her turn Dame Stuyvesant. But then Juffrouw Van Witt! What man, governor or not, could resist stroking a cheek like a peach blossom, when it may be said to have been a perquisite of his exalted station. There were certain heavy young mynheers who would joyfully have taken his place without his salary for the chance. But they were very shy of words, and their adoration only took the form of steady pilgrimages to Mynheer Van Witt's mansion, "Bovenkirk," just beyond Governor Stuyvesant's "Bowery."

Here of an afternoon they would find Wimpje Van Witt sitting by a window in the great living-room and spinning vigorously, while at another sat Juffrouw van Twist, and if there was a chill in the air a blazing fire on the hearth warmed the story of Daniel in the lions' den, in chilly Delft tiles about the chimney. Over it hung a time-dulled oil painting, " The Martrydom of St. Nepomuk," which made the sturdy table, bearing up under the weight of Juffrouw van Twist's choicest dishes, more comforting by contrast.

In the cosiest corner of the chimney, in a mighty leather arm-chair sacred to his use, reposed Cornelis Van Witt, alderman of New Amsterdam, chosen as such by Governor Stuyvesant for the curious merit in a legislator of being always asleep. Thus in assembling his council old Peter was always certain of one loyal, uncontradictory adherent, sound asleep in his high-backed chair, his pipe-stem firmly clutched between his teeth ; and this slumbering legislator was always acknowledged as being on the side of his Excellency.

Though Mynheer Van Witt wore six pairs of breeches and as many waistcoats, and represented the dignity of the town, it must be acknowledged that he had two mortal terrors—ghosts and Englishmen. He had been brought up with a ghost, so to speak, for there was a haunted graveyard only separated from his threshold by a spreading field and the public highway. It was Tante Jantje, his old darky nurse, who had educated him to a gruesome terror of that ancient graveyard beside the Church of St. Bartholomew.

It seems that many years before, a crack-brained sexton in a fit of madness took up all the headstones and planted them in straight rows in another part of the cemetery, whereupon he razed the quiet mounds and departed from the sight of men, and the worthy burghers, being unable to disentangle the ghastly result, left the stones standing in their straight, sad rows.

But that which really appalled Mynheer was that the figure of the mad sexton, in trailing white draperies, had been seen by credible witnesses at midnight gliding from stone to stone and wringing its hand in evident remorse. As Mynheer had retired to his couch at nine o'clock for fifty years, and as the ghost appeared at midnight, it is needless to say that he had not personally encountered the apparition, but on waking at night from a heavy sleep evolved out of sauerkraut, sausages, and cider, he would turn pale to the end of his red bottle-nose on hearing a rat scamper behind the wainscoting. Nothing in the world would have induced him to pass the kirkyard of St. Bartholomew at midnight, though he stood high in the esteem of the sacred establishment by reason of a ponderous silver communion service straight from Amsterdam, which had already excited the righteous longing of every rascal in town.

Mynheer's abhorrence of the British nation was patriotic. Great was his agitation when the belated tidings of the victories of the Dutch navy reached New Amsterdam. Mynheer was always a little behind time in everything, and this Juffrouw van Twist was obliged to acknowledge—she who had been waiting for eighteen years, since the death of Mevrouw, for Mynheer to propose.

Thus, from being a moderately young thing, sandy, and sharp of elbows, bony of ancles, and with colorless hair crowned by a stiff muslin cap, Juffrouw van Twist grew elderly and thinner, with all the other advantages unchanged, but with a heroic determination to marry Mynheer Van Witt sooner or later. If it be added that Mistress van Twist was not without a touch of romance, and that it was she who had educated Wimpje Van Witt, it will surprise no one to hear that young Wimpje's day dreams were enlivened by slimmer and more poetic figures than those silent young mynheers who trundled out to Bovenkirk of an afternoon, and whose only token of love was an abnormal staying power.

· II.

THOUGH Governor Stuyvesant had appointed Cornelis Van Witt to his high office for the original merit of being always asleep, there came a day when Mynheer for the first time wished he had been awake.

It was a Friday—a miserable, unlucky day, as every one knows. Governor Stuyvesant greeted his assembled council in full uniform and with a portentous frown, and at the end of a stormy meeting—in which he did all the storming—he gave such a thump to the table, that Mynheer Van Witt awoke gasping, and was with difficulty made to understand that something awful had happened. It seems that from private information the governor was warned that Great Britain was hungering for the Dutch possessions in America, and his Excellency was entreated to defend the colonies to the bitter end in case of invasion.

The aldermen's faces grew as long as their clay pipes and fully as white, and they answered with energetic silence his heroic appeal for support, and when it came to a vote it was found that only hard-headed old Peter and the gently slumbering Cornelis Van Witt were for a defence to the death.

This heroic, if unuttered, resolution being after vast difficulty imparted to Mynheer, that brave man staggered downstairs to the street, with dazed eyes and his knees quivering under his six pairs of breeches.

Such was the perturbation of his heroic soul that he ran afoul of one of the stone posts before the Town Hall, and only a grip in the rear saved him from the cobble-stones.

"Home, take me home," and Mynheer clutched the air for support.

"By all means, Mynheer, but where?"

The unhappy man took his gaze out of the future and fastened it upon his rescuer, who rested his forefinger with impertinent jocularity against the side of a very red nose.

"Too deep a glance into the eyes of the fair Ginevra, eh, Mynheer?" he remarked with shocking familiarity.

Mynheer was in no condition to resent this allusion to the national beverage, for he was fighting the entire British nation.   He leaned against the stone post and said, "Bring Powtje."

Powtje was a fat cob harnessed to a chariot without springs, and it may be considered a dispensation of Providence that Powtje should decline to do anything but walk.

Mynheer climbed in and was in danger of forgetting the obliging stranger, had he not patted Powtje's flanks with sudden enthusiasm.

"A beautiful creature, Mynheer; a veritable Arab steed."

"To be sure.   I'd forgotten you, my man.   Come home with me and you shall have a good supper.   I am Cornelis Van Witt of Bovenkirk."

After much coaxing Powtje decided to lift his Arab legs and crawl along, and thus did Abraham Baas, in moments of tenderness called "Brammatje," make the acquaintance of Mynheer, who sat beside him a victim to an active imagination which pictured to him all the horrors of war.

"O Lord, O Lord, have you heard," he groaned at last, "the British are coming?"

"Coming?" cried the valiant Brammatje, "Let 'em come!" and he slapped his threadbare doublet until the dust rose in clouds.   "We'll be ready for 'em. I've seen 'em in Boston, a lean lot whom a pottle of good Schiedam schnapps tips under the table."

"You are not afraid," Mynheer cried in undisguised admiration ; and a vague idea took possession of
him that it would be well to have so valorous a soul
always about, as a bodyguard for an evil day.

Thus it was, that Brammatje entered Mynheer's
service, not so much because he was asked as that
he declined to leave. And in return for his suste-
nance he gave Mynheer the comforting assurance of
his moral support in case of British invasion.

III.

THE first Mynheer Van Witt had chosen the location of his domain in fond remembrance of the
marshes about his own beloved Amsterdam. He also
constructed a canal behind his back door, which was
speedily covered with an aromatic green growth, the
smell of which positively made him homesick until
he built himself a windmill, and at sight of the slowly
turning sails his soul found some repose. Having
one day by accident discovered beyond his broad
fields a glimpse of the distant hills of the Hudson,
he had a high wall and a barn built to hide so obnoxious a sight. His son Cornelis inherited his father's
domain, his waistcoats, his breeches, and all his pre-
judices.

The day Cornelis Van Witt defied the British
lion, Wimpje Van Witt sat at the kitchen window
mending the household linen. Beside her, in speechless ecstacy, sat young Mynheer Wissenkerke watching a buxom darky in a scarlet turban, frying poffertjes. At the kitchen table Mistress van Twist was
preparing a roast of pork, and with the exception,
perhaps, of Wimpje, there was nothing Jan Wissenkerke loved quite so much. The situation was too
much for him ; he uttered these passionate words :

"When I marry, Juffrouw Wimpje, and am master in my own house, I shall eat pork and poffertjes every day—I just love 'em."

There is a picture of Wimpje, a slim young thing, yet with a suggestion of dimpling roundness, a sunny face framed by a tangle of short gold-brown curls held in place by a saucy muslin cåp. A gray home-spun skirt, a red-laced bodice, and about her pretty shoulders a ruffled kerchief tied in a knot at her breast. If it be added that the gray petticoat displayed the neatest of red stockings and a high-heeled shoe with a silver buckle, it will still be difficult to give to anyone a proper idea of young Wimpje Van Witt.

At Mynheer Wissenkerke's words the upward tilt of Mistress Van Witt's nose seémed to be accentuated ; but before she could utter a word the door was flung open and Mynheer Van Witt sank exhausted into the nearest chair, and it was only after several pulls out of a high-shouldered black jug that the good man revived. Then was a discreet cough heard, and Brammatje Baas was discovered lingering on the threshold.

"Give the man a drink," Mynheer murmured.

"Why, father, what has happened ? "

"These be terrible times, Wilhelmina," and Mynheer shuddered. "Invasion threatens—the British are coming. But it behooves us—to—to be brave. We'll all die together.

Here Jan Wissenkerke's legs shook so pitifully that he sat down, while Brammatje sniffed the aroma of the frying poffertjes.

"Who is that man, father ? "

Mynheer replied with elaborate caution : "A man of valor, whom it were well to befriend if the British are coming. A grateful soul who is, perhaps, destined to be killed in our defence."

They all turned to look at this prospective martyr to gratitude.

"At any rate count the spoons first," Juffrouw Van Twist said with a sniff.

"Jan, we depend on you," Mynheer continued tremulously. "A Wissenkerke never yields."

No description could do justice to the want of enthusiasm with which young Wissenkerke answered this appeal. Even Mynheer's moving description of the death of a hero had such a discouraging effect on him that he presently vanished, forgetful of love and roast pork.

There were for the present no further rumors of English invasion ; nevertheless Brammatje remained and attacked five mighty meals a day and waged a heroic war on the cider barrel and the gin bottles, mercifully unconscious that Mynheer proposed, if necessary, to make a rampart of his well fed body.

IV.

ONCE a year there was a kirmess in New Amsterdam.

In those days the market-place afforded ample room for the rude wooden booths built in narrow lanes and containing all manner of ware to tempt folks, from the governor down to the Indians. On one side stood the town-hall, and opposite was the Dutch Reformed Church, and in between were the dwelling-houses opening on the cobblestones and decked with flags and banners and evergreens. There was even a dance booth, towards which the exhilarating strains of Kristoffel Sauer's trumpet lured the juffrouws. A most delightful place to twirl about in if you kept clear of the posts. The sides were open to the summer air, and there were tables at which the exhausted could recruit their strength. At the table of honor sat Juffrouw van Twist, her eyes secretly fixed on the next table where sat a lithe and tall young stranger, who followed young Wimpje's evolutions in a country dance with smiling sympathy. He even bent forward to catch a glimpse of her slim form when a post, or the broader charms of some other damsel, hid her from view. Juffrouw van Twist rejoiced, for she had a grievance against man by reason of the belated declaration of Mynheer Van Witt.

Strangers were common enough in the town these kirmess days, but this one was altogether different from the ordinary variety. He had a handsome, frank face, and a brown mustache with an upward curl at the ends, that suggested adventure to Mistress van Twist. His knee-breeches and well-fitting doublet were black, and in pleasing contrast to the gray of his stockings, his broad silk sash, and the wide-brimmed beaver hat that lay on the table; and, as a good Dutch housewife, she noted how fine was the linen of his broad cuffs and collar.

It was Jan Wissenkerke who led Wimpje back, red as a June rose and pouting, for they had wrecked on a post.

There must have been some magnetism in the gaze of the handsome stranger, for Wimpje, looking up shyly, met his admiring glance, and with an involuntary smile her eyes sank before his, as he gallantly stepped forward and begged Juffrouw Van Witt for the favor of the next reel.

New Amsterdam was aghast, but Wimpje rose, shook her fair head and homespun petticoats in defiance, and lifted her pretty feet with renewed ardor to the tune of Kristoffel's most pleasing strain. Well might New Amsterdam stare; not even the posts were obstacles to this agile stranger. Neither did he grow red nor lose his breath; nay, when Kristoffel finished with a hilarious flourish, then did this obnoxious stranger stoop and kiss young Wimpje's hand in the very face of New Amsterdam, and lead her, blushing furiously, to Mistress van Twist, who acknowledged with a tender sigh that he was the belated realization of her youthful dreams.

Who was he and what did he want?   It transpired that his name was Cawardine—Captain Tom Cawardine; that he was staying at The Blue Grape; and, to explain his universal disfavor, that he came from Boston, though some experienced old burghers doubted if so much agility and cheerfulness could hail from a town famous only for the crookedness of its streets, the hanging of witches, the length of its sermons, and a certain unwholesome dish called pork and beans.

What Captain Cawardine wanted was plain.   It was a new way to lay siege to a peaceful colony by marrying its richest heiress, for it would be a municipal misfortune should Mynheer Van Witt's fortune leave the land.   So it was no wonder that all New Amsterdam shuddered when Captain Cawardine kissed the hand of Juffrouw Wimpje Van Witt, who—yes, who blushed and smiled.

V.

HOW describe the speechless amazement of the town when the rumor spread like wildfire that Captain Cawardine was courting Mistress Pamplona van Twist; but the most amazed was Cornelis Van Witt.   He had just prepared to take his afternoon nap under the protection of St. Nepomuk when that worthy damsel looked in.

"I—I—have something to say to you;" and she looked at St. Nepomuk as if for support.

Mynheer was in undisguised consternation.

"Mynheer Van Witt," she began, and paused; then there was such a terrible silence that a bumblebee straying in at the window where Wimpje was spinning, filled the air with its droning and flew out again.

"Mynheer Van Witt, I am going to get married."

Here Wimpje's spinning-wheel fell with a furious clatter.

Mynheer was speechless. Then he gathered his faculties together. "Juffrouw van Twist, are you—am I— Married? Did you say married? Blicksem, Juffrouw! When did I ask you to marry me?"

"You!" And out burst the suppressed resentment of eighteen years. "Not you, thanks be to gracious!"

"I don't believe there's another."

"There is!" she retorted in triumph.

"He waited long enough."

"He's in no hurry, he's young."

"Well, then, what the d—l is it to me!"

"I only want Mynheer to know that the young man is coming here—ahem!—courting."

"Courting!" Mynheer leaped to his feet and tore up and down the room. "Courting—I'll be hanged if he will!"

"Perhaps, then, you will kindly look out for another housekeeper."

Mynheer stamped with his feet.

"Donder and blicksem! I'd rather have married you myself."

"May the young man come?" Mistress van Twist's composure was unruffled.

Mynheer clenched his fists and spoke. "Tell him to come, or go to the devil;" whereupon he retreated to his favorite haunt, a Chinese pagoda on the canal, and tried to collect himself. This was truly a day of horrors. It began early that morning when Brammatje announced that, as he was a sober Christian, he had himself seen the ghost of the mad sexton just as the bell of St. Bartholomew struck midnight.

Mynheer thought of the apparition and shuddered, and he thought of Juffrouw van Twist and swore. How serene had been his existence these eighteen years, and how divinely she stuffed roast goose with chestnuts. He was unspeakably moved. Yes, Pamplona van Twist was fully revenged for the silence of eighteen years. And now all these beautiful accomplishments were to be devoted to a rascal who probably did not appreciate his blessings ; and when it seemed as if his cup of bitterness was full, who should stagger into view but Brammatje, and the valiant man's voice was all of a quaver.

"O Lord, O Lord, the English have come ! " he gasped, and fled to the woodshed.

A great sirloin of beef was roasting merrily over the kitchen fire as Mynheer passed. He paused at the door of the living-room with his hand on the knob. He heard voices, laughter, scuffling ; in fact levity out of place in these terrible times.

It was too true—the English had come ! On the other side of the door young Wimpje, playing with a red rose, smiled bewitchingly at the enemy through its leaves, while Mistress van Twist considerately nodded over a worthy book.

"Juffrouw Wimpje," the enemy pleaded, "give me the rose."

At this moment ponderous steps were heard approaching, and Wimpje, with a startled blush, drew back the hand which had found its way into British possession. The rose fell, both stooped to pick it up, and before Juffrouw Wimpje knew how it happened her head was on his breast, two dark eyes looked laughingly into hers, and—why explain ?

The next instant the door was flung open, and

Juffrouw Wimpje, as red as the rose safely tucked in the enemy's gray silk sash, looked guiltily down at sight of her father. Mynheer remarked with indignation that there was a jug of his best cider on the table.

"What—who?" Mynheer demanded, with a quavering voice.

"Yes, Mynheer; the young man of whom I spoke,"—and Mistress van Twist smoothed her best apron,—"Captain Cawardine."

"From where?"

"From Boston—an Englishman from Boston."

"I hate Boston and Englishmen," Mynheer muttered.

"So I hear," and Captain Cawardine smiled gently.

"A nest of Puritan bigots and hypocrites. What are you doing here?"

"Courting a wife, as you may have heard, Mynheer."

"'The more fool she," and Mynheer retreated to his sacred chair and pretended to take a nap, though he raged under his scarlet handkerchief until it rose and fell like an angry red sea.

But Mynheer was not the only one, for Brammatje sat on a woodpile in the shed and swore like a trooper.

"That hook-nosed Bostonian 'll bring you ill luck, Brammatje. He's seen you in Boston breaking stones on the highway with the rest of 'em, and all for the sake of that old mare. I know you, young sir, a king's officer fresh from England, famous at a sword thrust, a fandango, or a light ditty—they'd hang another on the Common for less. I've only to say 'British spy' to Mynheer and where'll you be, curse you!"

Nevertheless, Juffrouw van Twist's courtship prospered slowly and steadily; Captain Cawardine was at Bovenkirk every hour of the day, and poor Mynheer

Van Witt experienced symptoms of neglect, and to add to his wretchedness the ghost of St. Bartholomew had been encountered by several sober witnesses.

But as the proverbial worm turns at last, so did Mynheer, and he went in search of Juffrouw van Twist. He found her stirring batter in the pantry. From the solitary window there was a delicious view of the canal, the windmill, and the pagoda; this and the prospect of waffles moved Mynheer unspeakably.

"Juffrouw van Twist!"

The fair Pamplona paused with uplifted ladle.

"Juffrouw van Twist, what have we done that you wish to leave us? What is there so captivating in that young man, Pamplona?"

"He is a very pleasing youth, Mynheer."

Mynheer spoke with solemn politeness.

"Juffrouw, do not be offended, but how shall I put it to you? Shall I say he is too young for you, or that you are too—ahem!—mature for him?"

"It comes to the same thing, Mynheer."

"Then why do you marry him?"

"Because—because it is high time for me to settle. It may be my last chance, and the young man is willing. He likes me, Mynheer."

"So do others, Juffrouw van Twist," and Mynheer took the ladle out of her hand. "So do others, Juffrouw van Twist. I like you—marry me!"

"O Mynheer! why didn't you speak before?"

"Send him away, Pampy; send the youth away."

"And break his heart. No, I couldn't"—here she reflected—"unless—"

"Unless what?"

"Unless some one else could be found to take my place."

"We'll find some one," Mynheer cried with enthusiasm; and not only seized the fair hand of Mistress van Twist, but he was about to embrace her waist with one arm when the pantry door burst open and in flew Brammatje. "The English!" he roared, and vanished; and Mynheer followed.

This time it was true. That very morning on awakening, New Amsterdam was appalled by the spectacle of six English men-of-war anchored in the quiet bay, their guns pointed directly at The Blue Grape; and in the course of the day the English commander-in-chief, Colonel Matthew Borden, politely demanded of Governor Stuyvesant the surrender of the Dutch colonies in the name of his gracious Majesty Charles II. As further inducement, Colonel Borden added that if he refused it would be his painful duty to blow New Amsterdam into mince-meat. Whereupon the good burghers clamored enthusiastically to be surrendered. But old Peter Stuyvesant declined; he and that other patriot, Cornelis Van Witt, he declared to the deputation, would teach their fellow-citizens to be patriotic.

VI.

MYNHEER overtook Brammatje. "The English will rob and ruin me," he groaned.

"Of course they will, for he'll set 'em on."

"He—who?" Mynheer gasped.

"That long-legged British spy. He ain't been spying round here for nothing. With six ships down there to back him, he's only to say, 'Fork out, Cornelis Van Witt, or I'll—'"

"O Lord, what shall I do?"

"Make him harmless."

"But how, my dear, excellent friend?"

"When he comes lure him into the garret, that's safest; lock him in and make terms with him through

the keyhole. If he won't—" the rest Brammatje confided to Mynheer in a blood-curdling whisper.

"So, young man, you will spy on me, will you?"
he reflected with natural resentment. "Well, two
can play at that game. I'll be blessed if I want to
see your long legs round by the churchyard at night
any more. Grudge a poor man a trifle of luck, do
you?"

Late that afternoon Captain Cawardine appeared;
he looked preoccupied. "I have something to say
to you, Mynheer."

Mynheer grasped the arms of his chair. Did this
British spy mean to murder him or take him prisoner?

"Mynheer, I want to warn you against Brammatje
Baas. I have seen him in Boston; he is an escaped
convict."

Mynheer's muscles relaxed; he received this information with admirable composure.

"I have no proof, Mynheer, only suspicions; but
I am inclined to think he is planning a burglary."

"Indeed, where?"

"The old church over the way."

"Well, then, young sir, why don't you stop him?"
Mynheer retorted with unrepressed scorn.

"I can, if you will let me lodge in your house to-
night."

Mynheer Van Witt himself conducted his guest to
his room.

"Bolt yourself in, young man, and God rest you,"
he said piously, and when after two hours sleep Captain Cawardine tried the door he found that he was
locked in, for what reason he did not stop to consider.
Given a garret window, Juffrouw van Twist's home-
spun sheets, the roof of a broad veranda below, the
rest was a trifle for Tom Cawardine. He dropped
like a cat, still holding one of Juffrouw Pampy's sheets
in his hand.

"Now for a little fun," he thought with a twinkle in his eye ; and flinging the sheet about his shoulders he grasped the ledge of the veranda and swung himself into the midst of the famous Van Witt dahlias.

The bell of St. Bartholomew struck midnight. The pine trees cast black shadows across the old cemetery, and the weather-beaten headstones lay deep in the unmown grass. It required courage even in a ghost to break such profound silence. Yet the vibration of the bell had hardly ceased when something white, tall, and shadowy appeared against the darkness of the old church, crept along with flowing garments, its face hidden, but bearing in its hands a heavy burden ; progress was slow over the long grass. Suddenly through the silence there rang a cry of abject terror. The moment was unique in supernatural history : the ghost itself was haunted ; for before it, under the shadow of a pine tree, stood another apparition for all the world like itself.

"I have been waiting for you," an unearthly,voice spoke ; and at the words the first ghost dropped its burden and fell on its knees and shrieked.

"How dare you mock me, you wretch ? " the other demanded, and pointed to the flowing draperies.

"Forgive—forgive," the miserable mummer gasped.

"Brammatje Baas, you've been robbing the church. The communion service is in that chest."

"Ow-ow-ow!" and Brammatje bowed his rascally head in terror to the ground and made a discovery : the ghost wore spurs, and who ever heard of a mad sexton with spurs!

"The devil!" and he would have run, only his head came in smart contact with the muzzle of a pistol.

"I'd rather not blow your brains out," said Captain Cawardine, with a firm grip of Brammatje's collar, "never mind your plunder, I'll see to it."

Whereupon he trundled Brammatje to the damp

sacristy, dumped him in, locked the heavy door with Brammatje's own false key, and left that valorous soul to the companionship of the dominie's surplice and his own wrecked hopes.

Who will describe the condition of Mynheer Van Witt on discovering the captain's flight? He was now at the mercy of an implacable enemy. To add to his terror, rumor declared that New Amsterdam would be bombarded if the governor and Cornelis Van Witt did not surrender. Threats were uttered as to what would be done to Cornelis Van Witt if he insisted on being too heroic. Three times that day was he vainly summoned to attend the town council. Venture in range of the British guns and Captain Cawardine— never!

There being nothing else to do, a deputation of the worthy aldermen waited on Mynheer to remonstrate with him on his warlike folly.

"What is the use of being so heroic, Cornelis Van Witt?" they asked. Mynheer shuddered. With less trouble than they expected the deputation proved to Mynheer that it makes no difference whether you live under a Dutch or an English flag, if you have five meals a day.

So the common sense of New Amsterdam triumphed; Governor Stuyvesant gave way in a huff, and the British troops under Colonel Borden took possession of the town. The only apparent result of this bloodless victory was that in honor of his Majesty's brother, the Duke of York, New Amsterdam received the now famous name of New York.

VII.

THE evening after Brammatje's disappearance the sexton of St. Bartholomew's thumped against Mynheer's front door.

He was all of a quiver.

"O Mynheer, Mynheer! a great misfortune has happened."

"Another?" Mynheer spoke with stunned resignation.

"Your communion service, of which we were so proud, is—is—stolen!"

"Stolen!"

"Yes, Mynheer. I rang the six o'clock bell and went to the sacristy, and just as I turned the key the door flew open; some one knocked me down, but I recognized the rogue: it was Brammatje. I flew to the cupboard where the service is kept; the lock was broken and the silver chest gone."

Mynheer was left to his reflections, and they were not comforting. By the advice of a rascal, he had locked a blameless gentleman into his attic, leaving him no choice but to jump out of a garret window at the risk of breaking his neck. This same maligned gentleman was an English officer, who could make it very unpleasant for him in these days of British invasion. The communion service, which cost a small fortune, had disappeared. Juffrouw van Twist had been deprived of a bridegroom who was not yet definitely replaced, and Wimpje went about in tears. To add to his anguish the very next morning there appeared a musketeer on a brawny mare, with a command from Colonel Borden that Cornelis Van Witt should appear before him forthwith in the Town Hall of New York.

In this same town-hall, in Governor Stuyvesant's own chair, sat Colonel Borden, writing a letter and cursing liberally, for Colonel Borden was not as handy at a goose-quill as at a good stout sword.

"Confound it! Where's Tom? Here you, Cawardine!"

But no Captain Tom appeared. The colonel pulled a watch like a warming-pan out of his breeches pocket.

"Time for Tom's old man. So I'm to frighten the old chap a bit and make him mellow afterwards. Well, I'm willing."

Just then there was an awful scuffle at the outer door; it burst open, and in flew something ponderous followed by a musketeer.

"I've brought him, your Excellency. This is Cornelis Van Witt."

There was an awful pause, then Colonel Borden spoke.

"So you're the man who defied the British nation and refused to surrender these colonies to my gracious lord and master, Charles the Second, King of England!"

Mynheer stared at the colonel in silent horror. Why was he obliged to shoulder the entire heroism of New Amsterdam?

"The British nation"—here the colonel frowned majestically—"is not to be trifled with."

Mynheer grew so limp that he clutched at the nearest chair for support; it was the very chair in which he had once fallen asleep and awakened an unwilling hero.

Mynheer, your conduct has been such that you have aroused the —aw— the suspicion and resentment of the English government."

"Cornelis wrung his fat hands. "I'm only a peaceful citizen, your Excellency; and I—I—yes, I love and respect the English nation."

"Then why, Mynheer," Colonel Borden demanded, with singular abruptness—"then why did you lock
a beloved and respected Englishman into your garret?
A nice way to treat a guest, by Jupiter!"

Mynheer sank on his knees.

"Pardon, your Excellency!   I thought—I thought
the young man was a British spy."

So, then, it was out.   "A British spy!" the colonel
roared.   "Tom Cawardine, the son of my old friend
General Cawardine, a British spy!   I say, Tom, d'ye
hear?"   For Tom had come into the room, none the
worse for the tumble into Mynheer's dahlias.

Tom helped Mynheer to his feet and dusted him
tenderly.   "Why did you suspect me, Mynheer?"

Cornelis was silent, and then he stammered, "Brammatje Baas."

"Against whom I warned you.   Mynheer, why do
you believe the word of a ruffian instead of that of a
gentleman?"

"Young sir, why does a gentleman jump out of a
window at midnight?"

"Mynheer, since when does the host lock his guest
into his room?   But, pardon me, I owe you an explanation."

With these words Captain Cawardine pulled from
under the table a huge box with a broken padlock.
He flung the iron-bound lid back, and there, in all
its glory, lay the communion service of St. Bartholomew's.

"This," the captain said modestly, "is my explanation.   If I had not jumped out of the window I could
not have restored the treasure of St. Bartholomew to
its generous donor."

Mynheer beamed with joy, and he grasped both of
Tom's hands.

"I have done you a great wrong, Captain Cawardine.   Forgive me."

Tom smiled. " Tell me, Mynheer, why do you dis-like me ? "

Mynheer changed color, cleared his throat, and then he blurted out, " Why did you come courting Juffrouw van Twist, sir ? What do you, a young and handsome man, want with a woman old enough to be your mother ? " he urged. " The fact is, I have been meaning to marry the lady myself one of these days."

" Zounds, Tom ! If Mynheer is very anxious you might be induced to relinquish the older fair for one younger," Colonel Borden interposed, jovially. " So it seems the lady is a trifle mature for the boy, eh ? But if you take her and leave our young friend with an aching heart, sure it will be your duty to supply her place."

Mynheer looked dazed.

Colonel Borden continued, with some emphasis :

" It will be well for Cornelis Van Witt to be on good terms with the new government. As a Dutch-man who obstinately refused to surrender you may be heroic, my good sir, but you will certainly be—unpop-ular."

Mynheer changed color and cursed his own heroism.

" If, on the other hand, you can ally yourself with a good English family of undoubted loyalty, that will be a guarantee for your future patriotism. You un-derstand, Mynheer ? "

But Mynheer was all at sea.

" Listen," the colonel continued. " Here's a boy I love as my own," and he laid his hand on Cawar-dine's arm. " His people are the stanchest of good English folks, well to do and honorable. You, Myn-heer, are wealthy ; you have a daughter—"

" Yes, Wilhelmina ; a little maid with yellow hair and brown eyes," Mynheer murmured, absently.

" Perhaps you can persuade him to take the younger

maid for the older. What do you say, Tom, old fellow?"

Captain Cawardine watched Mynheer with breathless eagerness. Mynheer's perplexity was something painful. "This is so very sudden—so—so unexpected," he stammered.

"Sir," the colonel interposed, "do not forget my warning. I speak to you not as a prisoner of war, as I might, but as a friend."

"I—I—thank your Excellency,—I—I am deeply beholden to you,—but—you see, gentlemen, I must first speak to Wimpje—my little daughter. It will be for her to decide."

"Tell her to sacrifice herself for your sake, Mynheer, do you hear? And, I say, take Captain Tom with you. I don't trust you—you are a desperate character. You are the hero of New York these days, Mynheer. God be with you, gentlemen."

VIII.

MYNHEER rode beside the captain and pondered, and every moment he inclined more and more to the colonel's plan. As for its being an English government—mere prejudice; what had the Dutch government ever done for him?

Mynheer broke the silence. "It all depends on Wimpje, and whether her heart inclines to you. She's desperate woful since two days, and such matters as courting may come amiss. Such weeping and hanging round my neck when I left—why, blicksem! there they are running down the road to meet me. Why, Wimpje, child, and Juffrouw van Twist, here am I safe back;" and he held out a fat hand to each, while Powtje stood still and took a nibble of grass. "But there, child, don't you see the captain?"

Captain Cawardine swung himself out of his saddle, and with the horse's bridle over his arm he walked beside young Wimpje Van Witt.

"Juffrouw Van Witt," the captain said, softly, "have you missed me?"

There was no answer, only a sudden little sob.

"Why, Wimpje, my darling, so much?"

She turned upon him with a quiver of her pretty lips. "I must tell father. I can bear it no longer. To think that you are an Englishman, and that of all the world he should just hate Englishmen. I fear he will never pardon our deception."

"My darling, it will all end well, believe me. Perhaps it was a foolish plan, but how else could I have had my sweetheart? All's fair in love and war, and it was kind of Juffrouw Pampy to let me come courting her for the joy of seeing you. It was for the best, Wimpje, dear. Captain Cawardine was an unwelcome suitor for the hand of Juffrouw Van Witt."

"Oh, if my father will only forgive me for loving you! If he does not—why then I'll follow you to the end of the earth, for I cannot live without you. I'll go as far then as ever you wish—even if it is to Boston."

IX.

A PEACEFUL late-afternoon quiet rested over the living-room, and the holy saint was fading into twilight.

Two sighs broke the stillness.

"Why, Wimpje?"

"Why, father?"

"I wish to speak to you, Wimpje."

Wimpje brought the settle to the sacred chair, and rubbed her soft cheeks against Mynheer's hand.

"How old are you, Wimpje?"

"Eighteen, father."

"Now, Wimpje, did it—did it ever occur to you that young girls do sometimes marry ?"

Wimpje sighed.

A sudden thought struck Mynheer. You are not opposed to marrying ? Young maids have such foolish notions sometimes."

The answer was inaudible and yet satisfactory. Mynheer proceeded.

"Wimpje child, there now, tell your old father, is your heart quite free ? "

Here, to Mynheer's speechless consternation, she hid her face on his arm and burst into tears.

"What does this mean ? And just as I had a nice little plan."

" A plan ? " Juffrouw Van Witt murmured, sobbing.

"Well, child, you must be told.   Here is Pamplona —you always liked Pamplona, and some day I meant to marry her ; but there was no hurry, and all would have gone well, but just then there comes Captain Cawardine courting my Pamplona. And she took him, but only because I—I had not spoken."

Mynheer was unspeakably elated. "The fact is, child, not to hide anything from you, the decided stand I took in the matter of the siege of New Amsterdam (there be those who call it heroic) has been misconstrued. The English Government doubts my patriotism ; the English Government requires a guaranty for my—ahem !—loyalty.

"Now, Wimpje, tell me, what do you think of Captain Cawardine ? "

Wimpje controlled a sudden sparkle in her brown eyes, and hung her head discreetly. "He seems a worthy young man."

"He is more than that." Mynheer spoke with sudden impatience. "He is a young man of taste and discretion, or he would not have courted Juffrouw van Twist. That wound will heal. He is, besides, of excellent family and well to do, and he is as a son to Colonel Borden. Being so well with the government, young and sturdy, and pleasant to gaze upon, I thought—yes, I thought—"

"Well, father?"

"I thought, Wimpje, you might n't do much better, and you could do a great deal worse."

"But he is an Englishman, father."

"A mere prejudice, child. Through Captain Cawardine your old father could get many a good trading privilege. There, listen to me, Wimpje, do not sacrifice your father for a foolish fancy."

"So it would please you if I married Captain Cawardine?" young Wimpje said meekly.

"It would, child."

"Very well, then for your sake, you dear—" and before he could remonstrate Wimpje's arms were flung about his neck.

"I am so happy, so happy, !"

"Why?" Mynheer cried, struggling.

"Now you will have to forgive. Wait, I'll call him."

And Captain Cawardine came, smiling and eager.

"O Tom, I've promised to marry you," and before Mynheer could say a word, she was in his arms.

"This is very extraordinary, Captain ; will you explain, Wilhelmina? I thought, Juffrouw, you said your heart was not free."

"It wasn't, for there was Captain Cawardine."

"But there was also Juffrouw van Twist. Blicksem ! Whom did you come courting, Captain Cawardine?"

But Wimpje was already at his side stroking his fat cheek. "It was me he came courting, but it was all Pamplona's little plan, so you will have to forgive."

Of course Mynheer forgave, and before winter set in there were two fine weddings at Bovenkirk.

In the course of time Cornelis Van Witt's increasing wealth proved on what excellent terms he was with the government, while the wisdom and patriotism of Governor Cawardine of New York have passed into history.

As for the ghost of the mad sexton, it disappeared with Brammatje Baas.

Whoever doubts the truth of this narrative, let him take the elevated road in the great city of New York and search for the old church of St. Bartholomew not far from the Bowery. There will he find an ancient graveyard surrounded by time-stained warehouses. He will observe that the crumbling headstones still stand in straight rows as placed by the mad sexton. If he searches very carefully he will discover on one weather-beaten slab, beneath a solitary willow tree the years have spared, this half-obliterated inscription :

CORNELIS VAN WITT,

DIED AT THE GREAT AGE OF 90

IN THE TOWN OF NEW YORK.

1695.

REQUIESCAT IN PACE.